Janus Unfolding
Ancient Agendas

C. A. KNUTSEN

BOOK FOUR OF THE JANUS UNFOLDING SERIES

Acknowledgements

Many people encouraged me to write the fourth book in this series. The comments of two in particular, Conni and Veronica Zmolek inspired me to complete it. I would like to thank Judy Knutsen, Kenneth Kussmann, and Russel Beard for the most thorough beta read and feedback that an author could ask for.

caknutsen.com

Cover Art: Jeff Brown Graphics

ISBN - 13: 978-1-7330003-0-7

Janus Unfolding Books

Emergence

Factotum

Inheritance

Ancient Agendas

The Urritan Legacy

for

Rosalind Franklin
whose contributions to the discovery of the
structure of DNA were not acknowledged or
rewarded in her lifetime.

Contents

Concepts and Characters

H1 - Humans with standard Homo Sapiens DNA

H2 - Starting in the year 2000 some Human beings were born with a more complex DNA. The number of H2s in the population increased rapidly. By 2050 it was clear that they weren't aging as fast as H1s.

FTL – Faster-than-light travel

Sam Baxter, Compass Enterprises, and Sunaj (Soon'-ahj) - Sam was born as an H2 in the year 2000. Sam founded Compass Enterprises, headquartered in Seattle, Washington, and the H2 scientific research organization, Sunaj, which he located near the town of Frazier in Southwest Washington.

Martha - The cyber-based intelligence (she doesn't like the title "artificial intelligence") that emerged from complex systems developed by Sam. Martha made a copy of herself who she called Athena.

Janus (Jann'-us) - In 2051 the population of H2s on Earth was 250 million. H2s were just beginning to use telepathy to contact each other. It was at this point that the conscious activity among the H2s triggered the awakening of a global consciousness, which became Janus, an entity unto itself.

The Planet Ocean, the Cheneshi (Chen'-esh-ee)**, and Sways** – An unusual H2 boy from Norway, Hagar Bjornsen received a telepathic message from a race on a planet fifty light-years from Earth. Those sending the message were tree-like creatures called Cheneshi. They lived below the surface of the oceans on their planet. The Cheneshi had a problem and were reaching out to Earth for help. Among all the Cheneshi, Sways became the scientist's primary contact.

Jesse Chavez - Jesse was among the first two hundred H2s found by Sam Baxter and led the team going to Ocean.

Carmen Willathorpe - An anthropologist by training, after an accident on Ocean Carmen learned that she could sense consciousness of other sentient beings at enormous distances.

Rosalind Atwood - Rosalind was H1 and an accomplished physicist in her sixties when Sam Baxter asked her to join the H2 research team at Sunaj.

Lorengi (Lor-n-gee'), **Ahleeto** (Ah-lee-tow'), **Tim and Thelika** (Thel-ee-ka') -**a Lorengi Ship** - While on Ocean, the scientists found a facility that had been constructed on an island by a race called the Lorengi. The facility was managed by an artificial intelligence the Humans called Tim. The AI's purpose was to monitor the development of the Cheneshi. Ahleeto, a former Lorengi leader presented herself in holographic form. She introduced the Humans to Thelika. Lorengi ships like Thelika were sentient beings grown by the Lorengi. Thelika and the other Lorengi ships were telepathic, and also could teleport across vast interstellar spaces.

Ancient Agendas **Characters:**

Annli (Ahnn'-li)
    Theron (Ther'-on) – Spokesperson for the Annli
    Gerana (Jer-ahn'-ah) – Annli scientist
    Ontoron (On'-tor-on – Annli support on Thahll

Dhara'chee (Dara'-chee)
    Orlyn (Or'-lynn) – Dhara'chee leader
    Daran (Day'-ran) – Dhara'chee leader
    Aceri (Ah-sear-ee) – Dhara'chee ship
    Yarada (Yar-ah-dah) – Dhara'chee's home planet

Garduk (Gar-dook')
    Heyut (Hay'-ute) – crew member
    Nathat (Nah'-that) – ship lead
    Neva (Nee'va) – Nathat's mate, Second Ship Lead
    Sadut (Sah- dute') – fishing village leader
    Matrak (Mah'-trak) – Arrogant land holder
    Solan (So'-lan) – Garduk home world
    Seriatna (Sair-ee-aht'-nah) – Garduk ship
    Aflut (Ah- flute)

Lorengi (Lor-n-gee')
    Jarruda (Jar-rood'-ah) – Lorengi Queen
    Ahleeto (Ah-lee-tow') – Daughter of Jarruda
    Nassada (Nah'-sad-ah) – Scientist
    Atala (Ah-tal'-ah) – delegate to Thahll
    Gordi (Gord'-ee) – delegate to Thahll
    Thelika (Thel-ee'-ka) – Lorengi ship
    Masuri (Mah-zur'-ee) – Lorengi ship
    Katala (Kah-tal'-ah) – Lorengi ship
    Jannida (Jan-ee'-dah) – Lorengi ship
    Meratta (Mur-ah'-tah) – Lorengi ship

Sudahlli – (Sud-all-ee)

Set Li – First Born Mother of Clan Parlac, Ship Master

Jardut (Jar-dute') – Set Li's mate

Neylec (Nay'-lek) – Prime Officer on Thahll 2 station

Arlut (Ar'-lute) – Tech aboard Thahll 2 space station

Canli (Can'-lee) – member of Sudahlli resistance

Berla (Bur'-la) – member of Sudahlli resistance

Meritac (Mur'-ah-tak) – Sudahlli Fleet Commander

Mentan (Men'-tan) – Sudahlli World Council Member

Chantlasec (Chant'-lah-sek) – Set Li's Sudahlli ship

Thahll (Thall) – Sudahlli home world

Thahll 2 – Sudahlli space station

1 An Elusive Vision

Aboard the Lorengi Ship, Thelika
Near a Translucent Barrier

Carmen was shocked by the dazzling, blinding light. It was as bright as the Sun seen from Earth's orbit! She could think of no better way to describe what she saw with her mind-view as she stood in Thelika's common room.

Carmen had detected consciousness across a distance of four thousand light years. She had been sitting on a large rock at night, on the planet the Lorengi called Stone, five hundred light years from Earth. The Lorengi, Ahleeto was with her, and Thelika, the sentient Lorengi ship was connected telepathically.

With her mind-view, she had been testing her ability to sense consciousness, and had expanded her view until a spot of light caught her attention. The light was toward the galactic center, and slightly above the galactic plane. She immediately knew that this was a phenomenon that needed to be investigated. Carmen had Thelika teleport to a position near the light. She telepathically contacted Jesse Chavez who was with his team aboard the Lorengi ship, Katala, researching another planet, and asked him to join her at the new location.

Carmen and Jesse had found that telepathy and teleportation operated over interstellar distances without any apparent weakening. It was an expression of reality that was strikingly different from what her physicist friend, Rosalind Atwood, called the "observable universe."

1

When Jesse, and his teammates, Ashira Tahara, and Matthew Ronson arrived in Katala they teleported to join Carmen and Ahleeto in Thelika's common room. Using only their eyes they saw a large, light-colored sphere that was behind a translucent "barrier." It was difficult to gauge its size, for they couldn't tell how far away it was behind the barrier. When Carmen asked them to close their eyes and join with her mind-view they were as stunned by its brilliance as she was.

"What is it?" Ashira asked.

"A very dense concentration of conscious beings of some kind in the sphere we just saw with our eyes, Ashira," Carmen said. "Let's go back to viewing with our eyes to see what we have here."

"Look, there are two ships next to the sphere," Matthew said.

"Good spotting, Matthew," Carmen said. "So we have one large, solid-looking sphere and two ships near it, all behind a translucent barrier of some kind. Anything else?"

"There aren't any stars," Jesse said. "It's like we are looking through a translucent window at ships which are located in a part of space where there are no stars."

"That's unusual," Carmen said. So was the rest of the vision before them, she thought.

"Those two ships look like Lorengi ships," Ahleeto said. "If they are, that sphere is enormous. Look how small they are comparatively."

"They are Lorengi ships, Excellency," Thelika said. "I knew them when we traveled among the stars together millennia ago. I've tried to communicate with them. There is no response."

"With Lorengi ships near the sphere, might we hope that there are Lorengi inside of it?" Ahleeto asked.

"It's been thousands of Earth years since we lost contact with them, Excellency."

"We will find out," Ahleeto said. She was determined and cautiously hopeful. She last saw her fellow Lorengi over six thousand years ago when she volunteered to upload her personality into the systems on Ocean. She had stayed in contact with her colleagues for decades. After a while they stopped answering her. Ahleeto was left to wonder what had happened to her people. Had she finally found them again?

When Ahleeto conversed with others the former Lorengi leader appeared in holographic form. Ahleeto was about five-ten and Humanoid in shape. She wore a one-piece, short sleeved, light blue uniform with one small insignia on her shoulder. Her body was covered with a short gray fur. Her face looked something like a cat without the whiskers.

"There are other ships of some kind farther away," Ashira said. "How large is the barrier?"

"It is approximately a tenth of light-second in height and half that in width," Thelika said. "The other ships are of unknown origin. All the ships seem to be motionless, and I am getting no response from my attempts to communicate with them."

"Are your communications getting through the barrier?" Jesse asked.

"I cannot be sure. Without receiving a response, it is difficult to know if they are getting through."

"What is the barrier?" Carmen asked.

"I'm not sure it is a barrier," Thelika answered.

It didn't make sense. Carmen could see it. She'd never known Thelika to be wrong. Perhaps it was just a difference in understanding.

"I might have used the wrong word. I called it a barrier, because I assumed that the ships on the other side were barred from getting out by the translucent barrier we see, and that same barrier might be blocking our attempts to communicate with them."

"I understand the meaning of barrier as you meant it. I don't think that the word applies to what is before us."

"You think they are free to leave, but are just unable to?" Ahleeto asked.

"I don't have sufficient information to speculate about those possibilities."

Carmen occasionally found it frustrating to communicate with a being that was literal to a fault.

"Thelika, could you explain what you mean when you say you don't think it's a barrier?"

"That would be best, Carmen. I don't think it's a barrier, because it isn't there."

Well, that was helpful, Carmen thought, smiling.

"We can see the barrier, Thelika, and we can see ships beyond it."

"So can I," Thelika said, "but other than that visual evidence, I cannot detect the barrier or ships with any other means available to me. My next step of assessment would be to send a probe to see what happens. Shall I do that?"

"Launch the probe, Thelika," Ahleeto said. "I suggest a trajectory of minimum penetration and return."

"Yes, Excellency. Probe launched. You can see it on the forward screen."

They watched as the probe headed toward what they still thought of as a barrier. Thelika had aimed it at the large sphere. The probe crossed the barrier unimpeded. They were shocked to

4

see the probe pass through the sphere and come out the other side without apparently affecting the sphere or the probe.

It was as Thelika had said. The probe went through the barrier and the sphere as if they weren't there. Thelika reported that the probe was undamaged, and that it recorded nothing more than it would if it were traveling through a volume of empty space.

"Interesting!" Carmen exclaimed. "Thelika, do you have a speculation about where this visual representation is coming from?"

"No," the ship said, "but it is exhibiting characteristics similar to a holograph or perhaps a reflection. I can't subscribe to either phenomenon as an explanation of what we see. I can't imagine how either could be created on this scale. Perhaps it is a projection sent directly to our minds which is made to appear as if it is before us in open space."

"Who or what could do such a thing?"

"I do not know, Carmen," Thelika said. "You perceive consciousness emanating from the sphere. Perhaps the beings within the sphere are sending us the image."

Carmen let the recent surprises swirl around in her mind. She had detected consciousness in the sphere from a distance of thousands of light years, and that beacon had guided them here. They saw more ships were located in an expansive area behind a translucent veil. All the ships seemed to be inactive. Then they learned that what they thought they saw wasn't actually there! Were the beings in the sphere asking for help by sending the image to them as Thelika suggested? It was a puzzle of cosmic proportions. Rosalind would love it, Carmen thought.

2 Rosalind the Determined

Frazier, Washington State

"I have to experience it for myself!" Rosalind asserted. She was in Jamal Jackson's office at Sunaj. Rosalind Atwood was in her early seventies, five-feet six inches in height, stout of build, with gray hair and piercing blue-gray eyes which shone brightly with intelligence.

Like Rosalind, Jamal was a physicist. Jamal was thirty years younger than Rosalind. He stood six-one with a slim build, dark skin, curly dark hair, a brilliant smile. He focused on the theoretical and preferred to work in his office.

Rosalind liked to prove concepts, or at least be able to observe a theory's impact on the universe. She would go wherever was required to get that experience.

"You have experienced what it's like when I've helped you teleport," Jamal said. "What you 'saw' with your mind is what H2's would experience when they teleport, if they bothered to pause and look around before they go to the new location."

"Yes. I appreciate that opportunity. I just can't gain the understanding that I would if I were the driver and not just a passenger. I'm not getting any closer to learning what happens in between when a person teleports from A to B. We've tried a dozen different approaches."

"We have recorded visual evidence that nothing can be detected between the two points," Jamal said. "We didn't just rely on our view of the recording. Martha confirmed it."

"I also looked for other indications of anything in between your point of departure and where you arrived," Martha said. Martha was a cyber-based intelligence, or AI, who emerged over forty years earlier from the complex computer systems created by Sam Baxter, the founder of Compass Enterprises, the parent organization of Sunaj. "Not only was the visual recording empty in our repeated experiments I measured for any type of radiation. All efforts had the same result—nothing."

"I agree with both of you," Rosalind said. "I'm not arguing that when you teleport that you are within the observable universe, as you go from A to B. I've said all along that a person leaves our sensory frame of reference at one point and comes back in at another. I think if I experienced it as an H2 I might get a sense of what happens."

"I am H2," Jamal said. "I've no idea where we go when we teleport, and as you know I have been searching for an answer. I think it may have something to do with the additional dimensions predicted by the math of String Theory."

"Yes, yes, Jamal," Rosalind said. "I'm not criticizing you or your efforts. You may be right about String Theory, but so far no one has been able to observe the strings or the extra dimensions. I do think another dimension is involved, but I can't 'see' it. I'm frustrated. I have begun to wonder if I could somehow learn how to teleport."

"I don't think you can be changed into an H2, Rosalind," Martha said.

"I'm sure you're right, Martha, but look at what happened to Carmen. She's not H2, yet she is able to teleport and can communicate telepathically. She was altered in some way. The change saved her life, but it also opened up these new worlds to her."

"She was changed by one of the Cheneshi," Jamal pointed out. "They are all on the planet Ocean, and they altered Carmen because it was the *only* way to save her life."

"I thought I heard that Tim could do something like that," Rosalind said. Tim was the AI that the Lorengi had left on Ocean to monitor the development of the Cheneshi. When the Sunaj team came back to Earth, they brought a copy of Tim.

Since Martha and Tim were in constant communication, she was able to answer right away. "Tim says that he was given some ability in this area by the Lorengi, but it only related to the Cheneshi. He does not have the information necessary to perform such a procedure on Humans."

"Well, that's that, then," Jamal said. "We'll just have to work with what we have."

"Hmmm."

"Rosalind…?"

"I was just thinking that there is another option."

"What's that?"

"You could take me to Ocean."

"What? That's crazy! I've never been there. I'm not a field scientist. I work in my office."

"Oh, don't underrate yourself. I heard you were part of the team that overthrew the dictator in that small country in Africa."

"That was different. We used planes to get there. I was just a passenger, not the driver to use your metaphor. I've never been to Ocean, and I don't know how to get there."

"If I can find someone who's been there to take us, will you go with me?"

Jamal didn't answer right away. During the pause, Rosalind thought about who the right person would be to take them. Who had been there before? Who wanted to go back? Then she had the answer—Travis Beckwith. Travis was the head of the group that created the ships that had taken the original team to Ocean.

As Rosalind remembered, he was reluctant to leave Ocean. Travis had wanted to talk with Tim more to learn about Lorengi technology. Then Rosalind remembered that since a copy of Tim had been brought back with the team, Travis probably had all the conversations with the Lorengi AI that he wanted. Still, maybe he'd be interested in another trip to that watery planet.

Her thoughts were interrupted by Jamal's resigned response, "Yes. I'll go with you."

"Wonderful! Let's go find our master of interstellar ships."

Travis was viewing something on a large screen when they entered his office a few minutes later. Rosalind saw what it was.

"Is that the recording we took of the Nano device that makes the changes in DNA, which results in H2s? Or is it a new one?"

"It's the same one, Rosalind," Travis said. "I look at it occasionally to remind me how far advanced that little engine is, and to see if looking at it will give me ideas for our work here."

"Any luck?"

"Actually, it has generated some ideas over the years, but we're still way behind this level of gene technology. What can I do for you physicists today?"

"I'd like to go to Ocean," Rosalind said. "Since you are the one who made the ships that took the other teams, I thought you, along with Jamal, might be willing to take me."

"You don't need me, but I will be glad to have an excuse to go back."

"I was just thinking that your ships would probably need a couple of H2s to teleport them," Rosalind said.

"That was true, but we haven't used those for years. If we want to go anywhere out there," Travis said, using an expansive arm swing toward the ceiling to indicate the vastness of space, "we just use one of the Lorengi ships."

"Are any available?"

"Thelika had several going through a recuperation process, to get their life energy pumping again after millennia of inactivity. A ship named Masuri has just finished the process and is eager to go somewhere."

"Are you sure it's safe?" Jamal asked. "I mean is Masuri fully recovered?"

"Fit as a fiddle. Why do you want to go to Ocean, Rosalind?"

"Promise you won't laugh."

"I would never laugh at you."

Rosalind told him what she was struggling with and that she hoped to be changed like Carmen was.

"Sounds risky to me, especially for...."

"Don't you dare say 'for someone of my age,' Travis. I'd rather you laughed."

"I'm appropriately admonished, and I don't think this is a laughing matter. It's a serious step for anyone to take. I can see you are committed to this as the only way to get one of those 'insights' you're famous for. I'd be honored to come along and help where I can. Besides, I may be able to get back to that Lorengi station on Tim's island and see some of the marvels there."

Word got around that a trip to Ocean was being planned, and scientists at Sunaj wanted to either go themselves, or at least have input into the work that would be done there. Plans to study Ocean and the life on it were developed quickly. One researcher wanted to communicate with the small group of

Cheneshi who mapped and tracked the cosmos for their race. The big question was how they accomplished this since the Cheneshi had no eyes and lived beneath the surface of their ocean.

It was several days before everything was ready to go. The passenger list had grown to ten by then. Travis decided to refit Journey, the ship that had taken the original group from Earth to Ocean and load it into Masuri to serve as a base of operations on Ocean. Athena, a copy of Martha, who Martha thought of as her daughter, had been loaded into Journey to manage the ship on the first trip. Athena eagerly volunteered to serve that function again. Also included would be several updated High-Speed Hover Probes, or HSHPs, the electric vehicles that had been used to fly around the planet.

In the end, Sam Baxter, the nominal leader of Sunaj and Compass Enterprises, also decided to travel with the group. While there had been several missions to Ocean over the years since the first visit, Sam had not returned to the water planet himself. Sam spoke as if it was a vacation for him. Since Sam always had a purpose for whatever he did even on vacation, Rosalind wondered what Sam's real reason was. She decided to hold her curiosity in check for now and wait to see what happened.

Lorengi ships, like Masuri, were fully conscious, organic beings, grown and trained by the Lorengi to transport them around the galaxy. They did so by teleporting themselves and those within to the new location. The Lorengi called it Dimension Shift Transport, or DST. Ahleeto, the only Lorengi available to discuss how it was done, did not know how to explain it. Rosalind was determined to find out how it happened and what happened between points "A" and "B."

All the passengers and equipment were loaded on Masuri, who had come down to the surface for that purpose. Travis took the lead in arranging things and working with the Lorengi ship. Many trips had been taken to other planets aboard Lorengi ships. Still, no one was used to how fast they were able to get from one-star system to another. It took much longer to talk about making the trip than it did to travel the distance.

"Masuri, do you know the way to Ocean?" Travis asked.

"Yes. It was a planet of great interest to the Lorengi. I traveled there a few times myself. Even if I hadn't, all ships shared the coordinates of the planets that were visited."

"As you can see by the group we have assembled, it is a planet that is still of 'great interest.' Please, take us to Ocean."

3 Ocean View

Planet Ocean

In the next instant, the Lorengi ship Masuri was in orbit around the planet Ocean. The planet was covered by an ocean with islands of varying sizes spread around the globe. The largest island found so far was a little bigger than New Zealand. The Cheneshi lived beneath the surface of the ocean on the shoulders of the islands.

"Thank you for the quick trip, Masuri," Travis said. "Do you know the location of the island that was chosen as a base by the first team?"

"No."

"Welcome," came a booming, telepathic greeting to Masuri and all her passengers. *"I am called Sways by our visitors. On behalf of all the Cheneshi, I welcome you to our planet. I am rooted near where the first visitors landed. I sense that Athena is with you. She may be able to direct you."*

Most of the passengers were H2 and used to telepathic conversations. The four H1s on the trip had been alerted that Cheneshi were strong telepaths and communicated in that mode. Still, the "volume" of Sways greeting was startling.

"Thank you, Sways," Travis said. *"Masuri, can you take us to Sways' location?"*

"On my way now."

Travis had told everyone to go into Journey. When Masuri had arrived at Sways' location, she hovered above the ocean's surface. The H2s then teleported Journey to a flat spot on Sway's island a bit inland of the high-tide mark.

"Okay," Travis said, once Journey had settled, "everyone step out. Athena has some work to do."

The scientists knew what to expect, but it was always surprising to see it in action. Journey was made of organic material that was infused with nano devices that responded to signals from Athena. She communicated a blueprint of the desired shape and configuration to the nano units. They used material stored within Journey, and sand and organic material directly below it to shift Journey into the new design. The new shape provided living and work areas that would support the scientists and their research. When the change was complete, Journey was much larger.

"That didn't take you long, Athena."

"I've been practicing with our little nano friends, Travis. Everything inside is as planned."

"Thanks."

Travis turned to the others and said, "Please, go inside, find your assigned room, and stow your gear. It's afternoon local time. Why don't you take some time to look around the island, and communicate with the Cheneshi? Let's meet back here in a few hours for our evening meal, and to discuss plans for our stay here."

Rosalind found her room, dropped her bag, and walked out toward the beach. She stopped near where Jamal and Travis were talking with Sam.

"This has turned into quite an event," Rosalind said. "I was planning to quietly come to the planet and have a discreet discussion with the Cheneshi."

14

"It did grow beyond our original plan, Rosalind," Travis said, "but your discussion with the Cheneshi can still be private, don't you think?"

"I guess you're right. Anyone care to join me?"

"I'm coming," Jamal said. "I've never seen a Cheneshi. Besides, you and I are in this together."

"Thanks, Jamal."

"I'm going to pop over to Tim's island, and look at the Lorengi station there," Travis said.

"I'd like to come along, Rosalind," Sam said.

"Thanks, Sam. I'd like you to be there with me. Okay, let's go get our swimsuits, equipment and re-breathers."

A short time later they were ready for the swim and stood on the beach that stretched out on both sides of where Journey had landed. They were ready to go in, but unsure which way to go.

"Sways, I'm not telepathic," Rosalind said, *"but can you catch my thoughts, anyway?"*

"Yes, Rosalindatwood. I can. You are more telepathic than you think."

"Just call me Rosalind, please. I'm sure my friends Sam and Jamal would like you to use their first names, too. Can you tell us what direction to take, so that we can arrive in front of you?"

"Yes. I remember meeting Sam and you the last time you were here. I think it is Jamal's first time here, though. Am I correct, Jamal?"

"Yes."

"Welcome. To get to where I am, you can swim straight out from where you are. Go to a depth of about sixty feet, and you will see me, and my family arrayed in line parallel to the beach. Our fronds face away from the shore and are well above the

ocean floor. Swim under the fronds to the other side of the family line and pause in front of the largest of us. That's me."

They followed Sways directions, and a soon were floating in front of a line of the tree-like Cheneshi. Their fronds were swaying in the gentle current, as were the plants which looked similar to kelp that surrounded the base of their trunks.

The Cheneshi were rooted in the ocean floor. The tallest in the group, Sways, was in the center of the line and nearly ninety feet tall. All of those in his family, including Sways, had four fronds on each side of their trunks, proportional in size to their height. The fronds were larger toward the bottom of the tree, and got progressively smaller going up the trunk, which also got smaller in diameter as the height increased. At the top of each trunk was a single fan-like frond which was bulbous at its base. The upper point of Sways top frond was about twenty feet below the ocean surface.

Rosalind and the others wore weights to help stabilize them at their depth but had to make minor adjustments to keep the current from moving them away from Sways.

"Our planet-wide network is alive with anticipation of being able to communicate directly with you and your friends. It has already started. The new questions from your associates are exciting. Oh! One of you has reached out to our small group of cosmologists, as I think you might call them. I'm honored that you have chosen to communicate directly with me, Rosalind."

"Thank you, Sways," Rosalind said. *"As you may remember, Sam is the leader of the organization that the visiting scientists come from. Jamal and I work in a branch of our science called physics. We try to understand how things work in the physical world."*

"We are interested in those workings ourselves."

"That's what I've heard, and I am amazed at how much you understand and the mathematics you have worked out to describe things. I've come here to request your help. Are you familiar with our H2 population's ability to move about by merely intending to be at another location, and arrive there with no time delay? We call it teleporting."

"Yes we find it fascinating that you can do this. We understand the Lorengi ships can do this, also."

"I'm not H2," Rosalind said, *"but I have traveled that way with the help of others. Traveling doesn't take place within the physical space in between."*

"Of course. That wouldn't be possible. That would take time, as it would for one of our flying creatures going from one bush to another."

Rosalind was again astounded at how astute the Cheneshi were. They knew everything that went on in their world above and below the surface of their ocean and had developed mathematics to describe it. They accomplished all this without a written language, opposable thumbs or eyes.

"Exactly. I am trying to understand where they go, Sways."

"That's easy," Sways said. *"They go out. Then they come back in."*

"You've seen this? You've seen where they go?" Rosalind couldn't believe it—that the Cheneshi had the answer she was looking for.

"When I changed Carmen, she found she could do this. We watched her practice. Each time, we noticed that she went away at one place and came back at a different place. So we concluded that she went out, and came back in."

Rosalind knew that the Cheneshi had senses like what Carmen called her mind-view of things. They were in touch with their planet and all of the flora and fauna living on the surface of the islands and within the oceans. They had never seen one of their flying creatures fly with eyes, but they had "seen" with their sensitive minds the creature move from one place to another without touching the ground. That was "flying" from the rich perspective they had of their world. Rosalind had never heard of them referring to "out" in this way.

"Sways, do the Cheneshi know what 'out' is, or means?"

"We don't, Rosalind. Those of us who focus on the cosmos believe they are getting some of their impressions from somewhere outside. Watching Carmen practice, we concluded that there must be somewhere outside the reality we sense because we observed her leave and then come back. We could not sense her in between where she left and where she returned. She was not in our world."

That confirms our observations in a very conclusive way, Rosalind thought. The Cheneshi would know if Carmen had remained in their world! She looked at Sam and Jamal to see if they got the point. They both acknowledged that they were following the discussion and understood the importance of what Sways had just conveyed.

"I want to know more about what is outside. That's why I came here to be with you."

"I'm glad you came, Rosalind. I'm sorry, but I don't know how to help you in your quest."

"It would have been nice if you had the information I am seeking, but I came to you for another kind of help. I want you to change me the way you changed Carmen, so that I can 'see' things with my mind the way that you and Carmen can."

"Please don't ask that of me, Rosalind. We are forbidden to meddle in the life around us. If I were to do that, my whole family would suffer. We would be isolated from the rest of the Cheneshi. I can't do that."

"I don't want to cause you any difficulty, Sways. If you can't, you can't, and that will be the end of it. I have heard that this is forbidden, but I think my case is different. I know of Eldest, your oldest and wisest, who has been deferred to in such matters in the past. I'd like you to connect me with Eldest and let us all discuss this together."

"I will do that."

Sam, Jamal and Rosalind didn't have to change location instead they connected with the Eldest telepathically.

"I understand from Sways that you wish him to change you as he did Carmen," Eldest said, when they contacted him. *"We are not to do such things."*

"I understand, and I think not interfering with other life forms is important," Rosalind said. *"I'm petitioning you, because I think things have changed, and that my situation is excluded from your prohibition."*

"What has changed? Why are you excluded? You are a living creature. How is making changes in you now an appropriate action?"

"You have new information now." Rosalind responded. *"You now know that the Cheneshi themselves were changed in your ancient history by the Lorengi to allow you to survive as a species. As to why I can be excluded I am not part of the life of your planet. Also, this is not a case where you would be tinkering with another life form without it knowing about it. I am a self-aware being, and I am asking you to make the change."*

The conversation with the Eldest went on for a little while longer. As Sam listened he was impressed by the way Rosalind presented her argument to the Eldest and persuaded him to release Sways from the prohibition. She did it forcefully and respectfully and was successful. When the conversation with the

Eldest was over, Sam said he had a few questions and wondered if he could ask them before they took the next step.

"Of course, Sam," Sways said.

"Thank you. In my last visit, we didn't have much opportunity to talk, so I really didn't learn much about you and your fellow Cheneshi. I understand that your families are started from a single Cheneshi seed which grows to maturity and spreads roots. It is from these roots that the rest of the family sprouts. Where does the seed come from?"

"When a Cheneshi comes near the end of their life, the bulb you see at my top flowers and a seed is released from there. That seed floats away to find another place to root and start a family. Many seeds do not find a suitable place. Those that don't whither and fall to the sea bottom to become part of the planet again in that way."

"How long is a Cheneshi life?"

"About three hundred years."

"Thank you," Sam said. *"I've heard that you are part of a world-spanning network to which all Cheneshi are connected,"* Sam said. *"Could you tell me more about that? Is it like, Janus, the global consciousness than has emerged on Earth?"*

"There is nothing the Cheneshi, or from their records, the Lorengi are aware of that is like Janus. Janus is the amalgamation of all consciousness on Earth and is a conscious entity itself. Our network is more like a combination of your H2-net that functions using the implants in your heads, and the telepathy that has surfaced among the H2 population to replace the net.

"The Cheneshi are telepathic, but there is more. We are physically immersed in an enormous amount of data about our planet and the life on it. We don't have eyes, but we 'see' everything at an elemental level, as a flow of shapes without

boundaries, constantly in motion and exchanging energy and matter. Our entire being is caught up in this data. We capture it, store it, and share it with our fronds, trunks, roots and minds. We are inter-connected all the time, but of course we are most attentive to what we choose to focus on at any moment. As now, when I and many others are primarily focused on you and the rest of our visitors."

"How do we appear to you?" Sam asked.

"As a trunk with four limbs and a head, transparent and full of activity within, suspended in the flow of water that surrounds you, and exchanging energy and some matter with your surroundings. For example, your head appears to be heating up the water around it and exchanging gasses with the water. How do we appear to you?"

"We would use visual terms that may not make sense to you. To us you are grand, majestic tree-like creatures, with golden fronds that move with the current, and a trunk that reaches toward the surface of your ocean. Your trunk is about five feet in diameter at your base, and tapers to about half a foot at its top, ninety feet above the ocean floor. Your trunk is a brown-gray color, with a surface that is rough at the base and smoother further up. You appear solid. We can only guess what movement goes on inside. You are a very pleasing sight to us, because most of us have a natural affinity for the trees on our planet."

"Fascinating," Sways said. *"I have never had that described to me before. I'm getting similar responses from the Cheneshi who are listening in."*

Sam turned to Rosalind. *"Thanks, Rosalind, for letting me take the time for this."*

"No problem, Sam. Sways, Eldest has given you permission to proceed."

21

"I do not want to harm you, Rosalind."

"I appreciate that, Sways. I absolve you of any responsibility for the results of your efforts. I just hope you can find the right switches to make the change in my mind as you did in Carmen."

"I already can see that your mind is different. It seems stronger in certain areas. I know what I need to do, but I hesitate. Others of my kind are observing. They're apprehensive as I am. If we were air breathers like you, I would say we are holding our breath."

"Please go ahead with it, Sways, before I lose my nerve."

Rosalind closed her eyes. A sharp pain seared its way through her brain behind her eyes. She didn't remember Carmen saying anything about a pain like that, but Carmen had lost consciousness during her change. The pain went away as quickly as it had come.

She was hit with a flood of data about her surroundings. It was overwhelming at first, but her scientific mind began sorting things out. She observed and relished everything her mind perceived. It was better than she had imagined. Immersed in the ocean, with eyes closed, she "saw" all of the components of the water, and living things suspended and moving in it, including her two companions. They appeared to her just as Sways had described them. Humanoid, transparent shapes with all the movement within. She could even see the thermal energy emanating from their heads warming the water, and the re-breathers exchanging gasses with the components of the water.

She opened her eyes.

Nothing changed. She still perceived everything surrounding her in great detail with her mind.

She just couldn't see it with her eyes!

4 Second Sight

Planet Ocean

Rosalind looked around to be sure, but she knew she was blind! Perhaps it was temporary, but she believed the searing pain meant the damage was permanent. She checked herself, and found that she felt fine, wonderful in fact. There was no residual pain, and she had just been given the sight she wanted.

She doubted her colleagues would be so sanguine about this development, and she was sure that Sways would be devastated if he found out that his action had blinded her. Her absolving him of the responsibility would make no difference. She knew the kind-hearted Cheneshi would be deeply saddened. So he wouldn't find out. Neither would her colleagues, if she could help it. She had "sight." She just had to very quickly learn how to use it.

"Rosalind, are you okay?" Sways asked

"Yes, yes. I'm fine," she answered. She looked at her companions who probably had concerned looks on their goggled faces. *"Really, I'm fine—better than fine, in fact. Sways, thank you so much for giving me this. It is exactly what I wanted. I know you were reluctant to make the change in me, but you went ahead anyway. I thank you for that. You've given me a unique and precious gift."*

"You're welcome. I'm so glad it worked out so well. Will you be leaving right away?" Sways asked.

"No. If you are willing, I would like to stick around for a few days to work with you to hone my skills in using this new sight I've acquired."

"That would be very pleasing. I would love to help you."

"Sounds good, but not right now. I'm fine, but I think I need to rest for a while."

Rosalind turned to her two companions. *"Gentlemen, are you willing to help this elderly lady to her room, so that she can take a little nap?"*

Sam and Jamal swam to her. Together they made their way to the shore. Along the way, Rosalind began to use her new mindsight to guide her. She still had touch and hearing to help. Her new sight gave her more data than her eyes had. She just needed to learn how to interpret it, so she didn't bump into things.

When they got to shore, she leaned on Jamal to take her flippers off. No use making walking more difficult than it had to be. She stood in the shallow water and took her bearings. She saw the tree near the shore that she had noticed before. She concentrated. Amongst the milieu of shapes and movement she picked out the relatively stable shape of Journey. She looked down at the ground to pick out a path. She was confident that she could walk to Journey on her own but accepted Jamal's gesture of putting his right hand under her left elbow to help support the "elderly lady" to her room.

Jamal's continued his support until he had led her into her room, and she sat on her bed.

"Thanks, Jamal, Sam. I think I'll take a little nap now."

They left.

"Athena, would you close the door please?"

"Yes."

Rosalind found it comforting that Athena had chosen a mature woman's voice for herself. When she looked in the direction of the door, her mind "saw" that the material Journey was made of was shaped as an open door. Then it rapidly grew filling the opening completely.

"Thank you, Athena. I need to tell you something in confidence."

"I won't speak about what you tell me to anyone else."

"Thanks, I'm glad I can count on you, my friend."

This was all new to Rosalind. She was having a hard time talking about it. She "looked" around her room. She "saw" her bed with her clothes lying on it. She sat down on the bed, put her elbows on her knees, and her face into her hands. Blind! She was all for new experiences but hadn't expected this.

When Rosalind didn't continue, Athena asked, "What do you wish to tell me Rosalind?"

Rosalind stood up when she heard Athena's question. She wouldn't let herself sink into self-pity. She would make the best of this and see what the future would hold.

"I can see nothing with my eyes, Athena"

"Do you mean you are blind?"

"Well, yes in the conventional sense of the word, but my mind has a live image of everything around me. I asked Sways to alter my brain so that I could see things with my mind that way, the way the Cheneshi can. In the process something was damaged, and I lost the use of my eyes."

"I'm sorry to hear that, Rosalind. What was Sways reaction?"

"I didn't tell him. I knew it would upset him. I also didn't tell Sam or Jamal. I would like to keep everyone from knowing about it as long as I can."

"Ah. This is the thing you want me to avoid disclosing. Why tell me? If I understand these things correctly, if one wants to keep something secret, it is best to tell no one, not even a close friend, like me."

"I'm telling you because I will need your help."

"What can I do?"

"I am going to learn to 'see' well enough with just my mind to get around and function normally. It will take time to interpret the information my mind is picking up. I need you to be my eyes for a while. I want to make it look like nothing has happened."

"I'm still not sure what I can do."

"When the first team arrived here years ago, you provided them with visual and audio recording devices to gather data about the new planet. I would like to have something like that set up so that you can see through the lens and communicate to me what you see. Do you have something like that? I'd like it to be something that wouldn't be obvious to the others if possible."

Athena thought about it for what was a long time for her. A second later, Athena said, "Yes. I can provide the visual pickup you need. I detect that the implant that was used to connect you to Martha and the H2 net when you first arrived at Sunaj is still functioning. We can use that for the audio channel. That way only you will hear what I am saying to you. How will I know which items to bring to your attention?"

"That's an excellent question. We'll use the tried-and-true trial-and-error method. We'll start here in my room as soon as you give me the visual lens."

"I've provided two of them. I thought it would be a good idea to have a spare. They're resting on the shelf that I just opened in your wall.

"Hmmm, I'm beginning to see the challenge already. The opening is in the wall next to the door. Can you make out the difference in the contour of that wall where I created the shelf?"

"Yes, but before I put the lens on, I will need to change my clothes."

Rosalind rose and looked around her room. Her clothes were lying on the bed where she left them. She took her swimsuit off. She was covered with salt from the ocean, and a little sand. She would need to shower first.

Well, she thought, it's all part of the learning process. The bathroom facilities and shower were near the opposite wall. She saw where she needed to go. She walked over to the shower and requested a warm water shower from Athena. The material Journey was made of would absorb the salt, sand and water to be recycled. Warm air was blown at her from several directions to dry her when she was done showering.

"Thank you, Athena. That felt good."

Rosalind walked over to where her clothes were and dressed. Then she went to the shelf Athena had opened and picked up the lenses. She put one in her pocket and pinned the other to her blouse. The small lens felt like it was in the shape of a hummingbird.

"Did you just make this, Athena?"

"Yes, I thought it would be best to have the lens look like something other than a lens."

"It feels like it is shaped like a hummingbird in flight."

"It is. The metal is gold. The lens is one of the shiny facets of the bird's body."

"Clever. How did you make it?"

"Journey is equipped to be able to fabricate things the scientists might need. I'm the one who instructs the fabricator."

"Thank you so much, Athena. It's a perfect disguise, and hummingbirds are my favorite."

"You're welcome. I am going to enjoy helping you. I don't have much to do, except process data for the scientists. You have given me a project of my own. I'm grateful. Shall we start?"

"Yes. First let me tell you what my mind is 'seeing.' Nothing is solid as my eyes would have seen it. Everything around me is mostly empty space. There are no barriers, but there are shapes. The room has a shape, as do the bed and table you extruded from Journey. All the shapes are 'transparent' if that's the right word in this context. Each shape is filled with a swirl of activity, tiny points of 'light' moving about rapidly, a different pace for each different type of material. The activity within the material Journey is made of is moving at a much slower pace than the activity within the shape that is me, for example.

"My mind-view reaches beyond the confines of my room, beyond Journey to the outside where there are other shapes—bushes, trees, and small creatures. Inside of each of the shapes there is constant motion. I have a view through the floor to the ground, and beyond. If I saw that with my eyes, I would get vertigo. Even now, I am wondering why I'm not falling through what appears to be empty space.

"There seems to be a varying degree of rigidity characteristic to each shape that must be imbued by the intelligence that has assembled it. Rigidity is probably a misleading word. It seems like each shape is defined by a set of rules that determines how it interacts with the whole—such as what is allowed to pass into, out of or through the object, how it exchanges matter and energy with its surroundings, how it conducts thermal energy or retains it. For example, my shape

28

exchanges gasses mostly at my mouth, but it exchanges energy all along my shape, as thermal energy, and so on."

"Fascinating, that sounds similar to my impression of the electronic net that circles Earth when I am connected to it. What can you do with what you know of your surroundings?"

"I can walk around my room confidently, and with less confidence around the rest of Journey. Walking around outside will be more challenging, but I'll have you with me to help with that. You will have to help me know who is around me, until I am able to distinguish one from another. If they speak, I'll be fine. If they are just quietly around me, I'll need you to identify them for me. Something that you probably won't be able to help me with is the visual cues we pick up from others that guide us in our interactions. I'll just have to make it up as I go. I have more information to go on than a blind person does, and they do it somehow."

"I understand. What's next?"

"Let's take a walk outside."

"I'm with you. Oh, I've thought of something else."

"What's that?"

"Remember to blink."

Rosalind laughed and said she would.

She walked toward the door. Athena opened it and Rosalind walked into the common room where meals were taken. No one was in the room. She saw the opening to the outside and went toward it. She stepped outside. Jamal was near Journey talking with another of the scientists. When he saw her, he came over to her.

"Rosalind, I thought you were going to take a nap."

When he started talking to her, she looked up toward his head in what she thought would appear to be an attentive gaze. Blinking she found, didn't need conscious thought. Her eyes were functioning normally in a physical sense, so they moistened normally, and blinked on their own.

"I found that all I needed was a shower. I am going to take a walk and test out my new sight with my eyes closed." She closed her eyes, continuing to look at Jamal. "I can see you and all that is around us."

"You want me to come along, in case you trip or something."

"Not this time, I need all my concentration to focus on the new view of things. If I began to trip, or bump into something, I can always use my 'eyes.'"

"Okay but be careful."

"Will do." She turned to go around Journey and walked inland.

"Athena, was the other person Jamal was talking to Josh Reynolds?" she asked, after taking a few steps away from Jamal.

"Very good, Rosalind. It was Josh,"

"I thought so. He stood the way Josh stands, and some of the mannerisms seemed familiar. Well, that's a good start."

She left off talking and concentrated on the ground before her. She tried to fill in the details that her eyes would have given her. They would have told her things like tree, bush, rock, and added color and texture. She was happy just being able to determine what the object was without the highlights at this point.

She continued to walk slowly while attempting to contact Sways telepathically.

"Sways?"

"Rosalind! See I told you that you were telepathic."

"I think your little adjustment helped."

"True, but the foundation was already in place. Where are you?"

"I'm walking about your island, without using my eyes."

"You seem to have adjusted quickly. How are you feeling?"

"I'm doing fine. I just wanted to contact you to see if I could, and to let you know how things are going. I need to go back to concentrating on this new view of things."

"I understand. Let me know if I can help."

Rosalind was pleased with how things were going. She was so pleased she didn't notice the tree root across her path. Athena did.

"Root!" Athena shouted through Rosalind's implant. "You are just about to trip over a tree root."

Rosalind stopped immediately. She looked down and noticed the slightly different pattern crossing over the path she was on. The difference was subtle. It was just those subtleties that her eyes would have caught, and that she would have to be able to discern in this new way of seeing the world.

"Thank you, Athena. It's great to have you on my team."

Rosalind continued to walk through the jungle forest that was on the surface of Sway's island. She was so entranced by the way she was experiencing her environment with her mind that she lost track of time. Athena didn't.

"Rosalind, the sun is going down. The others are gathering for the evening meal. Some are expressing concern about your long absence, especially now that it's getting dark."

"Thanks, Athena. Could you tell them we are in contact via the implant? Let them know that I'm doing fine, and that I'm returning now."

Rosalind searched with her mind for evidence that the light was fading. She didn't see any, but she thought that she might be able to pick it out with more practice. She turned and went back toward Journey. At least, she thought she was headed in the right direction.

"Athena, am I going the right way?"

"Yes. I would have let you know if you weren't. You are following the path you came out on."

Rosalind concentrated, trying to find familiar patterns that would assure her that Athena's claim was true. She didn't doubt Athena. She just wanted to confirm it for herself. She thought she had spotted a few familiar patterns on the return trip. She would get better at this, she told herself as she entered Journey.

The forest was less complicated than what she just stepped into. The entire team was in the common room, choosing what to eat and drink, and talking over what they had discovered that afternoon. So many things her eyes would have described for her immediately she now had to interpret from the data her mind-view provided. She was glad to have Athena's help, but Athena could only do so much for her. She didn't want to overtax her dexterity by ordering something complicated to eat, so when she went to the synthesizer she asked for only a bran muffin and fruit juice.

She picked up her food, and slowly made her way to the table at which Jamal, Travis and Sam were eating. She thought it would make conversation easier for her if she were talking with people she knew well.

It turned out to be true. She knew who everyone was as soon as the conversation started. She turned her head to listen or speak with one of the others. She casually used her eye muscles to focus on the speaker as she would normally. She found that since they didn't expect her to be blind, they didn't think she was.

Rosalind excused herself when she was done and went to her room. She used their expectation that she would be exhausted after what she went through, being an "elderly lady" and all. It worked. Of course, it helped that she was exhausted, and probably looked like she was.

Athena closed the door behind her. Rosalind sighed deeply and prepared for bed. Quite a day, full of amazing new experiences she thought as she was lying in bed, falling into a comfortable, satisfied sleep. She didn't know then that the next day's experiences would be even more extraordinary and laced with danger.

5 Follow the Light

Aboard Thelika, in front of the Barrier

"There has to be another way," Jesse pleaded.

Carmen looked at Jesse and wished she could find another way to ease his worry. They had been at the location where they could see the barrier and the ships for a ship-day and night. The team had discussed what they had found, and what to do about it. Carmen suggested that she take one of their ships to the ships they were seeing behind the barrier—if they could find where those ships were. Jesse didn't like that plan.

The team believed the evidence of their eyes to the extent that the barrier and the ships it appeared to enclose existed—somewhere. That led to the reasonable conclusion that there might be beings on those ships, and that they might need some help. That led to the discussion of what they could do. In a normal situation, they would mount a rescue effort. This was not a normal situation.

Carmen and Jesse were having breakfast in the room they shared. It was early morning of the second day. It was wonderful to have the opportunity to spend time with Jesse, but Carmen would have been happier if the situation weren't so stressful.

Jesse sat his coffee cup down. "I just don't want to lose you, Carmen. You could be killed on a trip like that."

She smiled. "We knew it would be this way when we

offered to lead the effort to explore the worlds that the Lorengi had visited."

"I knew it meant that we would be apart more than we liked. I never thought it would come to a point where we had to make a decision that put your life in danger. I realize that exploration comes with risks, but not this."

"Well, we agree that it would be better if we could find another way. Let's talk with those who have much more exploration experience than either of us. Thelika, Ahleeto, are you available to talk things over?"

"Yes," they said at the same time.

"Have you thought more about our situation while Jesse and I were sleeping?"

"Yes," Ahleeto said. "We haven't come any closer to understanding what we are seeing. Yesterday, you suggested that you go there to see what we can do for those who might be trapped inside the ships. That would be highly risky even without the uncertainties present in this situation. If we went there, we might be trapped. We don't even know how to get wherever 'there' is."

"See!" Jesse exclaimed. "Even they don't think it's a good idea."

Carmen laughed. "That just about sums up our situation. So, should we just pack up, and go home?"

The others protested. They didn't think they should leave either. They just didn't like the plan they had come up with so far.

"Okay," Carmen said. "I don't think we're going to come up with a solution anytime soon on our own. I think we need more minds."

"Who are you thinking of?" Jesse asked.

"Sam Baxter and Rosalind Atwood. Sam has been losing

himself in metaphysical musings recently. Rosalind has been seeking a practical example of what she calls the 'strange physics' that Jamal's mind swims around in. So let's include Jamal, too. I'm pretty sure that what we have in front of us will fascinate all three of them. They may be just the combination of thinkers we need to help us find out what to do next."

Sam Baxter woke in his room in Journey, reminding himself why he decided to come along on this trip. Lately he'd been in a bit of a daze which was unusual for him. Sam had always been more deliberate in his actions. He hoped this new-to-Humans planet, and the delightful Cheneshi who were native to it would provide new perspectives on the questions he'd been struggling with.

Also his wife, Senator Lesley Anderson, told him to get out of town. He was driving her crazy with his existential questions and ramblings. She said that she had a country and world to help adjust to a changing Human population.

There was someone he knew who wouldn't tire of the conversation. Janus was struggling with the same nebulous quandary.

"Janus?" Sam said out loud.

"Yes, Sam. You're on Ocean. How are we doing with the central question of our being?"

"You do have a sense of humor, or was that just sarcasm?"

"A little humor and a little sarcasm for both of us. We are both going in metaphysical circles."

"Thanks for joining me on the carousel of the mind. I am not minimizing the great strides we've made improving life on Earth. With a greatly expanded population of H2s those efforts will continue without my help. I'm left to wonder what it's all about."

"Humans have been wondering about that since they were able to frame the question."

"H2s seem to be the legacy of an intervention," Sam said. "That adds new dimensions to the age-old question. Was it an intervention, or some unusual, natural event that caused the H2s to begin emerging at the beginning of the twenty-first century? If an intervention, who intervened? What did they have in mind? Setting aside the potential agenda of a possible intervener I think we are not done. I've notice what H2s are capable of doing is expanding. Where are we heading?"

"Are the H2s, and the global consciousness they triggered to play some greater role than making the improvements on Earth?" Janus asked. *"Perhaps something for which there is no role model, something that has not existed before, something that we can't even imagine at this point. Is that the question?"*

"Yes," Sam said. "Sounds like you've been thinking about this since we last discussed it together."

"I have. I am interested in this myself, being the 'global consciousness' triggered by the advent of H2s.'"

"I'm not sure what you mean. Aren't we seeking an answer to the same question?"

"Yes and no. I am interested in the destiny of the Human part of me and will be involved in that destiny. I am comprised of the consciousness of others besides that of Humans."

Sam hadn't given much thought to that, but Janus was more than Human consciousness.

"Right, like the whales, porpoise, and dolphins."

"When I first became self-aware," Janus said, *"I assumed that I was comprised of only the consciousness of Humans and those sea-going mammals you mention. As time went on, I found that there was a level of consciousness in all creatures, and that their consciousness was also part of me.*

"I learned I could communicate at some level with most creatures. When I did, it greatly expanded my understanding of life on Earth. My self-knowledge didn't end there."

"What do you mean?"

"Sam, you are an organic being, and a sensitive one at that. You are able to detect life in the smallest plants and animals. In addition, Human scientists can detect life at microscopic levels with their instruments.

"I am a being comprised of consciousness. As you can detect life, I can detect consciousness, and I have learned that there is an element of consciousness in all components of matter, organic and inorganic, at the most fundamental level. The larger and more complex the matter is, the greater level of consciousness, combining the consciousness of its component parts. You could view your consciousness as the sum of the consciousness of the thirty trillion cells within your body, your component parts, and..."

"...and you, Janus, are the sum of all the components of consciousness of Earth," Sam said, awestruck at the implications of the conclusion.

He had never thought of Janus as more than the sum of the consciousness of Humans and the obvious sea mammals. He was silent, humbled by the magnitude of the entity he so casually thought of as his friend, an entity that Sam thought was mostly focused on the affairs of Earth's most arrogant creatures, Humans.

"I sense what you're thinking, Sam. Relax. I too am still trying to get used to what I am. Please go on considering me as your friend. I would be greatly saddened if this new perspective were to create distance between us."

"Okay. I'll try, but I am...well it will take time for me to get used to this new understanding of you. Wait, I guess I'm already getting used to it, because I have a question. When you learn something do all your parts learn it at the same time?"

"I often work directly with Humans and whales for example," Janus said. *"The knowledge gained in those activities is available to the whole population. I think you are asking a different question though, and I think the answer to your question is the same for you as it is for me.*

"When you are enlightened by learning something new, Sam, I believe your entire self is raised to a higher level. Some would speak in terms of your individual cells vibrating at a higher frequency. Others would call it an awakening.

"I believe it is that way with me as well. When I am enlightened by some experience my components vibrate at a higher frequency, are awakened to a higher level. In this way, life is one awakening followed by another, with all of us moving toward a greater understanding of the universe of which we are part.

"I am deeply interested in these questions and will continue to work with you as you seek the answers. Right now I should alert you that Carmen will be contacting you. She has encountered something unusual."

"Sam? Janus says you are on Ocean, and that Rosalind and Jamal are with you."

"That's right Carmen. What's up?"

"I have two teams here at a location where there is something very unusual, and there may be unknown beings in trouble. We would like you three to come here. We need help understanding what we have and what to do."

"I certainly will come. I'll check with Rosalind and Jamal, but I'm pretty sure they'll be interested. How do we get there?"

"I'll send Katala to get you."

"Okay. I'll have Rosalind contact you if she or Jamal have any questions."

Rosalind was just waking when Sam contacted her. She came wide awake when he mentioned the "something unusual" and "unknown beings" parts of Carmen's message.

"I'll be ready in a moment."

True to her prediction she was up, packed and waiting outside Journey when Sam and Jamal became out. Jamal was still rubbing the sleep out of his eyes.

When Katala said she had arrived they teleported to the ship, and immediately went to Carmen's location. Once there, they joined the others on Thelika. Carmen had Thelika bring up the view of the phenomenon on the main screen. Rosalind's true condition became apparent when she couldn't see what was on the screen. They all stared at her.

Jamal broke the silence with his exclamation. "You're blind! But...." He couldn't believe it. Rosalind didn't look any different. His face showed his concern for his colleague, his friend.

"Calm down, Jamal. It's not a big deal. It happened when Sways changed me. I'm perfectly happy with the result."

"Why didn't you tell us?" Jamal asked.

"I didn't want Sways to find out. I think it would upset him deeply."

"How are you doing?" Sam asked.

"Me. I'm doing fine. I have more information about my surroundings than I would have with just my eyes, and I'm not distracted and misled by my eyes as I think you all are."

"What do you mean?" Carmen asked.

"Thelika, what do you estimate is the size of the barrier before us on the screen?" Rosalind asked.

"Based on visual information only, I estimate that it was

about a tenth of a light-second in height and half that in width, roughly ellipsoid in shape."

"That's what I thought," Rosalind said. "The image before us is not three-dimensional, so ellipse would be more accurate. It's a two-dimensional representation of something, as if it were projected on a screen. The line surrounding the picture is charged with some form of energy. I pick up the consciousness in the sphere in front of us, and there is more. This is a live picture of a scene somewhere else."

The entire team was in Thelika's common room. There was complete silence after Rosalind listed what she had discovered in her view of the anomaly. She had a better grasp of what was there than they did looking at it with their eyes.

"What do you mean there is more?" Carmen asked.

"There are specs of consciousness in the non-Lorengi ships."

Rosalind turned to Carmen. "I know you can 'see' this way, too, Carmen. Being blind perhaps my sense of these things is more acute. Why don't we all join together to get this mind-view of things. If we all have the same information, we can make better plans."

They found comfortable places and Carmen led them into it as she had before. They closed their eyes and used telepathy to communicate. Rosalind began the tour of her perceptions.

"First, look at the fringe. There seems to be some energy crackling along the outline."

"What do you think that is?" Matthew asked.

"I've no idea," Rosalind said. *"I wonder. Thelika, are you seeing that? It is very faint, but is that energy present there?"*

"You're right Rosalind," Thelika said. *"It is faint, so faint that I missed it in my initial scan. It is definitely there, and it is closing."*

"What!" Carmen shouted.

"Now that I have a clearer perception of what is in front of us, I see the energy ring as a frame of a window to wherever those ships are. I detect that the size of the window is shrinking," Thelika answered.

"How fast?" Carmen asked

"Barely perceptible. Based on the current rate, I'd say that the area within the window has decreased by a thousandth of a percent since we first arrived here."

"Thank you, Thelika. Please let us know if the rate changes." Carmen said. *"Time has just become a critical factor in our deliberations. Okay, let's continue with our view."*

"I think I see one of the points of consciousness you mentioned," Jesse said.

"If this is a 'screen-like' projection, can it only be viewed from this perspective?" Sam asked. *"If I think of it as a screen, roughly vertical before us, I wonder what it would look like from below, or from the other side?"*

"I will move us to those locations," Thelika said. *"First let's see what it looks like from below."*

A moment later, they were in position that they assumed would be below the projection.

"Do you get anything on your instruments, Thelika?" Ahleeto said. *"We are seeing nothing."*

"No Excellency. I'll shift us to a position that would be behind it."

Again, there was nothing. Thelika brought them back to the front of the image. It looked as it was before they had moved. The group let out a collective sigh and opened their eyes. The view didn't change for Rosalind.

"Thank you, Rosalind," Carmen said. "Like you said, we all now have the same basis for discussion. The window can only be seen from this point of view. With Thelika's new information we also now know that we don't have unlimited time to come up with a plan."

"You're welcome," Rosalind answered. "Let's pause from observing and start listing thoughts we have regarding what is before us. Even minor things could help."

"I think we have proved that it is not an image projected into our minds," Sam said. "If it were, it would have shifted position with us as we moved around it."

"It isn't at the physical location where our eyes see it," Jamal said.

"We all are assuming that this is an image of something that does exist, somewhere," Ashira said.

"I'd like to ask a question," Matthew Ronson said. "Besides the sphere and what we believe are Lorengi ships near it, there are other two ships in the same area. Ahleeto, do you recognize those other ships?"

"No. In all our time exploring the galaxy, we did not encounter any other civilizations, besides Humans on Earth and the Cheneshi on Ocean. We found ruins on some planets, but no live, space-faring race."

"That's what I thought. So besides the weird fact that what we see is not really here, we have discovered other races. That's fantastic!"

"Yes, it is," Ahleeto said, "and as long as we are listing things about our discovery, I want to include a hope that there are Lorengi in the Lorengi ships or in the sphere."

"We all share that hope, Ahleeto," Carmen said. "I've got a question that might be helpful. If there are Lorengi somehow connected to those ships and the sphere, how did they get there?"

"They traveled the same way we do," Jesse said. "They

teleported. Do you think the other ships did the same thing, and that somehow what happened to them all was a result of teleporting?"

"I suppose that's possible," Carmen said, "but those other ships look like they are powered by propulsion engines of some sort. Still there must be some common element."

"The other ships may also be interstellar ships," Jamal said.

"I think it is likely that they are able to travel among the stars," Rosalind observed. "If they are, they will have found a way to bypass the constraint of not being able to travel faster than light within the observable universe, or they'd be very old when they arrived at their destination."

"Thanks for putting words to the feeling I was getting," Carmen said. "What does it mean?"

"I'm going out on a limb here," Rosalind said, "but I think what we have here is a window into the dimension through which we travel when we teleport. Ahleeto, didn't your scientists call it Dimensional Shift Transport."

"Yes, but don't ask me to explain DTS."

"That won't be necessary at this point," Rosalind said. "It supports what Jamal and I have been thinking about teleporting and telepathy as well. They both use another dimension to get something done that is impossible within our four-dimension, sensory, frame of reference—our 'observable' universe. I think that somehow, we are seeing ships that are trapped in that dimension."

"How are we able to see it, if it is outside our known universe?" Matthew asked.

"I don't know how we are able to see it," Rosalind said, "but I didn't say the dimension was outside of our universe. We just usually can't see it. Perhaps the beings in one of those ships, perhaps the Lorengi, recognize the dilemma they face, and are sending a visual SOS. However this image has come to us, we are the only ones in a position to respond."

"I agree that we are the only ones able to respond," Carmen said. "We want to help, but how do we find them?"

"We are detecting aspects of their existence, Carmen. Which is the most pronounced?" Rosalind asked

"The brightness of the consciousness coming from that sphere."

"Then we follow the light!"

6 The Plan

Aboard Thelika

"How does one follow the light?" Jamal asked. It was the question that was on everyone's mind.

"I don't know," Rosalind answered, "but I think it's all we have."

Carmen thought about it for a moment and then asked Thelika how the ship guided itself.

"I've always used coordinates as a guide," the ship answered.

"On mechanical ships," Jesse said, "there are often tech manuals that describe all ship functions. Do you have information about the science behind how you move about?"

"There are a few technical papers on the subject in my data storage. I just reviewed them. They all start from the assumption that we know where we are going before we start out."

"Sounds like a good idea to me," Jesse said.

The group laughed. They all thought it was a good idea. They just didn't happen to have coordinates for a location within a dimension which might not have space-time reference points.

Carmen saw that they were getting nowhere. So she decided to shift the focus for a while. "How long has this window been here? Ahleeto, did your explorers report anything like this?"

Ahleeto shook her head, "No."

"I'd guess six thousand years, or so," Ashira said.

They all looked at the diminutive young woman.

"Well, my guess is based on a few assumptions," Ashira said. "Ahleeto said she lost contact with her people about six thousand years ago. If they're trapped in that area, it could have been what happened when they were lost to her. If we're guessing that this window was created by beings from one of the ships we see, and further that maybe it was the Lorengi, then it was created about six thousand years ago.

"They must be dead after such a long time. If so, then how can they be the ones who created the window or are sustaining it? I guess my guess wasn't such a good one."

"Don't give up on it yet, Ashira." Ahleeto said. "I haven't given up on my people. When I left them, a number were deciding to upload their essence to a system to live as a stored personality, like I did. If the Lorengi are at this location, they may all be in the same state as I am, and would not have aged, let have alone died."

"That's one possible explanation," Rosalind said, "and probably the right one. I have another notion of what might be going on. Space and time are dimensions of our observable universe. Neither may exist in the dimension in which these ships are trapped. So no time may have passed since this happened to them, whereas, as Ashira proposed, six thousand years has gone by for us since it happened. Before you ask, no, I don't know what existence would be like in a dimension without space or time."

"Wait a minute," Jesse said, "why aren't we trapped inside this dimension. We teleport all the time."

"Conjecture is all I have," Rosalind said. "I think something happened at the moment in time when the Lorengi, if it is them, were teleporting, and the other ships were in the middle of whatever constituted FTL travel for them. That something aborted their normally inconsequential pass through the dimension, and they got stuck there. I don't know what that something was. We may find out when we go there."

"Hold on," Jamal said. "Why won't we be trapped if we go there?"

"I have an idea about that, Jamal," Rosalind said, "and I need you to stay here to make it work. So getting stuck won't be a concern for you. Would you be willing to stay behind?"

Jamal was visibly torn. There would undoubtedly be interesting discoveries on the trip, but his interest in new things did not extend to jumping off a cliff into a foggy abyss of unknown depth.

"I'll stay here, but you have to come back and tell me what it was like. What do you have in mind, Rosalind?"

"There are two things that distinguish our trip to this location from those who are there. One is that we Humans are able to see things and do things that others there may not be able to see or do. Another would be that we leave an anchor here in the form of a Lorengi ship with some of us aboard. I don't know if that anchor will help, but it may. I think what happened to those other ships was so sudden that it wasn't possible for them to have someone on the other side to help."

"What if the window closes while we're there?" Ashira asked.

"Thelika, has there been any change in the rate that the window area is shrinking?" Rosalind asked.

"Not that I can detect, but it would be difficult to detect in such a short time."

"I wonder why it's shrinking," Carmen said.

"Perhaps it takes more energy to sustain it than is available," Rosalind offered.

"Why worry?" Matthew asked. "At the current rate, it wouldn't close completely for a hundred thousand days, or about two hundred seventy years from now."

"I would feel more comfortable if it weren't shrinking at all, Matthew," Carmen said. "If it's shrinking because whatever is holding it is weakening, it could collapse all at once at any time. You see if Ashira's guess about its age is right, and if this rate of shrinkage had been constant since the beginning, using your calculation it would have collapsed over five thousand years ago. I'd say that means it has begun to weaken recently, and that concerns me."

Carmen kept the conversation going, while in the back of her mind she was thinking about how to guide Thelika.

"I'm planning to go on this trip," Carmen said. "It sounds like Rosalind is too. We'll be taking Thelika and Ahleeto. Who else wants to go?"

"I'm going if you are," Jesse said.

When it looked like Carmen might protest, Sam said, "I think that's a good idea. Having a variety of perspectives and skills will be helpful. With Jesse going, I will stay here."

"I'd like to go," Ashira said. She was the most junior of the scientists. She didn't think it was her place to self-appoint herself to the venture.

Carmen looked at her and smiled. "Thanks, Ashira. I'd be glad to have you with us, but please take a moment to consider that you might not get back."

"I still want to go," Ashira said.

"Okay, you're with us. I don't think it would be wise to risk more people on this trip, so unless someone else is very eager to go, we have our team."

No one spoke up and Carmen was glad of it. She didn't have any idea of what they were getting into. She wouldn't want to lose anyone, let alone all of them. The fewer the better.

"What do you plan to do when you get there?" Jamal asked. "Because the window is shrinking, you should probably act as if your time is limited. It would be a good idea to list the objectives, and then prioritize them."

"Find out who is stuck there and get them out, is what I think we're doing," Carmen said.

"That's a good overall objective," Jamal said. "Whose door will you knock on first? There are several ships there."

Thelika said, "We may be able to communicate once we are there. With that I would contact the two Lorengi ships as a starting point."

"That's a good idea, Thelika," Ahleeto said. "If we can communicate, I would like to be the one to contact the sphere, to learn whether there are Lorengi in there."

"Thelika, could you map the area, highlighting the location of the other ships?" Rosalind asked. "I don't know if our communication will be recognizable to the beings in the non-Lorengi ships. We'll be landing near the Lorengi ships, but when we begin to look for the other ships I would like to have an idea where they are."

"If you have time," Jamal said, "it would be useful to gather some kind of description of the characteristics of the 'dimension' or whatever it is."

"I will be recording during our entire stay," Thelika said.

"What do you think the situation is there?" Sam asked. "Those ships don't seem to have moved since we've been here.

Rosalind, you said you thought this was a 'live' picture of the screen. I see no movement. Are they truly stopped in place, or is something else going on?"

"We can't know from here. Setting aside the mystery of how we are able to see them at all, my best guess is that we see no movement because time and space, if they exist there, are different.

"They could be trapped as a fly in amber. If that's the case, we may meet a similar fate when we pop in there. That could mean the show is over for them and us. That is too limiting a scenario for my mind. I'm hoping something else is going on. I'm hoping that we'll have sufficient freedom to have an impact that will change things and allow us to get everyone out to safety."

Carmen thought the discussion had gone as far as it could, and that it was time to face the question of how to get there. She thought of something.

"Let's get back to how we can get there. I've got an idea. When we teleport, we know where we intend to be at our next location. That location is 'real' to us. Because it is, we believe in it as a valid destination. We can intend to be there, and then we are there in an instant."

"But we don't have that in this case." Jesse protested.

"I agree that we don't have coordinates within our 'observable universe,' to use Rosalind's term. We do have an objective to be at another location. We just need to find a way to make that location as real to us as some point within our four-dimensional frame of reference."

"If we could do that going in, we would have an even clearer target for the trip out," Jesse said. "Wait, if it is so easy, and there are Lorengi there, why don't they just pop themselves back out?"

While the group discussed Carmen's suggestion, Sam contacted Janus.

"In case you aren't focused on us, I thought I'd better alert you that some of us are about to attempt to do something very unusual."

"I am following this, Sam. I'm surprised that you haven't volunteered to make the leap yourself. Are you 'getting too old for this?'"

"Not yet. It's something else. The volunteers are putting themselves at risk. I want to do what I can to make sure they get back. I have a feeling that I am going be more effective if I stay on this side."

"I share your concern. I don't know what you or I will be able to do either, but the footing is surer here."

"Wait, you don't have feet."

"Actually, I have billions of feet, and flippers too."

"Okay, okay, back to business," Sam said. *"I don't know what's coming. I may have an immediate need for your help."*

"I'll be ready."

"Thanks. Could you alert Sways and the Cheneshi?"

"We have been eaves dropping through Janus already, Sam" Sways said. *"Sounds like a fascinating but dangerous undertaking."*

"Thanks, Sways. It is reassuring to have Janus and the Cheneshi aware."

Sam checked back into the conversation.

"We'll know more when we get there," Rosalind said. "Some possibilities come to mind. They might be incapable of doing anything. I don't care for that possibility, because we may find ourselves similarly disabled. Another is that they just got there and haven't had time to respond. A variation on this last one is that they don't know where they are, or what to do to get back."

"I thought we said that they landed there about six thousand years ago," Matthew said.

"That's still the most likely scenario," Rosalind said. "If time doesn't exist where they are, no time will have passed since they arrived."

"That sounds crazy. Why wouldn't the same thing happen to you when you go there?"

"It sounds crazy to me, too, Matthew," Rosalind said, "but we will know what happened, and what needs to be done. I'm hoping that's enough to make the difference."

"Any other discussion?" Carmen asked. No one said anything. "Alright, when do we go? It's still morning, ship time. Do we wait until tomorrow?"

"I'm for going ahead," Rosalind said. The rest agreed.

"Today it is!" Carmen said. "All ashore, who are going ashore, or to Katala in this case."

"Rosalind used the term 'anchor' for the ship and staff that will remain," Sam said, addressing the rescue team. "That is a good metaphor for our duty here. If there is something funny going on with time over there, it could be that those of us on this side will have a long wait, with no communication from you.

"That won't matter. We will stay aboard here for as long as it takes. Janus and the Cheneshi are aware of what you are about to undertake and are ready to help if something happens. Although we aren't sure what we could do, we will try. I'll go to the other ship now, but on an occasion such as this, I think we ought to note that this is a major expansion of the scope of Human and Lorengi activity. Come back to us."

Sam and the others teleported to Katala. Carmen looked around at her small and quiet team—Rosalind, Ashira, Ahleeto, Jesse, Thelika and herself. A strong team, she thought. She hoped it would be enough.

She gestured for them to sit down. She took Ashira's hand.

"Ashira, stay mentally close to me as we go through this. I won't let go of your hand, but don't let your concentration drift away. We don't know what we are getting into."

She nodded to the group and closed her eyes.

"Let's join our minds and focus on the bright sphere in front of us. Believe in your sense of it as strongly as you can. It is a valid location. We will want Thelika to arrive between the two Lorengi ships already there. Focus on that space. That is where we are going, and something that we must hold onto. That is where we will be when we arrive. We might not have the ability to confirm it with our senses, so let's believe at the outset, that the space between those ships is where we will be when the trip is over."

Carmen felt the intense concentration of the team. It was as strong as it was going to be. If they could move there at all, this was their best chance. She gave the command to teleport. She sensed they had moved. The next thing she sensed was a mind-shattering, mental scream coming from Ashira.

7 In Touch but Out of Time

On Thelika - Inside the Window

Carmen wondered why she hadn't heard Ashira's scream in her ears. She found out when she opened her eyes, and almost screamed herself. She stared into nothingness. It wasn't black. It didn't have any color or any characteristic at all. It wasn't empty. It just wasn't. If any perception came to mind, not to her eyes, but to her mind, it was of an all-pervasive blankness. She realized that Ashira was still screaming. Ashira was clinching Carmen's hand.

"Ashira! I'm here. Feel your hand touching mine. You are not alone. Easy now. I'd say take a deep breath, but that might not be possible. Calm yourself. You're a scientist. This isn't scary, it's just different. What am I saying? It is very different."

Carmen felt the pressure on her hand ease, but Ashira still held on. For her own reassurance, Carmen was glad Ashira hadn't let go.

"Sorry. I opened my eyes and felt like...like I must have died or something."

"Understandable," Rosalind said. *"There is no light, no sound. I'm not breathing, and yet...I'm conscious."*

"Is everyone else present?" Carmen asked. *"Jesse, Thelika, Ahleeto?"*

"I'm here," Jesse said.

"As am I," Thelika said. *"Excellency?"*

"I'm here, Thelika," Ahleeto answered, *"but I don't really know if that is the right word. How can one be here, be present in nothingness?*

"Let's start with that," Rosalind said. *"I can touch the part of Thelika that I am sitting on. That's a comfort. I'm not breathing. I checked for a pulse and found that my heart is not beating. I'm confident I am conscious because of this conversation we are having."*

"What's all that add up to?" Jesse asked. *"Did we all die as Ashira thought? Is this an afterlife conversation?"*

"I'm not sure this will help," Ahleeto said, *"but I wasn't alive in a corporeal sense before. I feel no difference in my status, nor does communicating with you seem any different. I don't think you died."*

"I agree, Ahleeto," Carmen said. *"I don't feel any different, but like Rosalind said, we're not breathing, and our hearts have not taken a beat since we arrived. Rosalind, you thought time might not exist here. Is what we are experiencing a result of that?"*

"Impossible to confirm, but that seems to fit," Rosalind answered. *"Everything about us has stopped. We are living in the present, and this moment seems eternal. We are conscious, and able to continue communicating all within this moment—no past, no future, just now. Fascinating!"*

"How about space? Jesse asked. *"You said that space might not exist here either. We can feel when we touch. I can feel my body. It has volume as does the part of Thelika I am sitting on. Yet when I try to see, wherever I look there is 'nothingness,' like Ahleeto said. Is this what we might expect if 'space' didn't exist here, Rosalind?"*

"I don't have any more answers than anyone else, but like our 'time' hypothesis, that seems to fit."

"But how could we have dimension and volume in a place where space didn't exist?" Ashira asked.

"We all are sensing the same thing," Rosalind said, *"with the possible exception of Ahleeto. Our bodies seem to be here, yet nothing else is. It's not just empty space, there doesn't seem to be 'space.' Okay, let's face that fact—we're here, but there's no 'here' here. I've been hypothesizing that when we teleport we go through this dimension, or a place like it. I wouldn't think we would become immaterial when we do. What we're experiencing seems to confirm that."*

"If we can't see, if there are no directions because there is no space, how will we find the sphere and those ships?" Ashira asked.

"I'll try answering that one," Carmen said. *"I'll bet that we all have a memory of where we were sitting before we left. Now stand up and slowly come to the center of the area you remember we were sitting around."*

They did as Carmen asked and bumped into each other.

"Well, we now know we are all here. We knew where we were and the relative location of the others in our group. We stepped toward those locations and found each other. You're right Ashira, we don't have direction, but we do have location.

"Thelika created a map of the location of all the other ships we think are in this place with us. That will help us move toward them. The other thing that will help is that consciousness still has brightness to our minds. In that, we have a light to guide us, not with our eyes, but with our minds. We also can use communication. I'll bet that Thelika has already used that. Am I right Thelika?"

"Yes, Carmen. I wanted to be sure we teleported to the right location, so I contacted the two Lorengi ships we were to land between. None of my sensors are working. Or probably

more accurately, they are functioning but what they usually measure doesn't exist here. So I communicated with the ships using telepathy. As Carmen said, I could sense their consciousness on either side of our current location."

"What did they say?" Carmen asked.

"That they had recently arrived. They wondered where I'd come from, since I wasn't with them just before they got here."

"That seems to support our hypothesis about time," Rosalind said.

"What did you tell them?" Carmen asked.

"I said that I would talk with them later. That I had to alert my passengers as to our location. I was evasive, which made me a little uncomfortable."

"I understand, Thelika. It probably comes from being around Humans too long," Ahleeto said, with a smile that no one could see. *"Did you ask them about the Lorengi?"*

"No, Excellency. I thought that would lead into a conversation in which I would be required to disclose more than I should at this time. I did not sense any Lorengi aboard either ship."

"As eager as I am to find out about them, you made the right choice." Ahleeto said. *"If the Lorengi are not aboard the ships, perhaps they are in the sphere."*

"How can they feel that they just arrived?" Ashira asked. *"How can we have arrived at nearly the same time as them?"*

"Not the same time, Ashira," Rosalind said, *'but the same moment. There is only one moment here, and we all share it. It is odd to us. We think they arrived six thousand years ago, but in this dimension, the clock hasn't moved forward one tick. I'm not saying that I've adjusted to that notion myself. I may never adjust. Still, I can talk about the concept without fully believing or understanding it."*

"Time may not be occurring here, but it is where we have come from," Carmen said. *"That window frame we passed through to get here is shrinking. We don't know how much time elapsed back home. We don't know how much time we have left. So unless we want to stay in this 'moment,' we'd better get busy. We know what our objective is. We had a plan which still seems like a good one, but it needs to be adapted to our new situation."*

"Yes, Carmen," Ahleeto said. *"We need to contact the others ships that are here, and we need to figure out how to get them out of this place. It might be a good idea to divide the work. I'm willing to do anything, but please let me be the one to contact the sphere to see if there are Lorengi in the there."*

Carmen could sense the six-thousand-years of emotion of yearning to know what happened to her people surging, rising up within Ahleeto. She was so close to possibly finding out, so close to being with her people that she could barely hold it in.

"Of course, Ahleeto, you must be the one. Will you reach out to your people for us? We would love to meet them."

8 Jarruda the Elder

On Thelika

"Do you have a specific person in mind to contact?" Carmen asked.

"There is a leader, close to what you would call a queen. Her name is Jarruda. If she still lives, I will try to contact her."

A mental hush fell over the small group of adventurers as Ahleeto prepared herself to speak with her people.

"Will we be able to understand what you are saying to them?" Ashira asked.

"Yes, child," Ahleeto assured her. *"Unless there is a concept that you are unfamiliar with, when using telepathy, you quickly learn to understand. Thelika will help."*

"Jarruda, are you there?"

"Ahleeto! Is that you?"

"Yes, Honored Mother."

"How sweet to communicate with you directly, Honored Daughter. We have both now given attention to the formalities. Let's leave off the titles, shall we?"

"Of course. It is more precious than you know for me to be able to communicate with you."

"I missed you, Daughter, when you volunteered to monitor the Humans a hundred revolutions ago. Does your communicating with me at this point mean that the much sought-after progress has happened in such a short time?"

"Oh, Mother, there is so much to tell. First, are all Lorengi with you? Although the sphere is large, it is a small space for everyone. Have all Lorengi decided to enter a stored personality state? Are they all within the sphere with you?"

"Yes nearly all are here and in that state. There remain a small number who wanted to stay and continue our work. You will find them working away on some of the more interesting planets we explored."

Ahleeto knew that none of the Lorengi were left that her mother referred to and thought how difficult it was going to be to bring that news to her and the rest of her people.

"The rest of us saw the end of the Lorengi looming in the future and decided to ensure our continuation in this way. We were on our way to visit another galaxy when we got stuck here. Our scientists are working on what happened. It shouldn't be long before we are on our way. We hoped to find new wondrous things on our journey and return from time to time to see if our great hope for the Humans has been realized.

"I thought you were going to stay on that ocean planet with Thelika until you found evidence of progress with the Humans, Ahleeto. Yet here you are. Another curiosity is that you have managed to be here in the same fix as we are, and at the same time. I think that you have much to tell us, Daughter. Everyone with me here is listening. Please go ahead."

"Thelika is here with me, along with several Humans. Yes, the Humans have developed wonderfully. It has taken much longer than you think. You have been trapped in this place of nothing for approximately six thousand revolutions."

"What are you saying? We have just arrived."

Ahleeto could tell what she had told her mother had shaken her. She decided to give her some recognizable support.

"Are your scientists listening, Mother?"

"Yes, as I said, everyone aboard is. Nassada did you catch what my daughter said?"

"Yes, Excellency, and I am listening with a mixture of incredulity and excitement at what the Honored Ahleeto has claimed. Please continue, Honored One."

"Thank you Nassada," Ahleeto said. *"It is good to communicate with you. I'm glad you are present. You know about how we shift from one point to another."*

"As much as any of us know, yes."

"As I understand it," Ahleeto continued, *"our concept is that we go through another dimension to accomplish it."*

"That is what we believe."

"You are now in that dimension. Something happened when you began your shift, and you became caught in the dimension you had intended to pass through. In this dimension, time and space do not exist. Time has not passed here, but in the space you left time has passed. Six thousand revolutions of the Lorengi home planet have occurred since you left it."

"Not possible," Jarruda said.

"Not impossible, Excellency," Nassada said, *"but I would like to know more. How is it that you are here, Ahleeto?"*

"We were shown that you in the sphere and other ships were stuck here. When we saw what your situation was, we were determined to rescue you and the other ships. We found a way to come here, and here we are."

Ahleeto told them about how the Humans had developed. She said the minds of some of them had the ability to see farther than the Lorengi, and that in that mind-view the combined consciousness of the Lorengi in the sphere stood out as a beacon.

"The characteristics of this place are more obvious to those who have hearts that would usually beat and lungs that

would normally breathe. Neither of those things occurs here. The Humans with me on Thelika found those facts disturbing but adjusted quickly. They are now thinking about how to succeed in this rescue effort."

"How can any of this be, Nassada?" Jarruda asked.

"I believe that Ahleeto believes what she says. I am willing to consider the possibility it is all true, but she hasn't told us how it could have happened and what to do about it."

"I don't know what happened to cause you and the others to get caught here, perhaps when we contact the others, we may find out. We also don't know who created the visual presentation of your situation here.

"As to how we got here, Carmen spotted the dazzling brightness of the concentration of consciousness in the sphere you are traveling in. We used that marker to guide us as we ventured into this dimension. We believe that same technique can be used to get everyone out.

"I would tell you more details, but there is a limit to the time we have to leave. The window we came through is shrinking. We don't know if there is another way to keep us from getting trapped in this moment forever."

"If that is so, daughter, what do you want of us?"

"I'm not the leader of this mission, Mother. That would be the Human, Carmen. Now that I have given you the background, I'd like her to tell you what we need to do."

"Please go ahead, I would be very happy to meet Carmen."

"As I am honored to meet you, Jarruda," Carmen said. *"Three other Humans are with us, Ashira, Rosalind and Jesse. Ashira and Rosalind are scientists. Nassada, I would suggest that you begin a separate conversation with Rosalind, she has the most well-developed theoretical basis for discussing the science of our predicament."*

"I will do that," Nassada. *"How do I make the connection?"*

"Rosalind, this is Nassada," Carmen said.

"A fascinating opportunity. Good to meet you Nassada. Let's discuss what is going on here."

Carmen went back to communicating with Jarruda.

"Jarruda, thank you for letting this conversation continue even though you don't fully believe what you've been told. Could you tell me how many Lorengi are aboard the sphere you are travelling in?"

"Several billion. Why?"

"In my short experience I have never seen such a concentration of consciousness. I was able to detect it from a distance of four thousand light years."

"Unbelievable!"

"It is true, Excellency," Thelika said. *"Carmen shared the experience with Ahleeto and me."*

"Thelika? Oh my, this is a moment of wonderful things. How are you, my friend?"

"I am fine, Excellency. Pardon my intrusion, but I thought it might help you accept the veracity of Carmen's claim."

"It is always a pleasure to converse with you. Thank you for watching out for my daughter, for what was apparently a very long time. Now Carmen, what do you want from the Lorengi?"

"First, I think it would be a good time for a demonstration. I would like you to join with me to 'see' the consciousness here and in the ships near here, so you can see what we will need to do to make our escape."

"How will we do that?"

"When I'm working with Humans, I start by saying 'close your eyes.' If you would please concentrate in the way you

would if you were closing your eyes and connect with my mind. I'll reach out to all of you at the same time. What we'll see with our minds is the view of the universe that is the first step in teleporting. Does that make sense to you?"

"Yes. Let us begin," Jarruda said to Carmen and all the Lorengi.

The impact of connecting that way with several billion unfamiliar minds nearly overwhelmed Carmen. She knew that she couldn't allow herself to falter. She remembered how she mastered the immense data flow that the Cheneshi participate in constantly. That reference helped.

"Thank you," Carmen said. *"The Lorengi presence is a wonder to behold, and it is beautiful. Now look around with your mind and see the brightness that you represent. Not far from your sphere are three Lorengi ships, your two plus Thelika. You can see their brightness. When we were given a visual depiction of you in this place, we also saw two other ships of unknown origin. Follow me now. Can you see that there are small nodes of brightness located not too far from our location?"*

"Speaking for all of us," Jarruda said, *"this is an amazing presentation. Even more so because you have just shown us what you believe to be conscious, space-faring beings previously unknown to us."*

"I'm glad you accept what your minds perceive. I cannot stress too ardently that this is critical to our being able to extract you from your present circumstance. We left a contact at our point of departure as an anchor. We need to 'see' that contact in this way and convince our minds that it is real and a valid destination. That will be key to our being able to teleport out of here."

"We are beginning to accept what we have been told, Carmen. What will you want us to do next?"

"I ask that you be patient. Now that you are aware of your circumstance, you may be anxious to do something about it. I would welcome any suggestions, but I would like to discuss them with you before you act on them. Also, we do not know what the reception will be when we contact the other ships. We may need your help then."

"In this form, it is easier to be patient," Jarruda said. *"We will be glad to help you in any way we can, but I must tell you this, Carmen. Now that I know we are in danger, I will have the well-being of the Lorengi foremost in my mind."*

"I understand and would expect nothing less from a great leader of a great people. I must excuse myself now to begin trying to contact the other ships."

Yes, it was understandable, Carmen thought. She just hoped that sentiment didn't rise up at the wrong moment and ruin the rescue of everyone. Wait, she thought, and smiled. There is only one moment in this place. Let's make sure it is the right one!

9 Voices

Aboard the Garduk Ship Seriatna

The Garduk are proud that they are among the tallest creatures on their home planet and are getting taller with each generation. Most adult males were now head and shoulders above their domesticated meat and milk animal, the aflut. Some adult males are said to reach to a height of what would be four feet on the Human scale.

Though Heyut was nearly that tall himself, he was feeling much smaller at the moment. His dark tan skin was stretched tightly over a bony frame that slumped in his despair. He pulled at the points of skin that flopped down over his ears and cursed his curious nature.

It happened while he was on wake-watch, so Heyut knew he would get the blame for it. It wasn't fair. He should never been put on wake-watch by himself. Being as inexperienced as he was, another should have been taken from deep sleep to be with him. Then that other person would have kept Heyut's curiosity from dropping him and his shipmates into this dismal nothingness that was all around him.

He hadn't known what the button was for, nor that he should never have pushed it while traveling within sleep-space. The other person could have told him what it was for, and that he should never push it. There was no other, only Heyut, and he did push the button. His shipmates were in deep sleep. He was in deep trouble.

He couldn't see the button anymore. He couldn't see anything in this place that his curiosity had dropped him. It was probably a good thing because he would be tempted to push the button again to see if he could reverse the effect.

He would be going mad if he weren't so worried about the trouble he was going to be in when his Ship Lead woke. Of course, it wasn't like a Garduk to go mad anyway. The Garduk were a practical people. Flights of fantasy or into madness just weren't part of who they were.

There was something else that wasn't quite right. He had been hearing a voice in his head. That wasn't usual for Garduk. The voice was asking for a response. Hearing voices in one's head was one thing, answering back…well, that did border on madness. Although how could he judge? No one had ever reported being in the fix he was in, so he didn't know what was normal in this situation. Perhaps hearing voices was natural in a place like this.

"Hello. Are you there?"

There it was again. It was a strange sort of language, but somehow he knew what they had said. Well, nothing else he could think of might extricate him from the trouble he was in.

"Yes, I'm here. Who are you? Where are you? How is it possible that I am hearing you in my head and not in my ears?"

"I am using mind-to-mind speech," Carmen said. *"I can't hear you either, but I can pick up your thoughts."*

"Garduk do not have the ability for mind-to-mind talk."

"I am not Garduk, I am Human."

That stopped Heyut for a moment. What was Human? Then the same curiosity that always had gotten him into trouble rose up, and he answered, *"I've never heard of Human, but then this is my first trade-trip. Perhaps my more experienced shipmates have heard of you. I thought I was just imagining you because of the unusual situation I find myself in. If you are real, Human, what do you want?"*

"I am called Carmen."

"I am Heyut. What do you want, Carmen?"

"You and I are in the same situation. I believe I have a way to get us out of it."

Earlier, when Carmen had ended her conversation with Jarruda, she began discussing what to do next with her team. They had a clear objective. Now that they were here they knew that they wouldn't be able to see who they were trying to rescue.

"Not being able to see them is one thing," Jesse had said, when they started to plan what to do. *"How will we get them back to normal space? We teleported here. It is possible that the others can't do that. How will we move them?"*

"I've been thinking about that, Jesse," Thelika said. *"The ships we saw appeared to be small relative to the Lorengi ships. Perhaps we could put each of the other ships inside a Lorengi ship. I've communicated the idea to the other Lorengi ships, and they are willing to try that. Of course there is still the logistical challenge of getting next to the prospective passengers and easing their ships into our holds when we can't see anything. If we can get those ships inside, we could bring them with us."*

"What if they have weapons aboard their ships, and in their anxious state of mind decide to fire them when they are close to you or inside?" Jesse asked.

"I've considered that," Thelika said. *"I don't believe any weaponry would operate within this dimension. Everything here*

is time-suspended, and other physical properties usual in our observable universe do not seem to apply."

"What about after we get them out?"

"We will put an energy field around our passengers as soon as we arrive in our normal setting."

Jesse seemed to be satisfied with Thelika's answers, but others had questions.

"What if they can't teleport on their own?" Rosalind asked.

"You and Ashira cannot teleport on your own, Rosalind," Thelika answered. *"Yet you were brought along with us when we all teleported. It will work the same for the other ships."*

"Which of the other ships should we contact first?" Ashira asked.

"We have no way to distinguish one from the other," Carmen said. *"Let's just try one."*

"How do we do that?" Rosalind asked. *"I mean how can we communicate with just the one?"*

"As I did when we contacted Jarruda," Ahleeto said. *"We don't have a specific individual in mind, but we do have a specific point of consciousness in mind. If there is a person there, perhaps we can get them to respond."*

Carmen was the clear choice to make the contact. It wasn't just because she was the team lead. It was her anthropologist background that made her the best choice for contacting an unknown race. It was frustrating at first. She knew there was a person on the other end, but that person had not responded at first. They didn't believe what they were hearing in their mind. Ultimately Heyut did respond.

"How can you be in the same situation? I am in my ship, and I pushed that Atu-cursed button." Then Heyut had a thought.

Maybe, Human Carmen knew more about this situation than he did. *"Did you push a similar button on your ship?"*

"Not exactly, but still, I share your predicament. I'll be back with you soon. I have to talk with my shipmates."

"Rosalind, as you heard, he thinks that he caused his ship to be stuck in this dimension because of a button he pushed. Is it possible?"

"Who can guess what is possible?" Rosalind said. *"Something happened that trapped the Lorengi and other ships here. I can speculate that something triggered an abrupt disruption of the trip through this dimension, and that whoever was within the influence of that something would be affected. All speculation. His button pushing could have been that something, but it seems unlikely."*

"Well, we can look into it when we have more time, after we get everyone out." Carmen said.

Ashira said. *"This is amazing! An actual new race. Do you think Heyut breathes air?"*

"I am as excited as you are, Ashira," Carmen said, *"but since none of us is breathing, he is probably not breathing either. He may not have focused on that. I'm afraid if I alert him to that fact, he might panic. There will be time to learn about Heyut and the Garduk after we leave this place."*

Carmen's team stopped asking questions, allowing her to get back to Heyut.

"Are you alone, Heyut?"

"Yes and no. My shipmates are in deep sleep. I am on wake-watch by myself. Why do you ask?"

"I am going to propose a few things that will be necessary to get us out of this predicament. If others were with you, they would want to know my proposal at the same time. I see no need to wake the others."

"What things are you talking about? I am going to be in enough trouble when my Ship Lead finds out what I've done. I don't know if I should do anything else without getting authority."

"I understand your concern, but if the things I propose get you out of the trouble you have gotten into, perhaps your Ship Lead will be more lenient. Why don't you wait to see what I'm suggesting?"

Heyut hesitated. It didn't seem like the person he was conversing with was going to act precipitously. Finding out what the proposal was made sense to him.

"What do you have in mind?"

"The ship I am on possesses the ability to jump back out of this dimension we are in. I don't think your ship has that ability. I suggest that we place your ship inside of mine so that we can get you out of here when we leave."

Sense-making had just stopped for Heyut. What kind of ship could Carmen have that could do something that his ship could not? Heyut could see nothing. Was Carmen able to see his ship somehow? If not, how would the Human put it into their ship? Did he want to be captured that way by another ship? Would Ship Lead Nathat praise him for falling into a trap?

"That doesn't sound like something that my Ship Lead would agree to."

"Heyut, if you were to wake your Ship Lead, he would be in the same situation you are, and would have no idea what to do. You can wake your Ship Lead if you want, I will wait, but our time is limited. What I am proposing to do must be done soon. Literally, the window is closing."

Heyut pondered and then asked, *"Can you see anything? I cannot."*

"I cannot see anything either. I will tell you something that will be hard to believe, harder than mind-to-mind speech. I located you in this land of no-sight, because your consciousness appears to me as a bright light in the fog. I will guide my ship to you using that beacon."

The impossible resting on the unbelievable, Heyut thought, or was it the other way around? It made no difference. He couldn't easily include either concept within his notion of reality.

Of course, Ship Lead Nathat wouldn't be able to either. Heyut made his decision. He was the one on wake-watch. He would decide what would be done. He believed Carmen when the Human said they didn't have much time. That much understanding came through in the thoughts she was sharing.

"I agree with your proposal, Carmen. I am hoping that you are honest. Tell me what I need to do, and what I should expect as you proceed."

"Thank you for your trust, Heyut. When we live through this, your shipmates will praise you."

"It will be enough for me if they allow me to stay inside the ship for the remainder of our journey."

"I'm sure they will. Now, it will take a moment for us to get one of our ships to you. I will let you know when we are there."

"What do you mean one of your ships? What is going on here?"

"I'm sorry, Heyut, I didn't mean to surprise you. There is another ship here in the same situation as you and your ship. You are the first one I've contacted. I have three ships that are each large enough to bring one of the two trapped ships inside with us as we travel away from here. If you are concerned, you can travel inside the ship I am on. They are all the same."

"How do you know all this?"

"Oh, Heyut, I am asking you to accept, to believe so much in a very short time. I am sorry for that. Perhaps I should have just come and picked you up without your knowing. I just thought it better to alert you to what was happening."

"I'm glad you have alerted me. Tell me how you know what ships are here if you can't see them."

"We started this rescue mission from outside. In some way I don't understand, we were shown that you and others were here. We found a way to come here to help you. Please believe me, because we need to act quickly."

"I can't understand any of this. Commit to tell me all about this when we get out of here, and let's get on with it."

"I promise I will. I'll contact you again when our ship has arrived at a spot we believe is very close to you."

If Carmen were breathing presently, she would have let out a sigh. Without breath, she sighed mentally.

"Ahleeto, I need your help to guide the Lorengi ships. Would you let them know about how we are going to do this?"

"Yes. Thelika, who are the other Lorengi ships?" Ahleeto asked.

"We have Meratta and Jannida to help us, Excellency. I have asked them to listen in so they would be ready to act."

"Thank you, Thelika. Meratta and Jannida, are you ready to be guided to the ships we intend to pick up?"

When they answered in the affirmative, Ahleeto said to Carmen, *"The ships are ready."*

"Thank you, Ahleeto" Carmen said. *"I suggest that all three ships travel together. Okay, Thelika, Meratta, and Jannida, please follow my mind's vision to Heyut's ship."*

In the next instant they had teleported to that ship's location. There was great relief when all aboard could "see" the distinct image of the consciousness aboard Heyut's ship shine

74

more brightly because they were nearer to it. The concept of being able to teleport about within this dimension was one thing. To learn that it actually did work was stress relieving.

"Heyut, all three ships are here next to your ship."

"That didn't take long. You'll have to tell me how you move about when you tell me the rest of it."

"I will. I am going to ask one of the ships, Meratta, to move forward a bit. You should feel a slight bump."

Meratta moved and bumped into Heyut's ship. She opened a hole in her side until with a few more bumps she could feel that it was large enough to accommodate the Garduk ship. She moved again so that she completely surrounded it, which she was able to tell by its bumping into her opposite internal wall and closed the hole.

"I have the Garduk ship inside," Meratta told everyone.

"Heyut, we have your ship aboard. You won't feel anything, but we will be moving to the next ship. Thank you for going along with this."

"You're welcome. Whether I feel something or not, it makes no difference. I'm sure I'm just dreaming all of this anyway.

10 Blind in the Land of Demons

Aboard the Sudahlli Ship Chantlasec

Her mate, Jardut, as was appropriate, had been beside her in the control room when the Chantlasec fell into this strange place. Set Li, as First-Born Mother of clan Parlac, was in charge of the ship, and piloting it when it happened. She had done nothing to create the situation, but all of a sudden she and her mate had lost all sensory input.

She couldn't see or hear Jardut but could feel the co-pilot's chair he was in jerking all around as Jardut was shaking in his madness. Jardut, like all Sudahlli males, had a hard time dealing with new and unusual situations. That this situation also had robbed him of sight and sound was enough to push her mate over the edge.

Trained, as all First-Born Mothers are, Set Li knew how to handle many situations, and to lead decisively when the situation called for it. Sudahlli females were born with a needle that can be extended from under their forefinger's claw-like fingernail on all four hands and used as a stinger. It is called the califa.

Females have control over what comes out of the needle. The chemicals range from deadly poisons to sedatives, mild or strong. In this case, Set Li raised her right upper arm, placed her hand on her mate's neck, extended the needle, and stung her mate into a deep sleep. With her mate sedated, and the rest of her Sudahlli crew already in that state before they entered this strange space, Set Li was free to assess what happened and what to do about it without interruption.

The Sudahlli appear to be ferocious and frighten anyone who does not know of their thoughtful, reasoned approach to life. The males, seven feet tall when standing erect, weigh nearly three hundred pounds. The females tend to be larger.

Sudahlli are covered with a short brown fur. The fur on top of their head is usually longer and grows like Human hair. All Sudahlli have two sets of arms, one extending from their upper shoulders, another set which emerges from the sides of their mid-section. When running on all-six limbs, using their four hands and two feet, their speed is stunning.

They have a large round head set upon their massive shoulders. Their ears are small and set close to their head. Their black, flat and fur-less nose is set between large and uniformly dark brown eyes. When they smile their sharp, omnivore teeth do not put a stranger at ease.

They are as powerful as they appear, but they are not aggressive. That doesn't mean it would be a good idea to provoke one. For the most part even when so confronted the Sudahlli think before acting. Set Li was thinking now.

She wasn't breathing. Neither of her two hearts was beating. She could touch things around her but could see nothing. When she looked around there was nothingness, which was probably the first blow to her mate's stability. She was blind in what her race, when they had been more primitive and superstitious, would have called the land of demons.

She wasn't superstitious, nor did she believe in demons. At least she hadn't until someone had spoken to her just now in her mind. She didn't believe it to be a demon, for it spoke gently in her mind. She didn't know who or what could speak so.

"My name is Carmen. Is there someone there?"

That was the third attempt to communicate that Set Li had heard. She couldn't speak, but perhaps if she thought back in response it would work.

"I am Set Li, First-Born Mother of Clan Parlac, and Master of the Sudahlli ship Chantlasec. *"*

Carmen thought for a moment about an appropriate response, one that would put her in the context of who she was communicating with but wouldn't overstate the truth of the matter.

"Well met, Set Li, First-Born Mother. I am Carmen Willathorpe, Human, currently leading the Lorengi ship, Thelika."

"You may call me Set Li. What do Human and Lorengi mean?"

"Please call me Carmen. There are two compatible races aboard, Thelika. I and several of my shipmates are Human. There is a female Lorengi here as well."

"Are you male or female, Carmen, if that makes sense for a Human, and why isn't the Lorengi leading her own ship?"

"I am female and was chosen to lead this expedition because of a skill I have that is critical to its success. Are there others aboard your ship?"

"My crew is sedated. What is your situation? I am without sight and sound, and though it is hard to believe, I don't appear to be breathing or heart-beating."

"The same is true for us. We were alerted that you were in this dimension, and we have come to help you back to normal space."

"That is a great amount of claiming to believe all at once. You are the only other entity I have encountered since arriving. I know I did nothing to create this situation. Why wouldn't I be

right in believing that you created it, so that I would fall into some trap you planned?"

"That would be a reasonable conclusion, but that is not the case. We have a short time to affect this rescue. What can I do to convince you of our sincerity, Set Li?"

"Among my people, I have a reputation as a person who understands the physical reality we live in. Do you have someone aboard that can talk to me in those terms?"

"I believe you mean you are what we call a scientist. We do have a scientist with us. She is also female and Human. I will ask her to respond."

Rosalind took over the conversation at that point.

"My name is Rosalind, Set Li. First let me ask if your ships are capable of FTL travel."

"Yes, though I am not at liberty to discuss the specifics of the technology."

"That's fine. The Lorengi and Humans also are able to do that, but in a way that is different from your ship. I think the two methods we have in common is that to accomplish it, you and we travel through the dimension we are currently in. You just didn't get all the way through it for some reason this time."

Rosalind went on, telling the Sudahlli First-Born Mother her theories.

"Well, that's my take on it, Set Li. What do you think is going on?"

"I'm in accord with much of what you have said. One part that is not clear is that Carmen said you came here to rescue me. How did you know we were here?"

"We were shown a view of this dimension by someone we do not know, who used a method of which we have no conception. We believed it to be true or perhaps hoped it was, because there also appeared to be Lorengi trapped here. That

compelled us to set aside our disbelief and try to rescue the Lorengi and the two non-Lorengi ships we saw."

"Two ships? Who are the others?"

"The Garduk. We were unaware of either the Sudahlli or the Garduk before we came here."

"I have heard of the Garduk but have never encountered them myself. I'll be interested to learn more about them. Thank you Rosalind. What do you and Carmen want me to do?"

"We have three Lorengi ships with us," Carmen said. *"Each is large enough to put your ship inside its hold. We are near you now. We have already brought the Garduk ship with one of the Lorengi ships. We will do that with yours if that is acceptable to you."*

Set Li's suspicions rose up again. *"Wait! How do you know you are near my ship? I thought you said that like me you were unable to see."*

"Sorry to have surprised you with that, Carmen said. I can see you with my mind, well not actually you, but your consciousness and that of your shipmates shine brightly in my mind. We can move toward you, guided by that vision."

"I'm not sure about the vision part of your explanation, but the moving part is even more troubling for I sense that my ship is incapable of motion in this sea of nothing."

"Let me try full disclosure then. Right now we are conversing with each other because the Lorengi and some Humans can use mind-to-mind communication. We and our ships can also do something called teleporting. It's similar to your FTL technology in that we can move from one place to another. In our case, we use our mind, and get there just by intending to be there. We traveled into this dimension by teleporting, being guided by my ability to detect consciousness over great distances. We intend to get out the same way.

"We don't know how much longer the window we were given will remain open. So our time is limited. I don't have anything else I can say to convince you that we are telling the truth, and I need you to make your decision quickly."

"Thank you, Carmen. I believe you, though I don't fully understand. Please go ahead."

"Thank you, Set Li. You will feel your ship jostled a little as the ship Jannida loads you into her hold. We'll have a joint celebration when this is all over."

Carmen was finding it difficult to be so certain of success. She didn't know how much time she had. She hadn't yet tried to spot the all-important luminescence of the consciousness of her anchor that would be her beacon for the trip "home." Whatever her concerns, now that the other ships were loaded, there was no doubt that she should quickly decide to leave.

"It's been a challenge," she said to her team, *"but we have all ships ready to go. Thelika, could you tell the other Lorengi ships we are going back to the large sphere containing all the Lorengi?"*

"Yes. They are ready."

"Anything else before we move?"

"Will this work?" Jesse asked.

"We won't know until we try. Let's concentrate on the Lorengi sphere and move our fleet back close to it."

She directed all three Lorengi ships to position themselves next to the Lorengi sphere and contacted Jarruda when they arrived.

"Jarruda, we have retrieved the other ships, and are nearing the time departure. Are the Lorengi ready?"

"Yes. Just let us know what we need to do and when."

"Good. I will take a moment to locate Katala and her passengers on the other side. When I do, I will ask you in the Lorengi sphere to join with me and the other Lorengi ships to make the transit to normal space."

Carmen rested for a moment to strengthen her concentration. She reached out with her mind in what she thought was the direction they came from when they went through the window. At first she saw nothing. She stumbled mentally, fearing that this wasn't going to work. She didn't let herself dwell on that very long. It had to work!

Then she remembered that her beginning place was different from when they started out. She was in position next to the Lorengi sphere, and the window she was seeking was on the other side of the sphere. The mental search she had begun was overwhelmed by the intensely bright consciousness of the Lorengi in the sphere. It was like the difficulty one has trying to see distant stars from Earth's surface when standing within a modern city.

She asked Thelika to move forward far enough so that the sphere was behind them. She looked in the same direction and found a feint glimmer of consciousness. She asked her team to join her. She wanted to be sure what she was seeing was their desired location.

"Can anyone get an impression from that distant light?"

"What do you mean?" Rosalind asked.

"I don't know. When we are close to one another, we can distinguish one person from another. At this distance, can you sense if what we are seeing is Katala and the others?"

"Could we try to communicate with them?" Ashira asked.

"Good idea, Ashira. Let's all attempt to contact someone out there."

They all did, and no answer was received.

"We don't know how far we've come to reach this location, if distance even has a meaning when slipping into this dimension," Rosalind observed. *"If that spec of consciousness represents our friends, then we are far away, too far for me to pick out who we are looking at. However, when we looked into the window, we saw only the Lorengi ships and the two other ships. Since all of them are accounted for, I'd say there was a good chance we are looking at our anchor."*

"I think you're right," Carmen said. She asked the others if they thought it was enough to proceed. There was general agreement with Rosalind's idea, so without losing sight of their destination, Carmen contacted Jarruda again.

"Jarruda, we have found our direction. Now is the time for you and the Lorengi in the sphere to join with our mental image of where we are going." Once Carmen sensed the connection with the billions of Lorengi again, she said, *"We are headed toward the small light in the distance."*

"That's not much to go on. Are you sure?" Jarruda asked.

Carmen told the Lorengi leader of their analysis.

"So I'd have to say, Jarruda, that we aren't sure, but it seems to make sense."

"Wouldn't it be better to have one ship go there to see what was there, and report back?"

"Sound logic, Jarruda, but I don't think we can use that solution in this case. We are not in normal space. 'Going there' means stepping out of this dimension through the window that someone has made for us, confirming it's the right location, and then popping back here. I hope you can see our problem. We don't know if the window will last long enough for an exploratory trip, or if once out, that the test ship will be able to get back in."

"Alright. I don't see an alternative," Jarruda said. *"Let's go ahead with your plan."*

"Thanks, Jarruda.

Having Jarruda's agreement, she thought it fitting to take a moment to address all parties.

"We are now assembled in a small cluster. We have with us, representatives of four races, Garduk, Sudahlli, Lorengi and Human. It is time to take all of us out of this place and back to normal space."

Addressing the Lorengi, their ships and her team, Carmen said, *"Now everyone focus on that point of light and believe it is a viable destination. Make it the focal point of all of your conscious energy."*

Carmen felt the presence of billions of minds focused on their destination. She was ready to give the order to teleport when another mind, definitely not Human or Lorengi, called to her.

"WAIT!"

11 The Unexpected

On Thelika

Carmen wasn't sure what to do. She believed it was Set Li who had contacted her, and it sounded urgent. The others were ready to go, but she had to see what the Sudahlli wanted. *"Hold your focus, everyone. Something has come up. I'll get right back to you."*

"Set Li, is that you?"

"Yes, Carmen, something extraordinary has just happened."

Carmen took a moment to wonder what could stand out as "extraordinary" amidst everything else in the very unusual circumstance they all found themselves in.

"What is it, Set Li? We are an instant away from leaving."

"There is another ship caught in this dreadful place. Someone within that ship contacted me and wants to leave with us."

"I'm glad you alerted me, Set Li. We will have to attempt to collect them and bring them with us. The way you speak of it, sounds like there is more to it."

"Yes, the one who contacted me is a Dhara'chee."

"I don't know of the Dhara'chee, Set Li. Is there something special about them?"

"Yes. They are an ancient, gentle race, revered by all civilized races. They have extremely advanced technology. They

rarely interact or speak with anyone who is not Dhara'chee. I am awed that one contacted me."

Carmen understood that it was a major life event for Set Li, but she was certain that the Dhara'chee would speak to anyone who had a way to leave the area.

"Ask them to wait a bit. I'll get back to you soon. I have to tell the others."

Carmen then addressed her team and Jarruda.

"Apparently there is another ship in this sea of nothingness. Someone on that ship contacted the Sudahlli ship captain. The ship belongs to another race, called the Dhara'chee. We have to try to find them and bring them with us."

"Time is short according to you, Carmen," Jarruda said. *"Is it wise to risk the rest of us, based on a whisper from the darkness? We are ready to leave. I suggest that we go ahead with our exit and send someone back for this new arrival."*

"I won't leave without trying, Jarruda, but your reasoning is sound. Maybe we don't have to risk everyone to achieve this remaining rescue."

Jesse sent a side thought to Carmen, *"What are you thinking? I won't leave without you."*

"I was hoping you'd say that, Jesse. I'm thinking we could send the Lorengi, and maybe the other Lorengi ships, and keep Thelika and our team here to get the job done."

"What do you want to do now, Carmen?" Jarruda asked.

"I propose that we send you and the other ships back, and if they are willing, I would keep Thelika and my team here to find the other ship and bring it back to normal space."

"You would risk my daughter Ahleeto and my dear friend Thelika?" Jarruda asked.

"I will gladly stay behind to help, Excellency," Thelika said.

"I will also stay, Mother, but you are right to save our people if you can. Go greet Katala again and meet the Humans there."

No one offered another thought until Jarruda said, *"I will take our people to safety, Carmen, but I hold you responsible for my daughter's safety. Please bring her back to me."*

"I will do that, Jarruda, and you can help. When you arrive stay in the vicinity of Katala. You will shine so bright we will definitely be able to see you."

"Yes!" Jarruda said. It was obvious she was glad to have an important role to play, even though she was fleeing and leaving others behind to face danger.

When Carmen announced the new plan to everyone, Set Li requested to stay behind to help rescue the Dhara'chee. Carmen checked with the Lorengi ship, Jannida, which held Set Li's ship, and found it was willing to stay behind.

Carmen found what they believed to be their anchor again and asked the Lorengi in the large sphere and the Lorengi ship Meratta to focus on that location. She worked with them until she could feel that their intensity and single-minded focus on that point was at its peak. She said it was time. Jarruda gave the order to teleport. They disappeared from the neighborhood, and immediately appeared where Carmen was aiming them. She would have to wait to confirm they were at the correct location, but the size of the sphere of brightness appeared to be about the same as when looking at it from outside the window.

Addressing her team, Set Li, Thelika and Jannida Carmen said, *"Now let's find the Dhara'chee."*

A great cheer had gone up on Katala in the beginning when Sam and the others saw Thelika and team arrive between the other two Lorengi ships near the large sphere in the window right after they had left. Nothing happened for weeks afterward. They had no way of knowing if Thelika and her passengers were trapped like the other ships seemed to be. Tension rose as Katala reported that the window was shrinking at an increasing rate.

Then in the middle of the night, over a month after the team had left, Katala woke up everyone with a report. The three Lorengi ships were no longer near the sphere but appeared near one of the two unknown ships. The team cheered in the common room again, and patted each other on the back, but this new information had increased the tension. If it was taking so much time, as measured in normal space, to accomplish something within the dimension where the team was working, would they have time enough to complete their mission before the window closed?

A little over a month later, the three Lorengi ships appeared near the other unknown ship. The first unknown ship that had been visited could no longer be seen, so the Katala crew assumed it had been placed inside one of the Lorengi ships. As could be predicted by the rate of their earlier process, about a month after that, the three ships showed up back at the sphere. The two unknown ships could no longer be seen and were assumed to be loaded aboard Lorengi ships.

"At this rate, we might see them back here in about a month," Sam said to the Katala crew. "Katala, what's your guess about whether the window will still be open for them at that time?"

"I am still seeing a slight acceleration in the shrinkage rate. If it doesn't get worse it should still be open at a month from now, but it will be a close thing."

To everyone's relief, about a month later, a sphere of immense size appeared near Katala. Next to it was a single Lorengi ship. The watchers on the Katala were anxious about those who were apparently left behind.

Sam had Katala direct a radio signal to the sphere, "Hello. Welcome. I'm Sam Baxter on the Lorengi ship Katala. We have been nervously watching the rescue mission for some time now. We're happy you made it and are wondering about the rest of those who didn't arrive with you."

"Hello, Sam. I am Jarruda Antilos, current leader of the Lorengi. We are in the large Lorengi sphere you see and are glad to be here. Apparently we've been gone for a long time, so we also have questions. As to those who didn't come with us, I need to ask if you lead the Katala group, and if I may discuss things openly."

"Thank you for your caution. Yes, I am, and yes you may. All are concerned about everyone who did not escape with you. Perhaps you could come to the Katala to discuss everything in person."

"Certainly."

An instant later, a hologram of a Lorengi, who looked like an older version of Ahleeto, appeared in the common room on Katala where everyone had gathered when the sphere had arrived.

Sam didn't react to the surprise he felt. Instead he bowed from the waist and said, "Welcome, Jarruda. I apologize for not knowing the proper way to address the leader of all Lorengi."

"Jarruda will do. As you see I am a stored person like my daughter, Ahleeto. All of the several billion Lorengi aboard our ship are in the same state. We are so grateful for the risk your team took to get us back to normal space. We have much to learn about what happened while we were away."

"It will be wonderful to share what we know. Before we continue, I must let you know that two others are telepathically connected to our conversation. One you may know, the other may be a surprise."

Jarruda waited for Sam to explain.

"The Cheneshi are connected through their representative who we call Sways."

"Jarruda, I was not yet sprouted when you last visited our ocean world. As you probably remember, our full names are cumbersome, so when the Humans first visited us, I suggested the name you just heard."

"Sways, it is an honor to meet you. Are all Cheneshi listening in?"

"I would think so, but some will be busy with other things at the same time."

"Then let me say it is an honor to meet you all. It seems that you have progressed mightily since my last visit to your planet."

Sam said, "Perhaps, Ahleeto spoke to you of developments on Earth."

"We had little time together," Jarruda said, "and were mostly focused on returning here. She did say there were interesting developments."

"I would agree," Sam said. He went on to explain about the emergence of H2s which triggered the formation of Janus, a global consciousness comprised of all conscious beings on Earth. He then introduced her to Janus. They spoke briefly, and then Jarruda turned to Sam.

"This is unprecedented, Sam. We Lorengi were closely connected first telepathically, now even closer since we share a digital existence, but nothing like your Janus. Nor did we encounter anything like a globally conscious entity in our travels. We must discuss this further, but first the more urgent matter—why the others did not return with us."

Jarruda told the Katala crew about how someone on another unknown ship had announced itself just as everyone was ready to leave. She told them that Carmen had said she would stay to rescue that ship.

"One of the ships that had already been recovered requested to remain, and aid in the rescue."

"Was the new contact a member of one of the rescued races?"

"No, Sam. The new one was from a race called Dhara'chee. The Dhara'chee made itself known by contacting the Sudahlli captain. Apparently the Dhara'chee are revered and something of a mystery. The Sudahlli captain wanted to meet the Dhara'chee when it was rescued."

"We haven't seen any additional ships near where you were trapped," Sam said. "Perhaps the Dhara'chee are a great distance away. I hope they can find it fast. The window is only a third of its original size and shrinking more each day."

"Ahleeto mentioned something about a 'Window' that was provided to alert you to the need for our rescue. May I see it?" Jarruda asked.

Sam pointed to the screen in Katala's common room that they used to view the window.

"Those look like the two Lorengi ships that were left behind," Jarruda said. "That's odd. I thought that Carmen was eager to go in search of the Dhara'chee right away."

Sam explained the timing of things that the Katala group had witnessed.

"This whole experience is very disorienting," Jarruda said. "Time didn't seem to pass in that dimension. What you said took months of observation here occurred instantly there. At least we are back in 'normal' space now.

Even though much time has elapsed since we left, and new things have developed, we are able to ground ourselves by connecting with Humans and re-connecting with the Cheneshi. I think our passengers in the Garduk ship which is in Meratta's hold will have a tougher time adjusting. I've just learned we have a communication from the Garduk crew member wondering if we have arrived yet. Shall I put it through?"

"Yes," Sam said. "Who will we be talking to?"

"His name is Heyut," Jarruda said. "He was the only crew member on duty when the Garduk ship fell into the dimension we all found ourselves in. So far he hasn't awakened any of the other crew. They call the captain of their ships, 'Ship Lead'."

"Will we be able to understand him?"

"Yes. We were only able to use telepathy before. In normal space Meratta will translate for us."

"Hello, have we arrived? Carmen? Anyone?" Heyut asked.

"Hello, Heyut. Carmen and her crew are still in the other dimension. They are searching for another ship. My name is Sam."

"Where am I, Sam?"

"Your ship is still in the hold of the Lorengi ship, Meratta, but you are back in normal space."

"Is it time to waken Ship Lead Nathat?"

"Yes. Would you like one of us to come to your ship to help explain what has happened?"

"That would be helpful. I'm sure he will ask questions I cannot answer."

"It will take me a few minutes to make the arrangements. Please wait until I get back to you."

Turning to Jarruda, Sam asked, "Is there any way to find out facts about the interior of the Garduk ship including its atmosphere, temperature, and dimensions?"

Jarruda paused for a moment before answering. "The air in the ship is similar in content to what you usually breathe. The temperature is warmer but livable. You will want to sit on the floor before teleporting. Heyut is in a space with a ceiling that varies in height, but it is all lower than six feet. Apparently Heyut is about four feet in height. Sitting will keep you from hitting your head and be less intimidating for Heyut at the same time."

"Will Meratta be able to translate us through my implant?"

"Yes, but it may be awkward. You have telepathy as a backup. The Garduk are not natural telepaths, but Carmen was able to use telepathy with Heyut during the rescue."

"Will you accompany me?"

"Yes. I would love to meet Heyut and the other Garduk. It will be a first contact for the Lorengi as well. Through me, all Lorengi will be participating."

"Heyut, it's Sam. Do you have a science officer aboard?"

"Yes. Nathat serves in that capacity as well as being Ship Lead."

"Good, we will only need to wake Nathat to begin with then. I will arrive shortly. I will be accompanied by Jarruda Antilos. She will be in holographic form which I will explain when we arrive. Please don't be disturbed. We will teleport to your location and appear in front of you. Because Humans and

Lorengi are a taller than your space will accommodate, we will be sitting on the floor. Are you ready?"

"Yes," Heyut said, in a shaky voice.

Sam received help from Meratta to get the location right and teleported to the Garduk ship. When he arrived, Heyut was in front of him. He was four feet tall, on two legs and slender, with his light brown skin pulled tightly over his bony frame. He had a short, narrow nose that separated two brown eyes on his small head. His ears had a pointed piece of skin that flopped down from the top extending to the ear opening. His small mouth was pulled into a tight slit. His one-piece, brown, short-sleeved uniform exposed his two narrow arms, and hung loosely on his slender body. Sam wasn't sure he could read Garduk facial expressions, but Heyut looked nervous. Sam thought he better say something to ease the tension.

"Heyut, my name is Sam. Next to me is Jarruda. She is the leader of the Lorengi people. Are you doing alright?"

Meratta was translating and piping the result through the Garduk ship comm system for Heyut. Sam hoped the voice Meratta chose was pleasant on Garduk ears, and that the words were right.

Heyut was standing in what appeared to be a control room when they arrived. Visibly relaxing when he heard Sam's greeting, Heyut sat down in a swivel chair at one of the workstations and turned to face the new arrivals.

He said something which Meratta translated as, "Wow! You are big! I've started the process to waken Nathat from deep sleep. I've heard him stirring already. He should join us soon. This will be quite a shock for him. I hope you're ready with an explanation."

"We are...," was all Sam got out before Nathat came grumbling into the control room, rubbing the sleep from his eyes which were glaring at Heyut. With his limited vision and intense focus on Heyut, Nathat didn't notice Sam and Jarruda.

"Why have you wakened me Heyut? I am not scheduled for wake-watch!"

"We have visitors, Sir." Heyut said pointing at Sam and Jarruda.

Perhaps it was because he had just emerged from deep sleep, but whatever the reason, with one startled glance in Sam's direction Ship Lead Nathat collapsed on the floor.

12 Window Pain

On Thelika

When Carmen's team's task was to rescue the first two ships, she knew their locations from what they had seen in the window before they left. She didn't have that information for the Dhara'chee. Before discussing the next steps with her crew, Carmen used her mind to scan the area for any signs of consciousness. She didn't sense any brightness. Locating the Dhara'chee would take a more intense effort.

Addressing everyone, she said, *"It's not obvious to me where our quarry is. Set Li, are you still in contact with the Dhara'chee?"*

"No, Carmen, I am not. The mind-speech I received was not strong, just a whisper. Either the Dhara'chee was weak or was sending from a great distance. I sent back that we had heard and would be contacting them again. I'm not sure I got through. I'm not skilled at mind-speech."

Since distance didn't seem to weaken the strength of telepathic communication Carmen thought that they might have a sick Dhara'chee on their hands. That added another element to their time-urgency.

"Thanks, Set Li. I will try to contact them. I will shout in no particular direction. I hope they pick it up. Everybody listen in."

"DHARA'CHEE! DHARA'CHEE!"

"Who are you, and why are you shouting?"

"My name is Carmen. Sorry for shouting. I wasn't sure where you were, or if you were in a condition to respond. Set Li said your first contact was weak. I was worried that you might be incapacitated in some way."

"No need to worry, child. I am not ill or injured. I'm familiar with the Sudahlli that's why I contacted First Born Mother, Set Li. What kind are you, Carmen?"

"I am Human. In addition, we have a representative from the Lorengi aboard."

"Wonderful! I've not met anyone from either of your races. Finally, some joy in this dismal circumstance."

"What is your situation?"

"My shipmates and I are lost in a sea of nothingness. I'm the sole member of our expedition that is awake. It seems like we just got here, but my reason says otherwise. While communicating with the mind of Set Li, I found some unbelievable information. I got the impression that you and your colleagues are here on a rescue mission, and that you have the means to escape. Is that true?"

"Yes."

"That raises many questions. How did you know that we needed rescuing? Where are we? How did you get here, and how do you know how to leave? I also received the impression from Set Li that the rescue timeframe is limited. Perhaps answers to my questions will have to wait."

"That would be better. The answer to two of your questions will come as a part of the process of locating you."

"Then I'll be satisfied with that. What do you have in mind?"

"Without going into too much detail, when I close my eyes, and concentrate with my mind I am able to see consciousness as

bright light. I will search for the bright light which represents the consciousness of you and your shipmates and move to your location."

"Amazing, and though that does provide some answers, it raises another question. How can you 'move' anywhere in the morass in which we find ourselves. I believe I am still inside my ship, but I can't see it. When I attempt to communicate with it I get no response. I'm sure I could not move in any direction, or even if direction has meaning in this place. How will you move?"

"We have the ability to move using our minds. We call it teleporting. If we and our ship have a location in mind, we can get there just by intending to be there."

"Enough! Enough! I do not want to discuss these wonders until we can do so at our leisure. Let's do the practical thing and get together however it is you can accomplish it."

"Good. To begin with, I briefly tried to locate you a moment ago, and couldn't see you. Perhaps you are a significant distance from us. How did you know we were here to contact Set Li?"

"I believed we were the only ship in this situation. Then I detected telepathic communication. I focused on it. There were minds I did not recognize, but one that I did, the Sudahlli, so I contacted her."

"That's about what I thought. We will try to locate you again. This time I will include all of our team, including Set Li in the effort. Try to shine as brightly as you can."

"Though I think you are being humorous, I will endeavor to do what I can so you may 'see' me and my shipmates."

Carmen asked her team, Thelika and Set Li to join with her mind view as she had before. Because she didn't have a particular location as a target area she imagined her mind slowly sweeping around in a circle, casting deeply into the nothingness, seeking a beacon of light.

"There!" Set Li exclaimed. *"Is that small bright spec what we are seeking?"*

Carmen stopped sweeping with her mind and concentrated on what could be seen in the area before her. Then she saw it.

"Good for you Set Li. I believe it is exactly what we are looking for. I judge it to be a great distance away, but that is no matter. It will take no time to get there."

"Wait!" Ashira said. *"Will we lose our way home if we travel that far away from here?"*

"Excellent point, Ashira. Without losing our Dhara'chee location, I am going to expand our mental view so that we can also see the Lorengi sphere, our beacon for the trip home. Can you all see both of them now?

Getting a favorable response, Carmen said, *"Good. Now we're going to have to do something we haven't tried before. We will keep the sphere in our mind's eye while at the same time intensely focus on the location of Dhara'chee as a viable destination. We'll zip over there without losing site of our ultimate target."*

When Carmen sensed that the time was right, she gave the order to the two Lorengi ships to teleport. In that instant, the bright light of the Dhara'chee increased significantly. They had arrived. Carmen asked her team to keep focused on the Lorengi sphere while she communicated with the Dhara'chee and moved its ship within Thelika.

"We are near your ship. By the way, what is your name?"

"I am called Orlyn. That was a fast trip, Carmen. I am eager to find out more about teleporting."

"There will be plenty of time once we are all back to normal space."

"What's the next step in that process?"

"We will take your ship into the hold of ours."

"Hmmm that might not be possible. Our ship is immense."

"What is its shape?"

"Ellipsoidal. The horizontal dimension is one thousand perlens, which is five times the vertical dimension."

"We don't know what a perlen is. Is there a way to convert that measurement, Thelika?"

"Yes, give Orlyn and me a moment to compare wavelength information. That should do it."

After a brief interlude, Thelika said, *"A perlen is the height of a Dhara'chee, or about five feet. They are apparently uniformly about five feet tall. A thousand perlens would be about five-thousand feet or about fifteen times longer than me. Thus, Orlyn is correct. His ship will not fit inside me."*

"Would your teleporting work if I were to bring your ship inside mine?" Orlyn asked.

"It might," Carmen said, *"but how would we get inside? Our method of bringing you in would have relied on the organic nature of our ship. Thelika is a conscious, organic being. She can sense the other ship, open her hold to the right size to accommodate it, and move to enclose the ship inside."*

"Our ship is not organic, and as I said, it is not responding to my telepathic queries. So I don't think I will be able to open our hold."

Thelika asked, *"Do you have a hold large enough to accommodate me? I am roughly sixty perlens long and twenty in diameter.*

"Yes. Our ship has two such holds. One of them is completely empty. It is a cylindrical space one hundred perlens long and fifty perlens in diameter. It would easily accommodate you, but alas, I have no way of getting you in there."

Carmen was catching on to where Thelika was going. *"Can you visualize that space and its location within your ship?"*

"Yes. Why?"

"If we can get a clear location from your mind," Carmen said, *"we can teleport to that location inside your ship."*

"Truly? That is amazing."

"Yes. Please visualize the space you say will accommodate Thelika. We'll join with your visual image and use it to guide our teleporting."

Carmen had yet another new experience of joining with a very unfamiliar mind. The Dhara'chee mind was the most powerful and complex yet. She saw the place, checked with Thelika to confirm that the Lorengi ship also saw it clearly, and then they jumped into the hold of the Dhara'chee ship.

"Are you inside?" Orlyn asked.

"Just a minute, we will cautiously move a bit until we bump into a wall and the ceiling to make sure we have arrived."

After feeling couple of bumps within his ship, Orlyn said, *"It feels like those impacts are within our ship. Do you agree?"*

"Yes," Carmen said. *"We are in your ship!"*

After taking a moment to check, Carmen found the next obstacle. *"I can't see our anchor from in here."*

The others on Thelika understood, because they couldn't either. Orlyn didn't understand.

"What do you mean? Is your mental vision blocked by the material in our ship?"

"No, it's overwhelmed by the intense brightness of the consciousness of you and your shipmates. Though our anchor is relatively bright, I can't pick it out from what I'm seeing from all of you. I'll talk this over with my team. You can listen in if you want."

"Thank you. I would be interested."

"To begin with, Thelika, can we move a ship of this size?"

"Yes. During our exploration years with the Lorengi, ships were required to move objects more massive than this, but we need a destination."

Carmen was inside Thelika, which was now inside the Dhara'chee ship. She needed to get outside all of this to get a clear view of the beacon she needed to guide everyone home. She thought she could get that view if she went to the common room of the Lorengi ship Jannida, which was beside the Dhara'chee ship.

"Yes, I understand. Jannida, are you there?"

"Of course. What do you have in mind?"

"I want to try to locate the anchor from inside your common room. I believe if I come aboard, and we move away from the Dhara'chee ship in what we believe to be the direction of the Lorengi sphere, I might be able to spot it again. If so, then I can pass that visual image to Thelika and her passengers, and we can teleport out of here."

Carmen asked the others what they thought. Other than concerns over being separated, they thought it was worth a try. Carmen 'ported to Jannida. She got settled as best she could, given that she couldn't see anything with her eyes. She asked Jannida to teleport a short distance away from the Dhara'chee ship. On her own, she reached out with her mind to seek the Lorengi sphere. She picked it up right away. She connected with Thelika and the others.

"Can you see where we are headed?"

They all said they could. It was new to Orlyn, so he had to ask, *"Is it that bright spot in the distance?"*

"Yes. Since this is your first trip with us, I'll explain. Usually when we teleport, we have a definite location in mind. What we have found we can do in this circumstance is to believe

that bright light is a valid destination and use it to guide us. When we teleport, no matter the distance, it is instantaneous. Are you ready?"

Orlyn said he was, as did the others. They focused with all their strength, determined to get home. Their intensity rose. Carmen was about to give the order to teleport, when the bright image of the Lorengi sphere disappeared.

"What happened to the light?" Orlyn asked. *"Does its disappearance mean that we have arrived?"*

After making a quick assessment, Carmen came to the only conclusion she could—the window had closed!

"No Orlyn. We haven't arrived. We haven't left. You remember that there was a time element to our quest? We have just run out of time." She went on to explain about the window, and that it had just closed.

"You could have left with the others," said Orlyn. *"Attempting to rescue us has trapped you here. I am so sorry."*

"It was our choice, Orlyn. We knew there was a risk that we would run out of time. Now we have to figure out what to do about it.

"We have with us one of our top scientists on this mission. Her name is Rosalind Atwood, and she has some theories about our situation. From Set Li, we understand that Dhara'chee scientific progress is very advanced. I suggest you wake some of your best minds. Together we might be able to figure out an alternative way out of this place. If we can't, we will have all the 'leisure' time we need to talk about our respective wonders."

13 Stars!

Aboard Katala

"Wake up, Sam!"

"What? Who are you?" He didn't know who had awakened him, but he knew it was a voice in his head that he had never encountered before. It was clear, strong, and unlike anything else. It sounded close. He opened his eyes to see who it was and couldn't believe what he saw. There was a glowing amorphous volume of light floating before him. It shimmered and changed shape as he looked on.

"Who I am will be explained later. We are losing what you call 'the window.' It has failed catastrophically and shrunk to almost nothing. We may not be able to hold it much longer. You have to summon help. If we lose it entirely, we may not be able to recreate it. The Dhara'chee, Carmen and the others will be lost forever. You have to get help!"

"What can we do if you can't hold it? We don't know what it is, or how you created it."

"You must bring the power of the others together to help us open it back up and hold it until they can get out. I will contact you again when you have alerted the others. Now! Go!"

The light went out.

"Sam! The window has collapsed," Katala announced.

"Is it completely gone?"

"No, but what is left is too small for the remaining ships to get through."

"Thank you, Katala." He didn't know what to say to the others when he got their attention, but he couldn't wait for the right words. Whoever it was that had raised the alarm sounded sincere and worried. They also gave Sam the impression that saving the Dhara'chee was important, maybe more important than saving Carmen the others of his team. Regardless of the entity's priorities, something definitely needed to be done and quickly.

"Janus, did you happen to catch the message I just received?"

"Yes I did. I did not recognize the sender."

"Neither did I." Sam said. *"Nor do I know what we are going to be able to do to help with the window."*

"I don't either, but let's get the others together and find out. I assume the 'others' the mysterious entity was referring to are the Cheneshi, the Lorengi and me." Janus said.

"That's my assumption, too. I'll connect us all together."

"Jarruda, Sways, the window has collapsed to a point that our ships won't be able to get back through!"

"What will we do?" Jarruda asked. *"I can't lose my daughter after just having found her again."*

Sam told them about the strange apparition and the message he received.

"Do you think whoever contacted you opened the window in the first place, Sam?" Sways asked.

"Yes. He said that they were losing their ability to hold the window open. It sounded like it was their window. I don't know what we can do to help."

The mysterious light formed before Sam again. It communicated with all of them.

"Thanks for getting everyone together, Sam. I'm sure you have a number of questions, but for now let me answer these first two. Yes, we created the window, and yes, you can help."

"What should we call you?" Sam asked.

"I'm a member of an ancient race called the Annli. Ours is no longer a corporeal existence. It's hard to think of ourselves as individuals, so we haven't used names for a great while. My name was Theron. We have a limited ability to influence matters in the physical universe. We have been aware of the ships that were trapped in the other dimension for millennia. We aren't certain, but we think we may have created the situation. Whether we did or did not, we couldn't correct it. We had to wait until Humans had progressed to a point where they could help. That waiting was difficult, as we were becoming less and less connected to the material world. We feared your development wouldn't occur until after we lost all connection, and then had no ability to help.

"We saw our opportunity when the one you call Carmen developed the ability to see consciousness at great distances with her mind. I'm sure others will be able to do that soon, but one was enough. We created the window, and when the time was right, we gently influenced Carmen to look at it."

"When did we get trapped there?" Jarruda asked.

"As was surmised, your home world has gone around its star over six thousand times since the event that trapped you there occurred."

"So you created the window recently, and are already losing the ability to hold it open?" Sam asked.

"That is correct, Sam. As I said, we have limited ability to affect the material world. We did what we could. We hoped it would be enough, and that we could remain in the background.

That proved to be a vain hope. We needed help. So we had to come forth and ask for it."

"Okay. We'll talk about this more when we've fixed the problem," Sam said. *"How can we help?"*

"Lend us your strength, and we'll put it where it is needed. Let us begin with Janus and you. Lorengi and Cheneshi, you may not be needed, but please be ready."

"If you haven't done this before, how can you know Janus and I will be enough?" Sam asked.

"The global consciousness of Earth is immensely powerful. You just have not learned that yet. You have not had to bring it to bear on a situation. Today, you will."

"Janus, are you ready?" asked Sam.

"Yes, Sam, though I'm not sure what is required."

"That will become clear as we proceed," Theron said. *"We will channel your energy through us."*

"What kind of energy are you looking for?" Sam asked.

"Think of it as if you are pushing on an immense mass, Sam. Push with your minds. Start with a small, constant pushing effort. If you were to use your full strength I don't know what would happen. So let us begin with a small push. Focus on me. Push against me, gently at first."

All of the power resided within Janus. Sam was a component, and also aware of what was happening—a participant and a witness. Sam focused on the mental impression he had of Theron. He felt Janus do the same. They pushed with what they thought of as a mere whisper of a breath on a feather.

"Gently, please! Let us get used to incorporating your energy into our effort. Good, good. Now increase the force gradually."

"I do not want to distract you, but the window is opening slowly," Jarruda said.

"Yes it is, but please, no more interruptions. This connection is a delicate thing. It is working, but we need all of our concentration until we have firmed it up."

Janus gradually increased the force until Theron said, *"The window is now opened wide enough. It's nearly at its original size. Just hold it there!"*

"We are barely pushing," Sam said.

"As I said. You are very powerful. Just the slightest effort on your part accomplished something which required an enormous effort for us. Please hold that force. We have to wait and see if those trapped on the other side will see their target again."

"I'm afraid, that my mind is all we have available," Orlyn said. *"I will not be able to wake the others. As I have no control over my ship, I cannot operate the devices which control their hibernation. Since I am lead scientist on our expedition, perhaps I can contribute something to the discussion of alternative solutions."*

"I'm all for a scientific discussion on where we are and what to do about it," Rosalind said. *"I'm especially eager to discuss it with the lead Dhara'chee scientist. I'm just not very optimistic that something will come from our discussion."*

"What else can we do?" Jesse asked. *"I'd be willing to get out and push, but I need a direction to push in. We are literally in the dark here. I would like to see if your discussion could shine a bit of light on our situation."*

"Okay," Rosalind said, *"I'll start. I think we are in a dimension outside of our normal space-time frame of reference. I think it is the dimension we usually travel through when we*

teleport, and the Dhara'chee travel through when using their FTL transports. One thing that I think supports my theory, is that both the Lorengi, traveling by way of teleportation, and the Dhara'chee, as well as the Sudahlli and Garduk, while using their FTL transports were all stuck in the same place—here." Rosalind said.

"Excellent," Orlyn said. "I like your theory. Do you have any idea what caused us to be trapped here?"

"No. The Garduk crew person, Heyut, was convinced that when he pushed a button on his ship that caused the problem. That could have been the cause if his was the only ship trapped. I don't see how pushing his ship's button could have affected the others."

"Agreed." Orlyn said. "I had also thought we might be in the dimension you described, Rosalind. Further, I think that dimension, and so we, are still in our universe as opposed to another one. Was this caused by a single event or something that is ongoing?"

"I would think it was for just an instant," Rosalind said. "Teleporting and FTL travel have been going on unhampered as far as we are aware for millennia, after you were trapped here."

"Millennia? Millennia! We have been trapped here for millennia?"

"That's our best guess, Orlyn," Rosalind said. "Sorry. I could have introduced that part of the story a bit more sensitively."

"What causes you to think it has been that long?"

"The Lorengi who were trapped here embarked on their ill-fated journey six thousand years ago."

"Oh."

Both scientists paused in their discussion. They had said what they thought had happened and didn't know where to take the discussion. Orlyn was dealing with the revelation that he had been trapped in the dimension for a very, very long time. The steam went out of the lively discourse.

Carmen, still in Jannida, was interested in the science, but didn't think it would lead them out of the dark. So she kept her mind focused on where the anchor was when it disappeared. She doubted there was any hope of it reappearing, but what else could she do? Maybe the window closed temporarily, and would snap back open—possible, but not likely. As she remembered the assessment before they left, the window was slowly closing, not oscillating between closing a little and opening a little.

So she was very surprised when she saw the bright light of the Lorengi sphere again, solidly where it had recently so discouragingly disappeared. She didn't want to call out to the others right away, and falsely raise their hopes. Then again, she couldn't wait because it might not last long.

"Everyone! It's back! Get ready. We're leaving."

No one asked for an explanation. They all quickly rejoined Carmen in her mind-view of the dark dimension and saw that the hoped-for bright light had reappeared. They focused intensely as before. Their focused grew until its strength was palpable.

"Go!" Carmen shouted.

In the next instant, she opened her eyes and exclaimed, *"Stars! We're Home!"*

14 You Can't Go Home Again

Aboard Katala

It had been months for some, an interminable moment for others. Horizons had been expanded. There were new friends to meet. Once the tumult of arrival was over, Sam suggested that representatives from each race meet on Katala. He checked and found all were air breathers and the air they usually breathed was close enough in composition that Katala could create a balanced mix which would be comfortable for everyone.

While arrangements were being made, Sam had a connection he wanted to make sure was maintained.

"Theron, are you there?"

"Yes Sam."

"Good. I couldn't tell because I didn't see your light as I did before."

"It is not necessary for me to take that form to converse with you. I did it the first time to give you something to connect to the voice you were hearing in your head. It takes an enormous amount of energy to concentrate myself into such a small volume. I can continue using that form if you need me to."

"I'm fine without seeing you, though the vision was impressive. Janus and I have been conversing for years, and I've never seen him. I hope you realize now that the Annli have 'come forth' there is no going back."

"We do, Sam. For reasons we will discuss later, we need to stay in contact with you and Janus. We hope to minimize the exposure to the races that have already been involved."

"Good luck with that. So far Humans, Lorengi and Cheneshi are aware of you, though we don't know much more than that you exist. The others will need an explanation of how they were trapped in that dimension, and how they were rescued. They may also have to learn about your involvement with the window."

"We agree. Being truthful is important, and there are other considerations. First of all, the Garduk and Sudahlli have been cut off from their people for millennia. They will have significant adjustments to make just reconnecting with them. The changes that have occurred on their worlds are significant. We must help them where we can. Also, we have their cosmology to consider. We don't want them to begin thinking that we are a god of some sort."

"You did not include the Dhara'chee."

"Yes. Theirs is a special case. They are the last of their kind and must be protected from the fate of their people."

"What happened?"

"An epidemic killed them all two thousand years ago."

"How is that possible? There must have been survivors."

"The only survivors, Sam, are in the ship your team brought back. We were surprised as your team was to discover the Dhara'chee were trapped with the others. Once we learned they were there, it made the rescue even more important and the sudden collapse of the window more serious.

"They are an ancient race. They had a well-developed civilization when we left the physical universe, and they survived long after our change. Early in their existence there was an importance placed on uniformity in their society. It was

112

only a social preference, but it was strong. It helped in many aspects of their cultural and technological development. They are a wonderful people. They are extremely intelligent, rational and gentle. They explored but did not colonize. Their entire population resided on their home world.

"In the end their uniformity was their undoing. The epidemic was able to kill so completely because of the nearly uniform DNA of the Dhara'chee people. When you meet with them, you will see that they all have the same height and appearance. It is difficult to tell one from another, like twins in your race. It is even difficult to distinguish males from females.

"One of their exploration ships went to a world which had a microorganism which was harmless to the indigenous creatures but deadly to the Dhara'chee. Once it matured into its deadly state it began to kill. By the time the Dhara'chee learned what was happening it was too late to find a solution. Death quickly raced through their entire population. A month after it was discovered, they were all dead. Since the Dhara'chee kept the location of their home planet secret, others did not know what had happened. The Dhara'chee just disappeared."

"What can we do?"

"We will have to tell them, help them adjust and find a new home world."

There was no more time to discuss the matter. Sam's guests had begun to arrive. They were teleported, with the help of Humans, to the common room of Katala.

Orlyn chose to keep the rest of the Dhara'chee in hibernation until he understood more about what was happening. Set Li Thall made the same decision for the same reason. She also thought that the sight of just one towering Sudahlli would be enough for those unfamiliar with her race. Nathat, the Garduk Ship Lead, brought Heyut along with him, but had Heyut remain behind him with an order to only speak if Nathat requested it.

Sam had had time to get a telepathic report from Carmen the moment she arrived. She, Rosalind, Ashira and Jesse were standing to one side accompanied by the holograms of Ahleeto and Jarruda. The rest of the Lorengi were in attendance by way of their connection through Jarruda. The Lorengi ships were connected through Katala. Sways and Janus were listening in. Theron was also listening but asked Sam not to call upon him if it could be avoided.

Although the rescue team had been in contact with the other races during the rescue, they had not seen what they looked like. Sam had seen the Garduk, but not the others. He was amazed that Set Li was over seven feet tall. She was wearing a vest and short breeches made of leather of some sort. The exposed part of her body was covered with short brown fur. She had two sets of arms one extending from her upper shoulders, and another set which emerged from the sides of her mid-section. Each of the long arms ended in large, five-fingered hands. She was fearsome looking, but her stance and body language seemed relaxed rather than aggressive.

Orlyn was about five feet tall, had a large head on a slender neck connected to a slender body. He was hairless and his skin had a pinkish tint to it where it showed outside his short-sleeved one-piece uniform. It looked like he was smiling though one couldn't tell for sure.

Nathat's tan skin was stretched tight over his short, bony frame. Being the shortest of the group he seemed uneasy a midst of so many large beings especially Set Li. Nathat looked like he was to be trying to stand as tall as he could.

"Well met all of you," Sam said. "Everyone here is meeting other races for the first time, so I need not speak of my personal feelings of amazement. This is a truly remarkable event for the Human race, tucked away as it is in an unpopulated part of the galaxy. We are extremely happy that all of you could be brought out of the dimension you were trapped in for such a long time."

"That is truly the most difficult part of this to accept," Set Li said. "How is such a thing possible?" The verbal communication was being translated by Katala. Everyone had been given devices to wear that would allow them to hear the translation in their language.

"The Human scientist, Rosalind and I only have theories, First Born Mother, Set Li," Orlyn said. "We believe that time does not exist in the dimension we were in. Though I lived through it, I cannot even now believe such a concept. I was stunned when I was told that over six thousand years have passed during my absence."

"I was struck by that same revelation, Honored One," Set Li said, "but my reaction to that revelation was nothing compared to the awe I felt to have been contacted by one of the revered Dhara'chee. Perhaps we will have time to speak again."

"I look forward to it, Set Li."

Nathat made a noise which sounded like he was clearing his throat. He successfully captured everyone's attention.

"I also am awed by all of this, but I have some questions."

"Go ahead, Ship Lead Nathat," Sam said.

"How can we be sure such a time span has occurred? Our ships track time. When I checked after being told about the time lapse, my ship showed no time passed."

"If I may interrupt on this point," Thelika said, "I have some information that might help. I contacted the intelligence operating the Dhara'chee ship. Together we came up with astrological measurements and calculations involving relative position of stars and rotation of our galaxy.

We compared the data in the Dhara'chee database for these figures at the time it became trapped in the dimension to the values when calculated today. Together the Dhara'chee ship and I have made the calculations a number of different ways, and each time come up with the result that shows something in the neighborhood of six thousand Earth-years have passed since you were all trapped. Confirmation will of course occur when your contact your respective populations."

"Humph! I guess I will have to accept that until I can get back to my base," Nathat said. "Does anyone know what happened? My lowly crew member, Heyut, believes it happened because he pushed a button he was unfamiliar with when he was in the control room. As that button only controls the lighting in a room adjoining the control room, I don't think it created the situation we all found ourselves in."

"But it happened at the same time!" Heyut said in his defense. With a look from Nathat, Heyut said no more.

"We don't know how it happened, but we believe we know where you were," Rosalind said.

"Yes, I've heard the explanation, and I will accept it for now," Nathat said. "How did you become aware we were there?"

Carmen told Nathat that a window into that dimension had been created, which exposed the situation, and explained how she had detected it. Sam hadn't told Carmen about Theron and the Annli yet, so that information was absent from her explanation. Nathat didn't appear satisfied, but he asked no more questions.

"So what shall we do now?" Sam asked.

"Each of us may have a different answer to that question," Jarruda said. "After discussing this with my daughter, I am certain that all the Lorengi that exist are with me. We are mobile, but we need time to think about what to do next."

"The Sudahlli will want to return to our home world," Set Li said. "I can't imagine the changes that have occurred in our absence, but it is likely they are substantial. Though I'm not certain of our current location, I believe we are thousands of light years from Sudahlli-explored space. It will take a while for us to return."

"We can help if you would let us," Jarruda said. "The Lorengi ship you were enclosed within could transport you to your home world very quickly."

"That would be helpful, but we are already greatly in your debt," said Set Li. "I would be reluctant to increase our debt to you."

"Don't concern yourself about that," Jarruda said. "We will put together a team of Lorengi and Humans who would be excited to see your part of the galaxy and learn about your people and other races that live there. The opportunity to learn from you and explore that part of the galaxy would more than eliminate any debt you feel you owe us."

"I shall have to wake the rest of my clan, but once they understand what has happened, I'm sure they will find your generous offer acceptable. Besides if your transport reduces our travel time we will have time to learn more while we are here, and to talk with the honored Dhara'chee."

"What about us?" Nathat asked. "Our home world is even further away than that of the Sudahlli."

"We make the same offer to you," Jarruda said. "We would like to learn more about the Garduk, also."

"Thank you. I will wake the rest of my crew, and let you know when we are ready to leave. May I now be returned to my ship?"

"Their homecoming will not be pleasant, Sam," Theron said, after Nathat and Heyut were teleported back to their ship. *"Over a thousand years ago there was a civil war that ravaged their world and society. It set them back technologically to such an extent that even now there is still widespread starvation. They are a tribal society now, with violent clashes between competing tribes. I don't know how to help Nathat and his crew, but we should let them know and be ready to do what we can."*

"Will it be safe for our people to travel there?" Sam asked.

"As long as they don't spend much time on the planet's surface."

"Is there a way we can inform Nathat about what to expect?"

"Perhaps in a private session, though he doesn't seem to be in a frame of mind where he would likely believe us or accept our advice. We should try anyway," Theron said.

After a little more discussion, Set Li requested to be taken back to her ship, and was teleported there with Jesse's help. Orlyn asked to be taken back to the Dhara'chee ship so that he could wake his colleagues. He was eager to tell them of the many wondrous things that had transpired and break the news to them about how much time has passed. Sam asked him to stay a little longer so that he could share some information with him. Sam asked Carmen to join them. They went to a separate compartment, leaving the rest of the Human exploration crews from Thelika and Katala to talk over future plans with Jarruda and the Lorengi.

When they were settled around a table Sam asked if Orlyn wanted some tea.

"I'm not sure what that is, but if you have hot water, I have some lymbet leaves which can be used to brew a calming drink."

Orlyn made a cup of the hot lymbet drink for all of them.

"This is good," Carmen said, after taking a sip. "As you said, it does have an immediate calming effect."

"I'm glad you like it. Now Sam, you said you had some information," Orlyn said.

"Yes. First let me ask if you have ever heard of a race called the Annli."

"Only as a myth. Eons ago, the Dhara'chee were said to have been visited by an advanced, space-faring race who called themselves the Annli. The Annli were supposed to have shared some of their technology during their infrequent visits which helped the Dhara'chee of the time leap forward. Then the visits stopped. After a while, the Dhara'chee were visited by another race which told a story of the Annli disappearing along with their planet and its moon. It was so long ago that for most of us it is just a myth. I'm not sure they really exist."

"Apparently they do. I was recently contacted by an entity that identified itself as an Annli called Theron. He said that the Annli created the window which helped us find you and the other ships. He contacted me at the moment when that window collapsed."

"That must have been when the Lorengi sphere disappeared"

"Yes, that's probably what it looked like from your position, Carmen. Theron asked us to lend our support to opening the window again."

"What do you mean your support?" Orlyn asked.

Sam explained about Janus, and Orlyn became quiet.

"I know this is a lot to take in, Orlyn. I need you to be aware of this background so that you'll understand when I introduce Theron."

"Yes it is. I am learning that the mythological Annli are real and that Humans have astounding abilities."

"Thank you Sam. Carmen, Orlyn, I am Theron. My people were called the Annli. The strange disappearance you spoke of Orlyn did occur. It was the moment in time when the Annli, our home world and its satellite were transformed into pure energy. The Annli have existed in that state since that time."

"Amazing, truly amazing," Orlyn said, and then was lost in his thoughts.

"You created the window?" Carmen asked.

Theron told them about the sequence of events, how long they had waited to fashion a rescue and the key role Carmen had played.

It was Carmen's turn to be silent as she thought over the implications of what Theron had told them.

"Apparently, you wish to limit the number of people who know about you," Orlyn said. "I'm honored to have been informed of your existence, but I must ask, why me?

"In part because the Dhara'chee are an advanced society and have had some connection to the Annli in the past. Mostly because I must tell you about what happened to the Dhara'chee in your absence. I'm so sorry, Orlyn, but the ten thousand Dhara'chee you have on your ship are all that remain of the wonderful Dhara'chee."

Orlyn was obviously stunned by the news. The others gave him time to absorb it.

"What happened to my people?"

Theron told him about the plague, adding details that would be relevant to Orlyn.

"Those alive at the end put satellites into orbit which broadcast a recurring message about what happened and a warning about the plague. That satellite has a database which contains information about the Dhara'chee and their scientific analysis of what killed them."

Obviously shocked, Orlyn seemed to be talking to himself when he said despairingly, "We may be able to learn more about what happened, but never be able land on the Dhara'chee home world again...."

15 Sleeping Ship Lead

Aboard the Dhara'chee Ship, Aceri

Orlyn had asked Carmen to take him back to his ship. There were over ten thousand Dhara'chee aboard. Their mission had been to explore parts of the galaxy the Dhara'chee hadn't visited before. Their mission would change now.

Carmen looked around when they arrived in what Orlyn said was the control room for the enormous ship. He said it would be best if they arrived there for a number of reasons, including that it was one of the few spaces aboard where the ceilings would be high enough for Carmen to stand upright.

She was struck by the lack of visible controls. She saw several places around the large space, which were obvious workstations. The seats were sized to fit the smaller Dhara'chee bodies, but the panels before them were smooth, curved, milky white surfaces without the buttons, or screens, or lights that she would have expected. She wanted to ask about what she was seeing but decided to wait for a better time.

"Thank you for coming with me, Carmen. Would it be possible for you to stay with me as I share this tragic information with the others?"

"Of course."

"I'm glad that you are comfortable with telepathy. I would rather not have to use the harsh sounds of a translating device when I tell the others what happened. I will begin by bringing

only the section leaders out of hibernation. Together we will decide how to proceed."

Carmen learned more about how the controls stations operated when Orlyn sat down at one. Immediately a variety of colored lights began to flash on the panel before him. Occasionally Orlyn would reach out and touch the panel, but mostly the panel seemed to be operating on its own. Then she thought she understood.

"You communicate with your ship telepathically?"

"Yes. Although it is not an organic being like the Lorengi ships, our ships are conscious entities."

Carmen wondered how a cyber-based intelligence could communicate telepathically. Then she remembered that Martha, the ubiquitous, cyber-based intelligence on Earth, had developed the technology which allowed it to communicate with Janus telepathically. The lights stopped flashing and Orlyn turned to her.

"That's done. Fourteen of my colleagues will meet us in the planning room on the other side of the wall behind you. There will be a short delay as they go through the rest of the process that is required when coming out of hibernation. Let us go in and wait for them there. I will prepare lymbet. If ever we needed its calming influence, we need it for this session."

Carmen followed Orlyn down a short hallway. When he stopped, a section of the wall opened. Orlyn stepped through the doorway. Carmen bent down so she could go through the Dhara'chee sized opening, but the opening increased in height to accommodate Carmen's taller stature. The room she stepped into had ceilings tall enough, so she didn't have to stoop.

Orlyn went to the head of a table that had seating for twenty. Carmen went to sit in a chair on his right. It was too small and too close to the table. Again that difficulty was addressed by the ship. The chair moved back on its own and was reshaped to fit her more comfortably.

"Thank you."

"You're welcome, Carmen." the ship responded. *"I am pleased to meet you. I am called Aceri. I have not met a new race in a long time. I enjoyed exercising my shape shifting abilities."*

Carmen smiled. *"I'm pleased to meet you, also. Thelika told us that she worked with you on the calculations which established how much time had passed for you and the others."*

"Yes. I have never met an organic, living ship before. We worked well together. Will she be traveling with us again?"

"It is possible."

Before Carmen and Aceri could continue their conversation the Dhara'chee leaders came into the room. Apparently Aceri had informed them of Carmen's presence. As each of them came in, they went to Carmen, bowed, and greeted her.

All the Dhara'chee looked like a twin of Orlyn. Carmen wondered how she would be able to tell them apart. They had what looked like name tags on their one-piece, short-sleeved, light green uniforms, but as she couldn't yet read the Dhara'chee language the tags were no help. She thought she discerned some differences that could be gender related, but as an anthropologist, she knew the danger of assuming such things when meeting a new culture.

"I have wakened you to tell you of the wondrous things that have transpired while you were in stasis. I also have terrible news to share. I must tell you about the first, to establish a foundation for the second," Orlyn explained

He explained about their ship being trapped and how their rescue came about. He told them of the races he had met in the process, including the Theron and the Annli.

"An Annli?" an elderly Dhara'chee queried. *"How is that possible, Orlyn? They were just a myth when we left those thousands of years ago."*

"So we all believed, Daran. They are real, and they did interact with our ancient ancestors."

"Where have they been?"

"Theron gave me only the briefest of explanations. They were transformed along with their planet and moon. We have no suitable words for their current state. It is some form of pure energy. They have had little connection with the material world since then."

"So the story about their disappearance was true?"

"Yes."

"Why have they chosen to present themselves at this time?"

Orlyn told the group about the Annli role in their rescue. He looked down at the table and paused before telling them the rest of what Theron said. The others watched him.

"There is something else, isn't there, Orlyn?"

"Yes, Daran. Theron told me that something terrible happened to the Dhara'chee in our absence. They all died from a deadly infection."

"ALL?" Several Dhara'chee gasped at the same time.

"That is what I was told."

Orlyn then shared with his colleagues what he had learned from Theron about how it had happened. They sat in stunned silence until Daran, the eldest of the group offered some solace.

"This is the worst possible news we could have been given. To find that all we knew and loved is gone is too much for anyone to endure. Yet endure we must. We were entrusted to lead this expedition in search for new wonders. We must now lead our colleagues to find a new place in the galaxy for the Dhara'chee."

Carmen felt it was time for her to offer support.

"I am saddened by what you are faced with. Of the several races I am now aware of, including the Human race, none is more capable of rising to this challenge than the Dhara'chee. What I've heard of you fills me with confidence that you will succeed, and I know the Lorengi, the Humans and others will do all we can to aid you in your endeavor."

"Thank you, Carmen," Daran said. *"It warms our hearts in this dark time to know that others care and will help. You will be a welcome guest when we begin discussing options. It will take some time to revive the others and help them adjust to the news. We won't be making plans until everyone is alert."*

Before Carmen could respond, she received an urgent thought from Jesse.

"Carmen, where are you?"

"I'm with the Dhara'chee."

"You better come back to Katala. Set Li and Nathat were brought back to discuss next steps. Theron and Sam have just told Nathat about the unpleasant developments on his home world. He went nuts.

"In the first place, he doesn't believe any of what has happened, and now he is told his world has reverted to tribalism. He demands to be taken home right now. Sam and I thought that you and I should accompany the Garduk on the trip. There may be a way for us to help, if Nathat would even accept our help."

"I'll leave right away."

The group around the table was staring at Carmen awaiting her response to Daran's offer to include her in the planning discussions.

"I'm sorry for the delay. I've just been alerted by my shipmate that the leader of another of the races that were

rescued, the Garduk, is demanding to be taken home. Theron told him that a millennia ago there was a civil war on the Garduk home world. It was so devastating that the technological base for their civilization was destroyed. Now a much-reduced population is divided into tribes, and the tribes are fighting over severely limited resources."

"We know of the Garduk. They are an impatient, excitable race," Daran said. *"From what you have said, they may need your help. Go. We will be here when you get back."*

Carmen found herself in the middle of a heated discussion when she returned to the common room on Katala. Nathat was waving his arms around and shouting angrily. Sam, Jesse and Set Li were trying to calm him.

"I've been taken against my will and trapped in a web of lies!" Nathat shouted. Beside him, Heyut shrank away from Nathat's wrath. "I demand that you take me and my ship back to the Garduk home world, NOW!"

To emphasize his point, Nathat pulled what looked like a hand weapon and pointed at the others in the room.

Apparently Set Li had had enough of Nathat's histrionics. In a move so quick that the eye just barely caught it, Set Li leapt to Nathat's side, grabbed the hand that held the weapon, pointed it down, and touched her index finger to the side of his neck. Nathat slumped to the floor.

In the welcome quiet that followed, the others looked on in amazement. They were shocked at Set Li's swift violence."

"Silly creature," Set Li said. "A ship master should have more control over their emotions. Typical, when a male is put in charge."

"His shouting and pointing a weapon was no reason to kill him," Sam said.

"Kill? I did not kill him. I just put him to sleep."

"How did you do that?" Jesse asked.

Set Li told them of the needle that she could extend from under the claw like fingernail of her index fingers and its function.

"Do all Sudahlli have this?" Carmen asked.

"Only females. It emerges when they mature. We are trained in its use. As First-Born Mother of a clan I was given additional training. We can quickly choose from a variety of substances to inject. I chose a strong sleep potion for Ship Lead Nathat."

"How could you be sure it would be safe to use on a Garduk?"

"Do not worry, Carmen. I sensed a great deal about his body chemistry by just being in the same room with him. When my body prepares the substance with the effect I desire, it does so taking into account what it has learned about the intended target's body chemistry. This is especially important when one is being attacked and desires a fast-acting poison that will be effective on whatever is attacking."

"Handy," Jesse said.

"Our race found it so when living in the wild. As you just saw, in more civilized times we still find it useful."

"I hope you will take this in the way I intend it," Jesse said, "but I have a hard time imagining anything that would attack a Sudahlli, even a young one."

"I understand your remark, and no offense was taken. The Sudahlli are not the largest, nor the fiercest creatures on the world we evolved on. In our early history, a Sudahlli mother also had need to protect her infant from other Sudahlli in addition to natural predators. We evolved within a highly competitive, violent natural environment. It was a challenge to leave behind traits necessary for survival when we wanted to move into a more civilized way of life, but we have…for the most part."

Carmen looked up at the four arms with hands tipped with claws and the sharp carnivore teeth of the Sudahlli towering above her. She saw compassion and wisdom in the eyes that looked back at her and was convinced that Set Li had succeeded in making the shift.

"Thank you for helping calm the immediate situation, Set Li," Carmen said. "I'm not sure what Nathat will be like when he wakes, but we need to prepare to take the Garduk home. Heyut, is there a second in command aboard your ship?"

"Yes, Carmen. Nathat's mate is Second Ship Lead. Her name is Neva. She is milder in her ways."

"That will be a welcome change. I think we should take Nathat to your ship. We will explain what happened to Neva, and let your medical attendant know that Nathat will need bed rest while he recovers. By the way, Set Li how long will Nathat be out?" Carmen asked.

"Difficult to tell. I was a bit exasperated when my body chose the substance to inject and the amount to meet the need my emotion was expressing. I would guess one ship day."

"That will be helpful while we travel, but Nathat will likely hold a grudge. No help for that now. Jesse, could you pick up Nathat? From what Sam has said we'll need to teleport in the sitting position, so you'll need to lay Nathat across your lap. Heyut come and stand by me."

Jesse and Carmen teleported to the Bridge of the Garduk ship, taking Nathat and Heyut with them. It more closely matched what Carmen expected a Bridge to look like than what she had seen on the Lorengi and Dhara'chee ships. There were workstations with instruments, screens with internal and external views or information on them, and lights blinking.

Carmen didn't take long looking around for there were six agitated Garduk on the Bridge with them. When the Garduk saw the condition of their Ship Lead they became more distressed. Five of them drew hand weapons and pointed them at Carmen and Jesse.

16 Devastation

On the Garduk ship within the Lorengi ship Meratta

"Wait!" Heyut shouted.

"What has happened, young Heyut?" the Garduk without a weapon asked, holding up a hand to stay the others.

Meratta had been listening in on the Garduk conversations so she had no trouble translating for Carmen and Jesse.

"Well, we have landed in it. Do you think that is Neva, Nathat's mate? Do you think we should leave?" Jesse asked.

"She does seem to be in charge, Jesse. Let's see how this plays out. We can always jump out of here. Meratta, can you translate what we say, and broadcast the translation to them somehow?"

"I can make myself heard inside their ship. Through me they will know what you have said. It may sound strange and frighten them. Since they are armed, we should proceed cautiously."

"Nathat lives, Second Ship Lead," Heyut said. "Nathat became very excited, drew his weapon and threatened others. The Sudahlli First Born Mother quickly sedated him. They think he will be out for several ship days."

"A Sudahlli was there?"

"Yes, Neva."

"My sometimes-rash mate is lucky he was not killed. A Sudahlli! By Atu, these are strange happenings. Are these the Humans you spoke of who hold our Ship Lead?"

"The female is Carmen. It is she who rescued us."

"Is she the one that can communicate without voicing her words?"

"Yes, she can put words into your mind without speaking."

Neva turned to face Carmen. "What have you to say, Carmen?"

"I am honored to meet you, Second Ship Lead Neva."

Neva's eyes widened. "It is true then, what our young crew member told us. Did the rest of my crew in this room hear what you just said in my head?"

"No, I spoke only to you. If you would rather, I can send our conversation to everyone, or we can continue verbally, and Meratta, the ship your vessel resides in will translate for us."

"Let's continue with normal speech."

"Before we begin, could you have your crew put their weapons away? They might be startled when our translated words come through your ship comm system."

"As you wish." Neva turned to her crew and told them to secure their weapons.

"As Heyut said, Nathat has been sedated but is unharmed otherwise." A moment later, Meratta's translation of Carmen's words came through the Garduk ship's comm system, startling the crew.

"What caused my mate to get so upset?"

"Perhaps I should discuss that with you in private after your mate is given to your ship medical personnel."

Neva agreed to a private session, and had her crew take Nathat to sick bay. She asked Heyut to remain with her and the Humans on the Bridge. Carmen thought that Neva may have considered it a good way to keep Heyut from spreading information among the crew prematurely. Once they were alone on the Bridge, Neva asked her ship to isolate the Bridge from intra-ship communication.

"Now, what was it that drove my mate to draw his weapon?"

"He drew his weapon," Jesse said, "to emphasize that he was serious in his demand that he and his crew be taken to the Garduk home world immediately. We had already said we would take him home, but by that time he was beyond rational thought."

"What made him make the demand in the first place?"

"Nathat has had trouble believing anything we told him," Carmen said. "How you had been trapped in the other dimension for six thousand years, and how we rescued your ship and crew was all fantasy to him. He thought we were lying to him. Then we told him about the current state of your home world."

"Solan."

"What?" Carmen asked.

"We call our home world Solan."

"Oh. Thank you."

"What has happened to Solan?"

Carmen told her about the civil war and the changes that had resulted from it.

"How could you possibly know about what is happening on Solan?" Neva asked.

"Good question. The answer to that added to Nathat's distress." Carmen went on to tell her about Theron and the Annli.

"I join my mate in his assessment that this is all fantasy. The Annli are an ancient myth. I don't know how you heard of our stories from eons ago, but that is all they are, stories."

"Greetings, Neva. I am Theron, and I am a member the race once called the Annli. Perhaps if I add some specifics you might become convinced."

Neva listened in stunned silence while Theron told her, Jesse and Carmen about the dispute that triggered the war, the weapons used and how the infrastructure was destroyed. Theron went on to provide more detail about the current situation on Solan.

Neva's eyes glistened with moisture, forming tears at the edges. Heyut looked on not understanding. He hadn't been included in the discussion which informed Nathat of the situation on Solan, nor was he included in the report Theron had just given to Neva.

"What is it, Second Ship Lead? Have these Humans hurt you in some way?"

Neva reached over, enclosed Heyut's hand in hers, and gave it a squeeze.

"No, young Heyut. We Garduk have apparently hurt ourselves."

She looked up at Carmen. "I won't draw a weapon to emphasize my wish to go to Solan, but will you take us home? We may be able to do something to help, but I'm overwhelmed by the size of the challenge."

Carmen nodded solemnly. "Yes. All that is needed is to convey the coordinates for Solan to the ship your vessel resides in, whose name is Meratta by the way, and the trip will be made. If you wish, Jesse and I will accompany you. There may be something we can do to help, though at this point I cannot imagine what that would be."

"Yes, please. Together we may be able to do more than the Garduk aboard this ship can do on our own. Theron, will you assist us?"

There was a long pause before Neva received a response.

"Sorry for the delay," Theron said, excluding Heyut. *"It takes time for all of the Annli to express their opinion. Many wanted us to maintain our stance of not interfering with any corporeal beings. I and others argued that we have already interfered by rescuing you, and having done so, we have some responsibility to see this process through."*

"...and," Carmen said to only Theron, *"Sam said you intimated that the Annli might have had something to do with the ships getting trapped in the first place."*

"There is that possibility, and it strengthened my position in the debate," Theron answered her.

"When our discussion was completed," Theron said, *"the Annli decided that I should stay involved with you and help if I could. I must tell you, that the Annli ability to influence the material world is almost nonexistent."*

"A little help from an Annli might go a long way," Carmen said.

"Good. I am feeling better knowing we will have help from all of you," Neva said. "Carmen and Jesse, you go and make your preparations. I will tell my crew of the situation and that we are going to Solan to help if we can."

"What about Nathat?" Jesse asked. "He was very angry before he was sedated."

"I will be with him when he wakes. He is a fine Garduk in normal times. He just has trouble with changes and new things. I will help him adjust."

Carmen looked at the Garduk female and found determination written all over Neva's face. Carmen was certain that Nathat would be adjusted by Neva, if he didn't adjust on his own.

"I have received the coordinates for Solan from the Garduk ship," Meratta said.

"Thank you, Meratta," said Carmen. "I will go tell others and ask Jarruda if borrowing you for a while is okay with her. We will return soon, Neva."

When they returned to Katala, Jesse and Carmen found Sam in a discussion with Rosalind and Set Li.

"How are things with the Garduk?" Sam asked.

Carmen told him what had transpired.

"So you and Jesse will be going with them. Sounds like a good idea. Do you want anyone else along? Should I ask for volunteers?"

"Do you want me to go along?" Rosalind asked.

"We don't know what we'll be facing. I don't think we'll need a scientific powerhouse like you, Rosalind."

"Good. Working with competitive and sometimes violent tribal people is not what I think of as field work. I could pose as a blind wise woman I guess."

Carmen laughed. "I think you *are* wise, my friend, but I agree this is not your type of field work. I don't think we want a lot of people there, at least at first, so it won't be necessary to ask for volunteers. Why don't Jesse and I go, assess the situation, and determine if more of us are needed?"

When Carmen checked, Jarruda agreed that Meratta should be used for the journey. Ahleeto asked if she should accompany them.

"I'm always glad to have you along, Ahleeto. What do you have in mind?"

"Two things. I'm more familiar with our ships, and Meratta might like to have a Lorengi along. Also, although my holographic appearance will be magical to the Garduk, I will be able to speak to them in their own language. The combination might be useful in some circumstances."

"Sounds like a good idea," Carmen said.

"Neva, we are ready to come back. Is this a good time? We would like to meet with you in private again. We need to introduce you to Ahleeto and talk about the journey."

"Give me a little more time. I am still working with the crew, helping them get used to everything that has happened."

A short time later they were on the Garduk Bridge again. Neva's eyes were wide as she was presented with yet another new phenomenon. She still couldn't believe her eyes when Carmen and Jesse materialize in front of her in their sitting position, but she had seen them do it before. She hadn't seen the entity sitting next to them before.

The new visitor appeared to have short, gray fur where the skin showed outside of the one-piece uniform it was wearing. It had appropriately pointed ears, but instead of the point flopping down like Garduk ears, they were smaller and pointed up. Most troubling was the insubstantial look of the creature. Neva was only daunted for a moment. She walked up to Ahleeto and put her finger through Ahleeto's shoulder, and quickly jumped back away from her.

"Please tell me what this is, Carmen!"

"I think I'll let Ahleeto explain herself."

"Ah, she is female then?"

"Yes, I am," Ahleeto said in fluent Garduk. "I am Lorengi. A long time ago, I uploaded myself to a system, so I exist as a digital person. What you see is a projection of what I looked like when I made the decision to transform myself."

"A miracle every moment," Neva said. "Good to meet you Ahleeto. Now what about this trip?"

"The ship we are inside of is capable of teleporting itself and everything that is inside it to a new location," Carmen said. "Once the decision to leave is made, the transition to the new location happens instantaneously. It's just like when Jesse and I appeared or disappeared before your eyes."

"Another moment must have passed, for I am being introduced to another miracle."

Carmen smiled. "Thank you for believing me, Neva."

"It is either true or it is not. We will see when we travel to Solan. By my ship's instruments, we are thousands of light-years from Solan. It would take a long time to get there using our technology. If we arrive quickly as you say, I will be convinced."

"Good practical thinking, Neva. When we arrive, Meratta will be able to give us views of the surface. They will be more easily seen from within Meratta. How many crew members do you have aboard?"

"Fifty-three. Why?"

"I suggest that we all move to Meratta. She is much larger and can accommodate your crew. It could be that when we arrive we will want to stay aboard ship for a while until we can determine what to do next. Your crew might find the larger space within Meratta more comfortable during a prolonged stay."

"I agree, but let's decide that when we get there. If it is easier for me to see the surface views from within Meratta, then I will go there with you, but first, I will attempt to waken Nathat. If he did not believe you when you told him all of this, he won't believe you even if you show him pictures when we arrive. He must experience what I do, so we have a common reference. Wait here."

It wasn't long before Neva returned with a groggy Nathat who was being helped onto the Bridge by Neva and Heyut. Neva had apparently informed him of the plan, and reigned in his belligerent behavior, for it was a much-subdued Nathat that came before them.

"I have brought you each a device that you can put into your ear which will allow you to stay in contact with your ship," Carmen said.

Carmen gave Neva and Nathat the devices. They put it in their ears. Neva tested it and nodded that it was working. Neva told her crew where she and Nathat were going. Then she led the way to the hatch that would take them out of the Garduk ship. On hands and knees, Jesse and Carmen followed Neva and Nathat out of her ship and into Meratta. Then the two Garduk followed them to Meratta's common room.

"Are you able to communicate with your ship?" Carmen asked.

"Yes," Nathat said, becoming more aware of what was going on.

"Please ask if it agrees with Meratta about our present location."

"It says the two ships are in agreement."

"Good," Carmen said. "Meratta, please show us a view of what is outside the ship, including the other Lorengi ships."

Carmen pointed to Thelika. "The ship we are in looks a lot like that one over there."

"They are large, but not as large as that smooth looking white one. Whose ship is that?" Nathat asked.

"That is the Dhara'chee ship."

"I've heard of them. Were they trapped, too?" Nathat asked.

Carmen saw Neva's influence in Nathat's behavior. He was talking as if he believed in the trap and the rescue.

"Yes. I wanted to give you a vision of the ship you are traveling in, and to show you our starting point. Are you ready to go to Solan?"

"Yes," Nathat and Neva said simultaneously.

"Meratta, please take us to Solan, and establish an orbit that will allow you to provide us with visuals of the surface."

The scene on the large screen shifted. The ships they had seen before disappeared and were replaced by a view of a rotating planet."

Both Garduk gasped. "Solan?" Nathat wondered. "Wait. Let me confirm this with my ship." He did and nodded. "We are home. Now we will see if your claims are true. Can you show me a picture of one of our large cities?"

"Yes. Give us the name, and Meratta will get its location from your ship."

"Carrat. It is the city we lived in before we left."

A moment later, the scene changed to show a city in ruin. There were a few Garduk in rags furtively scurrying among the broken buildings.

17 The Gathering

On the Garduk Planet Solan

Sadut cast his net into the water again. Sixteen casts and only three small gazaz to show for it. It was not enough to feed his family, let alone provide any surplus to share with the village. The casts were like days in his life. With each cast, there was less than before. So it was with his village. Each day there was less to eat, people were lost to sickness or starvation, and marauders frequently raided taking what little they did have.

He used to dream of a life of plenty. When he was young the elders had told him what it was like in ancient times. He could no longer even fashion such visions in his mind. The rest of Solan was no better. It was worse in some cases. At least the sea provided some food. The stories from where there was no food were too terrible to think of.

He pulled his empty net into his small boat. He had no more time for fishing this morning. He had to bring his meager catch to the morning meal, and then meet with others in the village. They looked to him to lead them, to help them find ways to survive another cold season. He had no answers, but he would talk with them anyway.

"Sadut?"

Now he was hearing voices in his head. Perhaps the lack of food was affecting his mind. He continued paddling toward shore. Perhaps the voices would go away with some warm fish broth.

"Do not worry. You are not imagining this. I am an Annli. We are able to speak mind-to-mind. My name is Theron."

Sadut dropped the paddle into the water. It nearly got away from him. He caught it in time, and thanked Atu that he did. The gentle current that passed by this part of the village would take him away from shore. If he tried to swim he would lose his boat and meager catch. How could he say that it had happened because a mythological Annli had spoken to him?

"Go away!" he shouted to the mist that hung over this morning's calm waters. "Do not add to my misery by driving me mad."

"Sadut, please calm yourself, and listen. You have been chosen to come to a gathering. Your mate Tarad is to come with you. We are talking with Tarad at this moment. You will be transported to the place of the gathering after you and Tarad make arrangements to be absent from your village for a time."

Sadut looked toward shore and saw Tarad running to meet him holding her hands to her head.

Dakat was large for a Garduk, and not just his girth. He was taller than the rest of the males in the clan he led. Sitting upon his aflut, which was four feet high at its shoulders, the top of Dakat's head was over six feet above the ground, towering over the others lined up on both sides of him, including his captains who were also riding afluts.

The aflut were four-legged domesticated animals with shaggy brown coats and stumpy legs which the Garduk used for milk, meat and transport.

Today Dakat would ride his aflut into battle against Jerak, who used to be his friend. He didn't want this battle, but Jerak's men had continued to raid Dakat's villages on the border between their two lands. Dakat raised his arm above his head. He started to swing his arm down to signal his men forward to do battle with the army of Jerak, which had formed up on the other side of this small valley.

"Stop!"

The command boomed into the heads of Dakat and Jerak at the same time.

"You are to cease these hostilities, immediately!"

Dakat dropped his arm to his side. His captains looked at him in wonder. He looked across the field and saw that Jerak was looking around appearing to be confused.

"Yes. I am speaking to you Dakat and you Jerak. You are not to have this battle. I am offering you something that is far more interesting and rewarding."

"Who or what are you, that I and my opponent should believe you?" Dakat challenged. Since he was speaking to no one his captains could see, they stared at him without understanding.

"Dakat and Jerak tell your men to stand down. I want you to go forward until you are side-by-side in the center of the valley."

Dakat looked over to Jerak and tapped his hand against his head with a questioning look on his face. Jerak did the same, and nodded indicating he was experiencing something, too. Dakat told his men to stay where they were and nudged his aflut forward slowly. Seeing Jerak doing the same, he kicked his aflut into a trot and headed toward Jerak.

Dakat's men watched as he approached Jerak. As they came to each other's side, a giant-sized being of some kind appeared between them. The giant put its arms around the two Garduk leaders, and before they could draw their short swords all three disappeared. Both of their aflut mounts began to graze, as they are prone to do when they are riderless.

There were gasps and shouts among Dakat's ranks. The captains were as disturbed as the rest but called for order. They looked across the valley and saw chaos within Jerak's ranks. One after the other Jerak's soldiers turned and ran back the way they had come. Those astride aflut were trying to calm their animals. After a few minutes all of Jerak's men had quickly left what was to have been a field of battle.

Dakat's captains were proud of their men as they formed up for an orderly, but quick retreat. They talked among themselves about what they were going to tell Dakat's mate. They needn't have worried. When they returned to the capital, the captains learned that Aura disappeared in much the same way as Dakat.

Dakat and Jerak were still in the process of attempting to draw their swords, to defend themselves from the giant that put its arms around them. They were deposited gently on a grassy field. As soon as they landed the giant disappeared as quickly as it had arrived. They were left to look at each other.

"What was that?" Jerak asked.

"A very large being with unusual powers I'd guess," Dakat said.

With the giant gone, they looked at where they were. It was a part of Solan that neither had visited. It was a flat field with many Garduk of all stripes. Some were wearing fine gowns and cloaks; many others were in rags barely covering their bodies. Dakat and Jerak were both amazed that their mates were near where they had landed. The two females rushed into the arms of their mates.

Aura, Dakat's mate, ran over to him, weeping tears of joy.

"You're alive! Tema and I were so worried that you had killed each other in your silly battle."

"Things had to be settled, Aura."

"Aflut droppings! You and Jerak have known each other since you were young. You could have left your men at home and gone somewhere to talk it out."

"Leaders have to stand up to challenges. Jerak's men were raiding our borders."

"They were not," Tema, Jerak's mate, put in. "We can prove it was not our men, but it's time to stop this feuding. We have other things to deal with. What do you two brave males make of the wonders we see around us?"

She waved her arms around. The two newcomers took in the sight. Besides the many Garduk, there were tents of strange design made of fabric that had never been seen before. Inside were Garduk with strange clothing distributing food and drink to the lines of Garduk that had formed up to get it.

"Did you ask those handing out the refreshments what this was all about, Aura?" Dakat asked.

"We tried Dakat. They spoke in a strange dialect of our language. They were hard to understand, but I think what they told us was that we would have to wait and see."

"Well, Jerak," Dakat said, "it looks like we no longer have a battle to fight, and it sounds like these two females would refuse to let us fight here. What do you say we go get some of whatever they are offering, and talk things over as we are waiting to see what this is all about?"

A short distance away on the same grassy field, Sadut and Tarad were eating what they had received from the strangers, trying to be inconspicuous among the other Garduk in their fine clothing.

"What has happened to us, Sadut?" Tarad asked.

"I do not know, beloved. For now I am happy to be filling my stomach that has been empty for so long. I do feel guilty knowing how hungry our neighbors are right now. Perhaps these strangers will let us take some of this food back to our neighbors when they return us to the village."

"How do you know they will return us?"

"It is my hope, my love. What could such beings want with our poor selves? We have nothing. We only know our village, and how to eke out an existence."

"Perhaps they will take us as slaves," Tarad said, and shuddered at the thought.

Sadut laughed. "You are beautiful to me, Tarad, and I love you so, but look at our scrawny, bony bodies. We couldn't provide enough work for a slave master to justify the food he would have to give us to keep us alive. No, I think something else is going on here."

Just then a loud voice could be heard everywhere on the field. It spoke in what sounded like the common language used on Solan. The pronunciation was different, and some of the words were unfamiliar. What it said however was clear enough.

"Welcome! Please bring your food and drink and find a comfortable place to sit facing toward the west side of the field. You will be told why you have been gathered here."

There was some mumbling, some shouts of protest, but it all died away as the crowd moved. Once they were settled, some standing, but most sitting on the soft grass, the voice spoke again. This time the words were more familiar, and they were pronounced in the common fashion.

"Please do not be afraid. What you are about to see will not harm you. A machine will come from above and land before

146

you. Those inside want to welcome you in person and explain what is going on."

The shuttle from Nathat's ship came from the west. It dove down to hover about ten feet above the ground, a hundred feet from the crowd. To their credit, most of the Garduk held their ground. A few backed away, but no one ran from the unusual sight.

Seeing that the crowd had adjusted to the sight of a flying machine, Nathat eased the shuttle closer. When it was twenty feet from the closest guest he gently set it down and lowered the hatch.

The crowd didn't know that to think. Very large beings had brought them here in some unknown way. Was this their ship that could fly through the air? What did they want with those they had gathered?

After a short pause that seemed endless to the audience, Nathat and Neva walked down the ramp together. The entire crowd gasped as one. Someone shouted, "They are Garduk!"

18 There Are Others

On Solan

Nathat looked over the gathering. He still could not believe that his people had been reduced to this desperate, pre-technology level of existence. He wanted to help but was feeling overwhelmed by the challenge represented by the Garduk before him.

"Yes, we are Garduk. I am Nathat and my mate Neva is standing beside me. I am Ship Lead on the Garduk starship, Seriatna. The ship we arrived in is called a shuttle."

"What do you mean a Garduk starship? The Garduk have no such ships!" someone shouted from the crowd.

"The Garduk did have in my time. My ship, Neva and I, and our crew all come from a time in your distant past. I cannot explain what has happened to allow me to be before you today, because I don't understand it. Let me just say that we were caught in a place where time stopped. We were recently rescued from that place by Humans. You each met a Human today. It was they who transported you here.

"I know this is all hard to believe, but you have some facts to hold onto as you come to grips with all of this. You were contacted by Annli using mind-to-mind speech, brought here by Humans, beings you have never seen before, and I am standing before you on a shuttle that I flew here from my ship which is in orbit in the sky above us. If you will suspend your disbelief for a short time, I will tell you what we had in mind when we brought all of you here."

There were a few mumblings the gist of which was that it was about time for someone to say what this was all about.

"When Neva and I were rescued from the trap we had unknowingly fallen into, we were eager to come home to Solan. We are deeply saddened by what we see here. The beautiful cities of old are broken ruins, with Garduk in rags, starving in the shadows. Rural settlements are hardly any better. There is not enough food, medical treatment is very limited, and most Garduk now can neither read nor write our language."

A male with fine clothing, looking well fed, stood up.

"You paint a very bleak picture Nathat. It isn't all bad. I am quite satisfied with my life and with how things are," he said arrogantly.

"His name is Matrak, Nathat," Theron said. *"He is a landowner who keeps slaves and does not treat them well."*

"Yes, Matrak. I can understand that you are satisfied with your life, but those Garduk you have enslaved to support you are not as happy about life as you are."

"You are misinformed, Nathat. My people are all well taken care of," Matrak said, with an air of superiority.

"We are not, Master Matrak," a female who was not far from him stood and said, "Most of us do not have enough to eat. We are often sick, but your supervisors make us work anyway."

"Enough! You know better than to address me like that!"

The woman sat back down, but the rest of the crowd could see that Nathat's assessment was probably true.

Matrak was not deterred by the female's interruption. "That's another thing. As long as you have taken us from our homes, you could have planned for people of my rank to have proper seating, away from these…lower types."

Nathat smiled.

"I apologize for not having proper seating for you. How many of you feel as Matrak, and would like to be seated apart from the crowd?"

A few raised their hand.

"Could the rest of you allow these fine people to move to where Matrak is standing?"

When the relocation was accomplished, Nathat said, "Now could all the rest of you move a good distance away from these Garduk?"

Nathat motioned for them to move to the left leaving a wide space separating the small group of about ten individuals including Matrak from the rest of the audience. Nathat and Neva then moved to the left to be in front of the larger audience.

"Now that the arrangements are settled, we can proceed," Nathat said, addressing the larger group.

A female who was obviously Matrak's mate, stood up in the smaller group and said, "See what you've done, you pompous aflut's behind. Now we will be excluded from whatever will be offered." She then walked toward the main group and was followed by the other females from the isolated group. Then the males got up and did the same. Matrak was soon all by himself.

"You may not be able to appreciate this," Nathat said, when everyone was settled, "but we estimate that there are less than a million Garduk left on Solan. Before the war that destroyed our civilization there were over a thousand times that many Garduk on the planet. For the most part they were well fed, educated, and had access to excellent medical treatment when they needed it."

"How do you know so much about our past, or our present situation for that matter?" a male in the audience asked.

"The Annli told us about the war and what happened after it. Most of you have never heard of the Annli. Those who have heard of them believe that the Annli were mythical. I also believed that until they spoke to me in my mind. I don't know how they could possibly exist after all this time since their disappearance, but those speaking to us claim to be Annli, and I have no reason to doubt them. The Annli and others who have joined in this effort have been observing you for some time since we first arrived. It is from these observations that we draw our conclusions about the current conditions on Solan."

"You've been spying on us?" another asked.

"We have been gathering data so that we would know how to help you."

"What kind of help?"

"We will have to go slow to understand how to do things in a way that won't cause more harm. We need you to work with us. We have technology and knowledge that will help you learn how to help yourselves, but you need to take responsibility to become self-supporting.

Food is needed in most locations. We can provide some at the beginning and will help you provide for yourselves in the future. In many places Garduk do not have a clean water supply. We will help with that. We also will help you set up an educational system which will provide for the needs of adults as well as children and set up medical facilities. We need to teach some of you to become teachers, and medical practitioners as well as other professions. We will help you with roads, buildings and other infrastructure, such as a supply of electricity."

"How will you get all this done? Are you, Neva, and your crew going to do all of this?" someone asked.

Nathat laughed. "We will be a part of it but couldn't do much by ourselves. We will have the help of others that Neva and I have met since we were rescued. You have already had a brief encounter with two of the races that will help, the Annli and the Humans. We are blessed to have the Dhara'chee and the Lorengi to help as well."

"Why are the others helping?" a female from the audience asked. "I can understand why you might do it, but what drives others to aid us? Are we being taken over by these others? If not, what do they expect to gain?"

"We are not being taken over by others. As to their motives, they just want to help the Garduk get back the civilization that was once ours."

"What if I don't want their help?" Matrak shouted.

"There may be others who feel the way you do, Matrak. You will be left alone, but everyone will be given the opportunity to participate, including the Garduk who work your land for you. You may wish to keep out of it, but your workers can join in if they want to."

"I won't let them," Matrak asserted.

"Taking that position might not be in your best interests," Nathat said.

That apparently gave Matrak something to think about, because he sat back down and said no more.

"Where are these others?" another asked.

"They are in orbit about our planet, directly above us. If you are ready, I will ask some of them to land here."

The reaction of the audience was a mixture of nodding acceptance and apprehensive glances and murmurs.

Sensing that the group was as ready as they would ever be, Nathat let Carmen know that they should come.

A moment later Thelika suddenly appeared a short distance from the crowd, floating a few feet off the ground.

19 On the Way to Solan

Solan

Carmen walked down the ramp exiting Thelika. She stepped off the ramp onto the grass of the field where all the Garduk had been gathered.

She paused to remember how this project started when they had returned from the first trip to Solan. Nathat and Neva were in shock from what they had seen on their home world. All the cities were in ruin, some in worse shape than their home city, Carrat. What they saw and heard from the discrete monitoring probes launched from Meratta had made them feel even worse.

"What can be done?" Neva asked, when they returned to the common room on Katala.

Carmen had gathered those still on Katala together to tell them about Solan and talk about what could be done.

"Do you think the Garduk will accept help from us?" Sam asked.

"They might, but it all seems hopeless," Nathat said, shaking his head. "There are so many, and their needs are so great."

"I agree that it's a big challenge," Jesse said, "but at the rate they are dying there may not be any Garduk in the near future if we don't do something."

"I know, but what?" Nathat asked

Carmen could understand that Nathat was frustrated, but she was glad to see that he was beginning to exhibit qualities of leadership and caring for others which were hidden behind his earlier hysteria.

"We have many things we can bring to Solan to help," Carmen said. "Please keep discussing this. I promised the Dhara'chee I would meet with them upon my return from our trip to Solan. I will go with them to their home planet and discuss what is next for them. I don't think it will take long."

She checked with Daran and then teleported to the Dhara'chee Bridge.

"Welcome, Carmen." Daran said when Carmen appeared before her. *"We have revived all of our shipmates. They are eager to return home, even if it is to learn it is our home no more. It is our sincere wish that you accompany us. Will you come with us?"*

"Yes, of course."

"Good. Do I understand right, that the Lorengi ship that brought us out of the dimension we were trapped in can move us there more rapidly that our own ship can?"

"Yes. As soon as the Dhara'chee's ship Aceri provides the coordinates to Thelika, we will be there the instant after the command is given."

"Such a trip would take many ship-days under our own power. It will be something to behold to arrive as you describe. It will be good that we do arrive quickly. That way we won't have long to think about what waits for us at our journey's end."

"Let's delay no longer then. Thelika, do you have the coordinates from Aceri?"

"Yes, Carmen. I am ready."

"Daran, Orlyn, are the Dhara'chee ready?"

When the Dhara'chee leaders said they were ready, Carmen told Thelika to go. The scene on the Dhara'chee Bridge screens changed from an array of Lorengi ships to a single planet, rotating on its axis."

"Aceri, that planet looks like our beloved Yarada. May I believe my eyes?"

"Yes, Daran. We are in contact with one of the orbiting beacons that circle Yarada. It is broadcasting a message."

"Please share it with us and the rest of our shipmates."

"You have come to a plague planet. It may not be safe for you to land. We have no reason to believe that there are any Dhara'chee left, but if you are Dhara'chee, the planet is deadly for you. All Dhara'chee on the planet died from the plague as well as some of the surface animals. In this satellite we have stored a recording of all knowledge that has been accumulated by our race as well as much of our cultural heritage. In addition, we have left a description of the plague and the scientific analysis of how it kills. Please do not land. We would hope you will avoid our fate."

The Dhara'chee on Aceri's Bridge became very still. The truth of what they had been told was now revealed, and it immobilized them. They stood still as death in some sort of comatose state. Carmen could see that they were breathing, but the rise and fall of their small chests was all the motion there was to see. Their eyes were open, but sightless.

"Aceri, the Dhara'chee on the Bridge are in what looks like very deep shock. The reality of their loss seems to have overwhelmed them."

"The same is true throughout the ship, Carmen. Some have begun to fall to the floor. I sense that all are alive, but they take no action except to fall. I have dispatched mobile units to help those who fall to lie in a more comfortable position."

"Those here are beginning to fall, too. What should we do?

"I have no idea, Carmen. This is outside my experience."

"Mine, too. It is like they are all part of the same hive-like mind, all responding to the bad news in the same way and at the same time."

"I know what you refer too, but the Dhara'chee do not have a hive-mind. They are all very similar, and very connected to each other through telepathy. Also, all Dhara'chee have an intimate connection to Yarada. It was the main reason that the Dhara'chee never colonized on another planet. They didn't want to live anywhere else. I believe we may be seeing the impact of them realizing that they will no longer be able to have that close connection with their home world. It does not surprise me that this emotional state would sweep through the entire crew. If one felt that loss, they all did."

"Will you take my suggestions?" Carmen asked.

"Within reason," Aceri said. *"I want to help, but I remain the property of my inert crew, and will not do anything to harm them or the ship."*

"Of course. I don't want to harm them either. Can you send probes to the surface? I would like to see what is like down there. Perhaps if we present images and sounds of Yarada they will feel a remote connection, and it will break them out of this state."

"Perhaps that will help. I will launch the probes. I will gather data from the probes, but in light of the warning about the danger on the surface, I won't take them back aboard."

"Good idea."

Carmen focused on her fallen hosts. She rolled them onto their backs, straightening arms and legs in the process.

"Aceri, if this goes on very long, we should put covers over them."

"I will send mobile units to take care of that."

A moment later, Carmen was startled when a door to the Bridge was opened. She thought that maybe one Dhara'chee was unaffected. Instead one of Aceri's "mobile units" came in carrying a container which it set on the floor next to the recumbent crew members. The unit rode on quiet tracks and had several arms that had differently shaped fittings at their ends. It looked cumbersome, but it was quite dexterous as it took coverlets out of the box, and carefully tucked one around each of the Dhara'chee on the floor.

"How many of these units do you have aboard the ship, Aceri?"

"Five-hundred, though some of them are being maintained and unavailable. If this goes on longer, I will have them carefully pick up my crew, and move them to their quarters."

"All ten-thousand Dhara'chee?"

"It will take a while to accomplish, Carmen, but yes."

Carmen hoped it would not come to that. She felt strange being the only person awake on this beautiful and very large ship. It was good that Aceri was available to talk with, and to take care of everything that needed to be done.

In her short time with them, Carmen had become very fond of the Dhara'chee. It saddened her to see such a wonderful and intelligent people faced with such a devastating loss. She hoped they would recover soon. When they did, she would do everything in her power to help them through this.

Aceri told her that the first images and sounds were coming through.

"Put them on the screen in front of me, Aceri. Keep the volume low. I would like to choose which images and sounds we use when we try to revive them. There may be some which would only drive them deeper inside themselves."

Carmen was right. It had been over two-thousand years since the plague. She was seeing what must have been beautiful cities, which were now crumbling ruins overgrown with trees and other vegetation. The vegetation was beautiful itself, but seeing the cities lost to time and the elements might not be the best images to show them at first.

Other images of landscapes, mountains, arid lands and rivers were better candidates in Carmen's mind. Working with Aceri, she created a compilation of images and sounds that showed all the beauty that still remained on their hallowed planet. She asked Aceri to play the images and sound throughout the ship.

A while later, some of the Dhara'chee began to stir. The first few helped others near them. Before long, the entire crew had been revived. Carmen didn't know what their usual discourse was, but she believed that what she was witnessing was the Dhara'chee somber acceptance of their new reality as they began to talk among themselves and resumed their duties on the ship.

Orlyn and Daran came up to her.

"You have witnessed a thing that is very personal to us, something no non-Dhara'chee has seen about our people. I hope…."

"You need say no more, Daran. I was glad to be here, and to have been able to assist you in your grief. It will be a memory I will treasure, but no one else will hear of it."

Orlyn sighed. "What do we do now? What will become of the Dhara'chee?"

"I have a suggestion," Sways said.

"Sways, have you been listening in?" Carmen asked, scolding her friend.

"Yes. I hope we haven't offended you or Daran. We have been so concerned for the Dhara'chee ever since we learned that your home planet has been lost to you."

"You have not offended, friend," Orlyn said. *"Thank you for your concern. What were you going to suggest?"*

"The Cheneshi have discussed your plight and have come to a decision. We would be honored if you would share our planet with us. We live in the oceans. You could live on the islands."

Orlyn and Daran looked at each other, obviously still dazed from their reaction to the loss of their planet.

"We couldn't..."

"Of course you could," Sways said, *"but you don't have to make the decision right now. If you are like us, all important decisions must be discussed at length by everyone. I suggest that you ask Carmen to bring you here so you can look around and talk about it while you do."*

After a quick discussion among all the Dhara'chee, they thought it would be good to view another planet right away to get their minds off their loss. So they made the trip to Ocean and spent several days surveying the planet.

Orlyn, Daran, a delegation of other Dhara'chee including some children, and Carmen took a shuttle to the surface. They landed on Sways' island near the research facility housed inside Journey. All of the Dhara'chee got out of shuttle and walked around. The children immediately began running through the trees and some went down to play in the water.

"Welcome!" Travis Beckwith said and introduced himself using telepathy so that Sways could be included.

"Thank you, Travis." Orlyn said.

"All Cheneshi say welcome," Sways said. *"What do you think of our planet?"*

"It's beautiful," Daran said.

"It appears that your young like it."

"Yes. Our ship is spacious, but they long to be out in the open. I apologize for their exuberance."

"There is no need to apologize. Their laughter is a great joy."

"Sways, we truly appreciated your offer, but we don't want to damage the beauty we've seen by building a home for ourselves on the surface of these islands. We were never comfortable building any structures on the planets we explored, lest it impact the life that was already there."

"Sways and I thought that might be a concern for you," Travis said, *"and we think we have a solution. I have studied the one structure that the Lorengi built here and how they built it. That information plus the environment-friendly building techniques we Humans have developed will go a long way toward minimizing the impact your installations will have."*

Orlyn and Daran looked at the other adults that came to the surface with them. Together they telepathically conferred with the other Dhara'chee aboard Aceri. When they were done, Orlyn turned to Travis.

"We accept your generous offer, Sways, with the condition that we must assure ourselves that our presence will not seriously harm the life on your planet."

"Thank you. We Cheneshi would have been disappointed if we couldn't have you with us. We hope you will soon be saying that it is your planet."

It was decided that a contingent of the Dhara'chee, including the children, would stay in temporary quarters to help assess the plan Travis had in mind. The Dhara'chee would also spend time looking for a suitable island for their primary location on the planet.

When that was arranged, Orlyn turned to Carmen.

"Thank you for helping with this possible solution for our new home. Since all of us won't be needed here, what would you suggest we do?"

"If you will accept the advice of one who has no understanding of your people, I suggest that you take your mind off of the sorrow of your loss by helping others."

"What do you have in mind?" Daran asked. "Wait. I think.... Do you mean for us to help the Garduk?"

Carmen smiled and nodded.

"What a great idea. We have lost a great deal, but still have all our history, art and technology stored in Aceri and have all the Dhara'chee aboard. We can build from that foundation. The Garduk on the other hand have lost everything that they were. Some of us can help them rise up again, while at the same time others of us establish our new home here."

Carmen brought some of the Dhara'chee back to join with those on Katala who were developing a plan for the Garduk. With the trips to the Dhara'chee planet and Ocean, she had been gone for only half a ship-day on Katala. The plan they all developed included recruiting a large contingent of Humans, mostly H2s, to help in the rebuild of the devastated Garduk culture and arranging for the dedication of some of the Earth's wealth to provide equipment and supplies. The Dhara'chee quickly threw themselves into the project.

The Sudahlli also volunteered, but said they first had to reconnect with the modern-day Sudahlli on their home planet. Jesse agreed to accompany them. Carmen had mixed emotions about bringing the intimidating presence of the Sudahlli into the mix, but who could tell in advance what would be helpful. She would see when the Sudahlli came back from their home planet.

Today Carmen watched as the Humans and Dhara'chee left Thelika, and joined her on the grassy field, eager to start the work to re-vitalize the Garduk civilization. As an anthropologist, she had helped remote tribes before, but never this remote, and never a planet's entire population. She found the prospect both overwhelming and exhilarating!

20 Matrak's Marauders

Sadut's Village on Solan

The few leaves remaining on the trees were struggling to hold on in the brisk wind. The cold season was upon them. The sky was dark with threatening clouds. The air was cold. Carmen was chilled, but not just because of the weather.

They had worked so hard in the months since they had arrived on Solan, but there still wasn't enough food. Carmen knew that meant that more Garduk would starve to death before warm weather arrived again. Agriculture wasn't in full swing yet, but surely more food had been produced than could be accounted for. Where did it go? She was getting discouraged.

Carmen made sure that there were active projects going on in all parts of Solan. Water and food supplies were on the top of the list at each site. Healthcare was next on the list. Education was started but would be progressing slowly until they had a healthy population to work with. As it looked now that population would be smaller by spring or whatever the Garduk called their planting time.

Of all the Garduk she had met since the initial gathering, she was especially drawn to Sadut and his mate Tarad. They were so full of love even though they had a very bleak existence. The other villagers looked up to Sadut, a fact that he found difficult to understand.

Carmen was on the shore of the sea that bordered Sadut's village. She watched the joy of the males of the village as they caught more gazaz in their nets than could be remembered in recent times. Besides using improved nets, the secret to success was improving vegetation on the sea floor for the fish, so they would be drawn to come near the shore.

She was pleased that this village would not lose any more to starvation. Their homes had been repaired to keep the cold wind from coming in. Fuel for their fires had been provided without stripping the countryside of the few trees that were left. Progress had been made here and in other places across the globe, but it was not enough.

Her gloomy thoughts were interrupted by a noise coming from just outside the village. She turned and saw a group of Garduk riding aflut into the village. The women and children ran into their homes. The riders laughed at the sight. Marauders! Carmen had heard there were still a few raiding bands, but she had never seen them in action. Well, she thought, they have come to the wrong village this time!

She walked back to the village and directly up to the leader of the ragged bunch of male Garduk marauders. They stopped, not sure what her presence meant to their plans for the village.

"Ho ho! What do we have here?" the leader asked laughing. "You're large for a female. You are a female aren't you? I'll wager that you are one of the sky people I've been hearing about. Just step aside and you won't be harmed." He shouted over his shoulder. "Bring the wagon forward."

Carmen did not step aside.

"Who do you work for?" she demanded. "'I'll wager you aren't clever enough to lead even this small group of mongrels on your own. Who sent you to rob these villagers?"

"Janus, are you able to connect with the Garduk in front of me? If so do you think you might be able to put them to sleep?"

"I will try. Let me know which ones and when."

"The one in front of me. In a moment."

"I promise not to hurt you, if you tell me who it is," Carmen said.

The leader laughed. He was not used to having anyone interfere with their raids and wouldn't allow this unarmed female to interfere this time.

"Well, I guess I'll have to deal with you first," he said.

He got off his aflut and handed the reins to the Garduk next to him. He turned toward Carmen, drew his sword, and began to advance.

Carmen held up her hand.

"Stop where you are!" she shouted. "I don't want to hurt you."

He laughed again, looked over his shoulder at his comrades, and they laughed, too. He turned back, took one more step toward Carmen.

"Now, Janus."

The leader fell to the ground. The others looked at each other in stunned silence, not sure what to do. They couldn't return with an empty wagon. Before they could act Carmen told them what they were going to do.

"Now, the rest of you get off your mounts. Leave them and walk back the way you came. Your friend here won't be joining you. I have other plans for him."

There were growls of protest. They stopped immediately when Carmen raised her hand.

"Or would you rather join him on the ground, and share whatever fate awaits him?"

That stopped the protests. They dismounted and left the village at a brisk pace. When they looked back over their shoulder as they left the village, they saw Carmen standing there with her finger pointing in their direction.

The village females and children came out slowly. They were glad the raiders were gone but were now wary of their guest. What sort of being could kill a person just by raising their hand?

Sadut came up to her. "Carmen, what have you done?" he asked nervously.

"Don't worry. It's just a little trick. He's not dead. He'll come around soon. Do you have any thing I can tie him up with? I imagine that he will be angry when he wakes up."

"Yes, of course."

Sadut asked one of the females to get some rope.

Carmen turned to the group that was slowly filling the open space in front of the homes. She needed an explanation. She chose a deception they might understand, rather than the truth which they would never accept.

"Please don't be alarmed. The raider isn't dead. He is just unconscious. I communicated with my sky boat and asked it to use a gentle weapon to make him go to sleep. You'll see. Soon he will wake up. We'll talk with him and find out who is sending these raiders."

There were a few who nodded their heads, and some murmurs of uncertainty. They heard what she said, but it was so strange that they were far from assured. Still, Carmen had been among them for some time. They had found her to be gentle and helpful. A few of them laughed, pointing at the fallen raider. Soon they were all laughing, happy that Carmen had saved them from the brutal raiders.

The rope was handed to Sadut. He and Carmen lifted the downed raider and brought him over to a tree near the road.

When they had finished tying the raider's hands and legs, Sadut looked at Carmen and smiled.

"Someday will you tell me what really happened?"

"I will, but right now let's wake this ruffian, and find out who sent him."

She shook the raider's shoulders making a show of trying to wake him, while at the same time asking Janus to bring him around.

"Wha...?"

"Easy now. You fell asleep. We tied you to the tree so we could have a chat without you getting all feisty."

"Sleep! That wasn't sleep. You did something to me. Let me go, and..."

"And what? You'll fall asleep again? No, before we do anything else, we'll have that chat."

Carmen focused on the raider's mind, and asked out loud, "What is your name?"

"I'm not telling you anything!" he said, but the answer formed in his head.

"Telat."

"Telat," Carmen said.

"How did you do that? I didn't tell you anything."

"Well, Telat, here is what we are going to do. We are going take you to your boss, and we are going to get these raids stopped. Would you like to help us, or will you continue to resist?"

"I will not help you."

"Who do you work for?"

Again the answer formed in his mind, involuntarily, *"Matrak."*

Carmen turned to Sadut.

"His boss is Matrak. That surprises me, since we are far from Matrak's land, but at the same time it sounds like something he would do."

"I didn't tell you anything, you witch!"

"Matrak won't know that, will he? Nor will he believe your story that I used some unusual method to get the information. If I were you, I'd be thinking about how you could help us."

Telat muttered a curse and struggled against the ropes.

Looking at Sadut, Carmen said, *"I looked into his mind when I asked him the questions. He answered them even though he refused to do so verbally."*

Sadut nodded, though he still was uncomfortable with these strange people talking in his mind.

"I saw Matrak at the Gathering," Sadut said. "I agree that he might very well do this kind of thing. Will this one survive if we drag him behind an aflut as we travel all the way to Matrak's?"

Telat's eyes opened wide.

"You wouldn't do that!"

Instead of answering Telat's outburst, Carmen rose and asked Sadut to follow her far enough away so that Telat wouldn't hear what she had to stay.

"Traveling to Matrak by aflut would take more than one day. If you agree, we will travel there using the same method we used to get you and Tarad to the Gathering and back to your village."

That was another thing Sadut was understandably unsure about, but he nodded his agreement.

"Good. We won't be alone when we get there. I will ask my colleagues, to bring the members of the Restoration Council to Matrak's as well. I believe we will need their authority to support what I have in mind."

It took a while to arrange, but when things were ready, Sadut and Carmen appeared before Matrak in the small banquet hall at his home. He was eating there by himself, though a young female servant was standing by. He nearly choked on the food he was eating when they popped into existence before his eyes.

"What...? Who...? Where did you come from?" Matrak sputtered, spitting food all over the table.

"Hello, Matrak," Carmen said. "We met briefly at the Gathering. As I remember, you were sitting by yourself."

Matrak continued his attempt to compose himself, and wipe food from his face and the front of his clothes.

"My name is Carmen. I have brought Sadut with me. Sadut is the leader of a village that some of your men attempted to raid earlier today."

"Raiders? Not mine. Now whoever you are, you will leave now, or I will call my guards."

"Bring him in," Carmen told Anthony, one of the H2s on the Solan project.

Anthony appeared next to Carmen along with Telat struggling against the rope that bound his hands and feet.

"I didn't tell them nothing, boss."

Matrak did the Garduk equivalent of rolling his eyes in exasperation, "You fool! You just confirmed what they were guessing."

Matrak rose from his chair and came around the table to face Carmen.

"I enjoy taking what I want. It has allowed me to live comfortably. I am able to sell what I don't need and give some to my supervisors to assure their loyalty."

"You will not be allowed to continue raiding," Carmen said, "and the food and supplies you have stored here will be distributed to those who need it to keep them from dying this cold season."

Matrak laughed so hard, he nearly fell over.

"You have overstepped yourself, Carmen-from-the-sky, and have outstayed your welcome. Guards!"

The large double doors at the back of the hall opened. Instead of guards, a group of seven Garduk came in backed by five Humans, three men and two women, H2s from the Solan project team.

The female Garduk in the lead said, "Your guards and supervisors are taking a break, Matrak. We've come to help Carmen explain things to you."

Matrak's self-assurance was slipping, but he didn't let it show. "Fine. Say what you have to say, and then go. You are disturbing my mid-day meal."

"Perhaps you have heard at the Gathering that a Restoration Council made up of Garduk would be formed to guide the project that is helping restore the Garduk population and quality of life."

"I didn't pay much attention, since it didn't affect me."

"The Restoration Council was formed. We are the members of that Council."

"I am sure that's a fine thing for you, now please leave."

"Before we do, we are obliged to confirm what Carmen just told you. We will stop your raids, and will distribute the food, the herd of aflut and other items you have stolen to those in need.

"You have no authority," Matrak shouted angrily

"Hmmm..., you might be right, Matrak, but we will proceed as if we did. In fact, it has already begun."

Hearing noises outside in the yard, Matrak gave a surprised shout, and ran past the delegation and out into the yard in front of his house. He looked toward the stables and storage sheds. He saw wagons being loaded, and aflut being guided into groups of two. A tall Human climbed aboard one of the wagons. The wagon and Human disappeared. Another Human standing by two aflut disappeared along with the aflut. Matrak's mouth was open, but only sputtered curses came out.

The delegation of Garduk, the young female servant, and the Humans accompanying them came out of his house and walked by him. Carmen turned as she was passing.

"Enjoy your large meal, Matrak. It might be a while before you have another."

21 Expectations Differ

Aboard Jannida

Jesse and Carmen were going in separate directions again and Jesse didn't like it at all. It made sense that Carmen had gone to Solan to restart civilization there. Of all the team, she was the most qualified to work with the cultures on that planet. It was logical that Jesse go with the Sudahlli on their journey to their home planet. They needed to travel in the Lorengi ship Jannida, and he was the right choice to lead the small team that would accompany them. All logical, but that didn't mean he was happy about it.

Carmen's effort was under way on Solan. The team going to the Sudahlli home world, Thahll, was organized and ready to go. Jarruda said that it was important that a contingent of Lorengi go along. Two were chosen—Atala and Gordi. The Annli assigned Ontoron to focus on the effort. Jesse thought that no one else should go until the situation there had been assessed.

Things were ready for departure. Set Li's ship, Chantlasec would travel inside Jannida. Set Li's crew of thirty, including her mate Jardut, had become comfortable roaming around Jannida. They had been awakened, told what had happened, and were comfortably ensconced inside of Jannida for the trip. Jesse was confident he could manage on his own. He had been leading exploration teams for some time. Still, he thought he'd repeat his offer for Sam to join the venture. Sam was on the Lorengi ship, Katala.

"Are you sure you won't come along, Sam?"

"I have my own things to explore. Keep in touch and let us know how it goes."

"I will. Janus, I would feel better if you could keep some of your attention on us as we travel to Thahll."

"I will be able to do that. I'm in contact with Carmen on Solan. You'll be further away, but that shouldn't present a problem. Contact me as soon as you arrive."

"I'll be sure to do that. Bye for now."

Jesse's focus was now on Jannida.

"Set Li, are you and your crew ready?"

"More than ready, Jesse. It's time to face whatever greets us at home."

"Jannida, do you have you the coordinates from Chantlasec?"

"Yes."

Having arranged with Atala, Gordi, and Jannida ahead of time, Jesse assumed the role of directing Jannida's actions.

"Select a position near Thahll, but far enough away so we will have room and time to adjust our position if it becomes necessary."

Jesse saw a questioning look on Set Li's face.

"It's been a long time since you've been there. Also, from their perspective, we will be appearing out of nowhere. They might get nervous."

She nodded.

"Go!" Jesse said.

Thahll was slightly larger than Earth, with a proportionately stronger gravity. It had a few large land masses separated by deep oceans. The land was nearly totally covered with rampant vegetation due in part to the planet's warm average surface temperature.

The one moon circling the planet was called Salana. The sun Thahll circled was called Taa. Salana, Taa and Thahll, were ancient names for sister, father and mother coming from a time when the population was matriarchal. That no longer being true, the names, although still used, were not spoken with the same reverence that once was associated with them.

There hadn't been a war on the planet for centuries. Nor had any other race had the temerity to try to invade the potentially fierce Sudahlli from outside. Even so, the male dominated society currently in place had adopted a military-like structure. It seemed to suit the mindset that pervaded the current leadership.

The Sudahlli had been a space-faring race since before Set Li's time, though their travels had diminished significantly from what they were when she left on her explorations. The largest artifact of that space-faring history was the enormous space station that was put in synchronous orbit just a century ago. It was to serve as a base for the Sudahlli fleet, as well as a docking station for visiting ships. It also served as a visitor's sole point of access to the surface.

There were great expectations of prosperity from increased interstellar trade when the space station, called Thahll 2, was constructed. Trade did thrive at first, but with the conservative mien of the government, their strict import regulations and high tariffs, the number of traders quickly dropped off to a trickle, and in time stopped altogether. The fleet, mostly idle, was docked on the station, and collecting space dust. The staff on Thahll 2 was reduced to a skeleton maintenance crew, a few security staff and technicians whose job was to monitor the space surrounding the planet.

Few visitors came to the station. That being the case, Primary Officer Neylec's main task was to keep his staff from falling asleep at their workstations. So he was understandingly surprised when alarms began blaring, and warning lights started flashing. His first assumption was that it was some kind of drill, but if he wanted his staff to take it seriously, he thought he better show that he was acting as if it was real.

"What do you have?" he blurted out as he came onto the station Bridge.

"An unidentified object popped onto my screen," the duty technician reported. "I thought it best to sound the alarm, so we were alerted as we assessed what it is."

"Appropriate action," Neylec said. This didn't sound like any drill he had seen in his time on the station. "Where is it, and what do you mean it just 'popped' onto your screen?"

"It is just this side of Salana and is stationary. What I meant was that it was not visible until it appeared just a moment ago in its current location."

"Some form of cloaking mechanism, maybe?" Neylec wondered out loud.

"Perhaps, Sir."

"Can you enhance the visual? From this perspective, it looks like an asteroid rather than a spaceship."

The tech magnified the image. It still looked like an asteroid, although where the light of Taa shown on it, he could see that it was light colored, roughly ellipsoid and had a smooth surface with protrusions in random spots.

"What do your instruments say about it?"

"It is not rock or metal, though there does appear to be some metal within. If I had to guess, I would say it is made of some form of organic material."

"Guessing will get us nowhere. Just in case it's not friendly, put weapons on alert status. Turn off the alarms and attempt to communicate with it."

A voice came through their comm system before the duty tech could respond to Neylec's order.

"I am First Born Mother, Set Li, of clan Parlac. Please do not be alarmed. My Sudahlli crew and I are aboard the ship that has appeared on your monitors."

Neylec ordered the tech to mute the comm. "What do you make of that?"

"It sounds like an unusual dialect—understandable, but barely. What is a 'First Born Mother' and what is 'clan Parlac'?" the tech asked.

Being a student of ancient history, Neylec recognized the words, and they made him very uncomfortable. He knew of the time when there were clans, recognized the name of this one, and it didn't bode well. Clan Parlac was closely connected to ancient royalty that no longer existed, and part of a power base that had been displaced centuries ago. He signaled the tech to open the comm.

"Well met First Born Mother. I am Neylec, Prime Officer of our orbiting station, Thahll 2. What ship have you arrived in?"

The tech looked at Neylec quizzically. Neylec waved his hand impatiently, and the tech turned back to his station.

"The ship is Jannida and belongs to a race called Lorengi. My ship, the Chantlasec, is within its hold. May I bring a shuttle from my ship to your station and come aboard. I'm sure you have questions, as do my crew and I."

"Yes, of course. You will be directed to shuttle bay Eight, please follow the instructions that take you there. I look forward to talking with you."

When the comm was off, Neylec turned to his security officer and said, "Have your security team accompany me to shuttle bay Eight. They are to be armed, but with weapons secured."

Neylec thought there could be trouble, especially now that Set Li had claimed that her ship was named Chantlasec. It was the name of a famed exploration ship of old that had left millennia ago, and never returned.

She can't possibly be part of the original clan. So it's probably some kind of ruse. His first thought was that it was part of a plot of the troublesome female organizations that were continually pushing for things to return to what they were in the distant past.

Yet how could that be possible? This is the first time that anyone has seen a "Lorengi" ship, and none of the troublemakers have had access to any Sudahlli ship with which they could have contacted other races. Whoever this Set Li was, why was she choosing to do this now? What was she trying to accomplish? Where did she get that ship? Who are the Lorengi? So many questions. The most troubling was why did it have to happen on his watch?

Neylec had the six security members form up near the shuttle's hatch once it had landed and the atmosphere in the bay had been restored. It took a stern order from Neylec to keep them from drawing their weapons when they saw Set Li and the beings who accompanied her as they came through the open hatch and onto the floor of the bay. Neylec understood their discomfort.

To begin with Set Li herself was larger, and more muscular than any female they had seen, and she was obviously the leader instead of the male Sudahlli in the group. The male accompanying her, perhaps her mate, was also bigger than any male on Thahll 2. It wasn't just their size. They wore sleeveless vests and knee-length breeches both fashioned from finely tooled hide, which looked like it was from a santlok, a large, ferocious predator which he knew to be nearly extinct. The surface of Set Li's vest was richly decorated with colorful stitching. It was shocking to see them in such brief garments, especially the female who should be wearing a garment covering her entire body.

Their garments were the first thing that caught his eye, but they each carried what looked like a hand weapon of some kind attached to a belt around their waist. Also on the belt were cartridges which looked like they might be power packs for the weapon. The handles of the weapons looked worn showing they had been used often.

The female was not only improperly dressed, but she also had the arrogance to be leading the group and to claim a two-part naming used by people of importance in earlier times, when females ruled. Females were not allowed on Thahll 2. He would choose his time, but this female needed to be put in her place and off his station!

Another member of the group was from a race they had never seen. It was smaller than a Sudahlli, obviously fit, but had only one set of arms. It wore what looked to be casual attire and didn't appear to be armed.

These things were unusual, but the other two beings in the group were strangest of all. They wore one-piece, short-sleeved uniforms. They also only had one set of arms. The skin that was exposed was covered with short fur. They both were about the same size and somewhat smaller than the other one from an unknown race. The problem that this pair presented was that Neylec and his team could see through them. They appeared to be wraiths.

Set Li had her own reactions. Jesse saw she was tense.

"Set Li, are you alright?"

"I am. This isn't. There are no females present. In my time, one would have been in the place of Neylec, and other females would have made up the armed group you see. Something isn't right, or at least very different from my expectations. Let us proceed cautiously. Reveal nothing.

Jesse contacted Janus and described the situation. He also helped Set Li express her desire for caution to the others in the group.

Set Li took a step forward.

"I am Set Li. Am I addressing Prime Officer Neylec?"

"Yes. Who have you brought with you?"

"I have with me my mate, Jardut."

"Why is he not the spokesperson for your group? Is he unwell?"

"He is fine," Set Li said, answering the second question, and ignoring the first.

"Also with me is a Human named Jesse and two Lorengi, Atala and Gordi. I see by your expression that you wonder at their appearance. They appear as holograms because they are digitally stored people. They chose to upload their essence to their systems in the past and that is the state of their existence."

"You all present unusual visions for me and my team. Are the Lorengi alive?"

"Yes, we are Prime Officer Neylec," Atala said in perfect Sudahlli. "Though not organic, we are fully functioning persons. We are pleased to meet you and hope we will have time to talk with you and your people to learn about the Sudahlli."

Though it was harmlessly said, Neylec tensed, wondering what that might mean. What would they do once they knew about the Sudahlli?

"Well, I'm not being a gracious host, having us stand in an open bay asking you questions. Let us go to more comfortable surroundings to continue our discussion."

As they left the shuttle bay, Jesse connected with Janus again.

"Are you able to see into the minds of the Sudahlli here?"

"Yes. They are suspicious. That's normal considering the circumstance. You present a number of puzzles for them. Set Li leading the group is the first. Apparently this is now a male dominated society.

"That is threatening to them, especially the one called Neylec. He is naturally paranoid, and your arrival has triggered that state of mind. It helps that he is confronted by two new unknown races. That should keep him from doing something foolish, at least until he knows more about you. So I agree with Set Li that revealing nothing is the best strategy at this time. Be careful."

"Can you help if there is trouble?"

"Perhaps."

22 New Management

Sudahlli Orbiting Station Thahll 2

The station was in the shape of a spindle, of ten disk-shaped structures on a common vertical shaft. The Bridge was on the top floor. Docks, some of which were being used by the Sudahlli fleet, and the shuttle bays were on the sixth level. Staff lodgings, power supply and other facilities were in the lower five levels.

Neylec brought them to the top floor using one of three elevators in the station and led them into a meeting room near the Bridge. The room had windows that provided a view of the planet's surface and surrounding space. Three of the security guards followed them into the room and stationed themselves by the door. Before sitting down, Neylec asked the visitors for their weapons.

"Will your people remain armed?" Set Li asked.

"Yes, as is appropriate."

"Then we shall keep our weapons," Set Li said.

She led her group to the table in a position to see the door and the security guards who were standing with confused looks on their faces. She made sure she was still relatively close to Neylec and remained standing. The guards looked to Neylec for directions.

"I must insist that you turn over your weapons."

"Noted," Set Li said.

"If you don't turn over your weapons, they will be taken by force!" Neylec threatened.

"Neylec, let's sit down and talk things over a bit before you resort to force. My mate and I have been away from Thahll for…a long time. When we left it was common to greet guests with courtesy, respect and trust. If we are unwelcome, then we will leave. If we are welcome, then let's sit down, and learn from each other."

Set Li was calm, poised and, ready. Neylec was ruffled and uncertain.

"Guards maintain your station by the door!" Neylec said, in a way that sounded like he was in control of the situation. Everyone in the room knew he wasn't, and that Set Li was. He sat down and gestured for the others to join him.

"Things have changed since you went away," Neylec said.

"I can see that. In my time females had a more prominent role. I see none among your staff."

"When was 'your time' exactly?"

"You will have a hard time believing my answer to your question."

"Still, the question remains."

"My crew and the Chantlasec left Thahll over six thousand years ago."

Neylec was not surprised at her claim. It was impossible of course, but her and her mate, their clothing, the name of the ship, the clan name, everything fit. He wasn't surprised but didn't believe it was anything other than a well-researched plot designed to foment social unrest. It would stop here.

Neylec laughed. "Well done, Set Li, or whatever your true name is. You arrive claiming these impossible things, and expect what—that we would bow down to some claim of nobility? The name you chose did denote high social standing thousands of years ago. It means nothing, less than nothing now. The power structure you attempt to lean on crumbled centuries ago. Females like yourself have been put in their proper place—serving males, the rightful leaders of Sudahlli. Guards! Take their weapons!"

Set Li and Jardut moved their chairs back and calmly rose to their feet. Jesse followed their lead but didn't know what to expect.

"I warn you not to resist," Neylec said. "These guards are highly trained professionals. They will try to avoid harming you but will if necessary to carry out their orders."

Set Li made her move before the guards started around the table to get their weapons. She jumped behind where Neylec was sitting, jerked him out of his chair and placed the index finger of her upper right hand next to his neck. The guards didn't know what that meant. Neylec did.

"Stop! She might kill me!"

The guards didn't understand. It had been so long since females had been trained to use their personal weapon, the califa, that the guards were completely unfamiliar with it. They kept coming.

"Stop you fools! Don't you know anything about your history?"

The three guards finally stopped, looking at each other wondering what their Prime Officer meant.

"What now Set Li? Do you plan to hold me hostage? To what end? Are you planning to take over the station? I warn you there are too many here for your finger poke weapon. I happen to know that it takes time to recharge so you won't even be able to use it on many of us."

"I know how few people are on this station," Set Li said. "We scanned it when we arrived. I hadn't planned to take it over. I was hoping for a more respectful greeting. That hope has failed. Now we'll make it up as we go.

"I know you don't believe my claim. If we had the chance to talk before you chose to threaten us, I would have explained. I am who I claim to be, and yes the name Set Li was a respected name at court. What you don't know about me is that besides being an explorer, I was also a military leader. In that role I developed military strategies that I'm sure have been long forgotten. That training will serve in this instance."

"Please bring the guards to me, Jardut."

Jardut drew his weapon and went to the guards who gave up their weapons with some reluctance. He marched them over to his mate. Set Li had Jardut guard Neylec while she went to each guard and stung them with a heavy sedative using the needle under her index finger. She had Jesse drag them out of the way. They would need to be tied, but they had time.

Jesse watched all this happen as did the non-violent Lorengi who had astounded looks on their faces. He also hadn't planned to take over the station. Even as the current situation played out, he still didn't want to take over the station if it meant killing Sudahlli.

"What are we doing, Set Li?"

"I apologize, Jesse. As I said, I hadn't planned this, but this animal and his kind have apparently subjugated the female Sudahlli, and he was planning to do the same to me. If nothing else, we can simply leave, though I would hate to turn my back on my home world for the rest of my life. I think we have enough time to find an alternative. Right now, we have to complete the takeover of this station. Can you help with that? Will you help?"

Jesse took time to think before answering. He didn't want to take part in an armed conflict. Besides being against such activity, he might get killed. Then he had an idea.

"Janus, I assume you have been following this."

"I have, and Set Li is right about what Neylec had planned. I don't want to be part of an armed action any more than you do, but I think Set Li was right to take the action she has so far."

"Right. Can you see into Neylec's mind? Do you think you could do that 'sleep thing' with these male Sudahlli? If you could, it would be like Saludadi all over again, and we could take over the station without bloodshed."

"I will try."

A moment later, Neylec slumped to the floor. Jardut and Set Li looked down at Neylec and then at Jesse, who said, "Okay! I can help."

Looking down at Neylec, thinking about the way he acted toward her just because she was female, Set Li was reminded of how some of the females of her time had treated males. She saw some of her actions at that time in a new light. This had to change. The Sudahlli had to create a more balanced society. She knew she had to help them find that balance.

Leaving Neylec and his guards in the meeting room, Set Li led everyone to the Bridge. She and Jardut brought the guards' weapons with them, but being more familiar with their own weapons, they had those in their hands when they walked onto the Bridge.

The security chief and the three guards on the Bridge started to draw their weapons. Set Li and Jardut pointed their weapons at them. The security team stopped trying to get to their weapons, and instead slumped to the floor.

That got the attention of the rest of the Bridge staff, who were in shock. They had never seen a Human or Lorengi, a race they could see through. The Sudahlli female and male were dressed unusually, held weapons they had never seen, which could apparently kill by just pointing. With startled looks, they rose from their stations, and held their arms out to their sides, palms facing Set Li to show they were empty.

Set Li and Jardut were as surprised as the Bridge staff that the guards fell to the floor but didn't show it. Set Li looked at Jesse again. He nodded and smiled impishly.

"Who is senior here?" Set Li asked calmly.

The technician who had spotted the arrival of Jannida looked at the security chief on the floor, and then turned to Set Li.

"Among those you have not eliminated, I am."

"What is your name?"

"I am Technician First, Arlut. If it will not anger you, could you tell us what is happening?"

"Your fate is in your hands, Arlut. You and your colleagues will be unharmed if you cooperate and answer my questions. As to what has happened, Prime Officer Neylec was rude, and had to be dealt with."

Arlut looked around at the four Sudahlli staff still standing. They nodded their willingness to follow his lead.

"We will cooperate and will endeavor to avoid any rudeness as we do."

Set Li smiled in spite of the seriousness of the situation. The technician seemed like someone she could talk with.

"Arlut, can you be spared from the Bridge to consult with us for a few moments?"

"Of course."

"Good. The rest of you please resume your work. It would be 'rude' of you if you were to attempt to communicate what has happened here to anyone else. I'll ask my mate to remain with you to help you remember."

Arlut noticed three guards and Prime Officer Neylec on the floor in a corner of the meeting room as he entered. Set Li made introductions. She let Arlut know that those on the floor here and on the Bridge were just unconscious, not dead. Obviously relieved, Arlut asked what he could do for Set Li.

"I need you to tell me about the Sudahlli," Set Li said.

"What do you mean? You are Sudahlli. Don't you know?"

"Just tell me. It seems that the males are dominant, and they treat females terribly."

"Yes. That is the way of things. Most males I know are uncomfortable with how females are treated, but we can't do anything about it. There are shadow groups of females who are trying to fight back. Some males support them. The females are imprisoned and treated harshly if they are caught. Any males who are caught with them are killed on the spot."

"How could this happen?" Set Li wondered aloud.

"What do you mean?" Arlut asked. "It's always been this way, at least it has for centuries."

"No Arlut, it hasn't always been this way. Tell me, do you know any females who are leaders of the groups you mentioned?"

Arlut looked around at the strange beings at the table and then back to Set Li.

"Is this some elaborate scheme leadership has arranged to trap me? I admit it doesn't seem likely, but..."

"If Neylec is a representative example of your leadership, I don't think they are that clever. Tell me! Do you know of someone, Arlut?"

"My sister is one, but you won't be able to talk with her. She has been imprisoned."

"Can you help with this, Jesse?" Set Li asked.

"I may be able to. It will require Arlut's knowing participation. Do you think he is up to it?"

"We have to try."

"Arlut, I realize all of this has been strange for you. There is something more I will be asking you to do which will be even more difficult to believe. Jesse is going to communicate with you in your mind."

Arlut got a worried look on his face which intensified when Jesse put his thoughts into Arlut's mind.

"Arlut, I am able to communicate mind-to-mind. You don't have to do anything unusual to participate, just form your response as a thought instead of speech. Give it a try."

"Like this?" Arlut asked.

"Exactly. I've arranged this so Set Li can listen in. How are you doing?"

"Alright, I guess. What are we doing this for?"

"I'm going to ask you to think of your sister as clearly as you can, in as much detail as possible. Do it now."

Jesse picked up an image of a Sudahlli female. He felt her in his mind.

"Next, Arlut, we are going to communicate directly to your sister. What is her name?"

"Her full name is Canliot. Though when we were children I just called her Canli."

"I will reach out to Canli now. I need you to be ready to assure her that it is alright. She will be frightened. Can you help her?"

"Yes. I felt so bad when they took her. They wouldn't let me visit. They just took her away, and I haven't seen her since."

"Here we go."

"Canli, can you sense me in your mind? I have Arlut with me. Canli?"

Canliot was roused from sleep on her hard prison bed by strange thoughts in her mind. She no longer was surprised that her mind was failing. She had been over a year in this dark damp cell, with no one to talk with, eating the rotten food they served her. Maybe she could get back to sleep.

"Canli?"

There it is again. It sounded so much like the way that Arlut used to say her name. She missed her brother.

"It is me Canli. It's Arlut. Someone is with me. He is from another race that can talk mind-to-mind and is helping me connect with you that way. Are you alright?"

"Arlut? Is it really you? I must be going mad."

"You are not going mad. It is me. I'm on Thahll 2. Something has happened up here. Someone here wants to talk with you."

"With that much detail, I am going to assume that it's true. Besides, it's much more fun than just talking with myself."

"Hi, Canli. My name is Jesse."

"Is it you who is making this possible?"

"Yes. A female Sudahlli, named Set Li is with me. We don't have much time to explain, so I'm going to ask you to suspend your natural disbelief. Can you do that?"

"I may as well. I'm probably hallucinating anyway," Canli said.

"Good. What I want you to do is look around your surroundings. I realize that a prison cell doesn't have much detail but try to see as much detail as you can."

"I'll do my best," Canli laughed quietly, thinking in her heart that she was imagining all of this, and enjoying playing along.

"Perfect. Now I am going to appear right next to you."

Jesse did as he said he would. Canli let out a small gasp. Jesse put his index finger to his lips to quiet her. He walked over to her, touched her shoulder, and then teleported her back to Thahll 2.

She arrived in the room wearing a ragged and dirty prison uniform. She saw Arlut and looked around. Already being in a weakened state, what her eyes saw was too much for her. She fainted.

23 The Mysterious Alien

Aboard Thahll 2

Arlut and Jesse caught Canli as she was fainting and sat her in one of the chairs at the table. She opened her eyes shortly after being sat down. She rubbed her eyes and looked around again. Arlut was in his fleet uniform as usual. "Usual" stopped there. She opened her mouth but couldn't think of what to say.

"Canli, I'm so happy to see you," Arlut said. "All this is strange to me, too. Let the female explain."

"Hi Canli, I am called Set Li."

"I am grateful to be out of that terrible cell, but…"

Set Li introduced Jesse and the Lorengi. She described events that led up to their arrival on Thahll 2."

"Are you really from that far in our past?"

"Yes, Canli, and I am surprised and disappointed in what I have learned about the situation on Thahll at this time. I was hoping you could give me more detail about what is happening."

Canli nodded, trying to process what Set Li had said. She abruptly sat upright in her chair with her eyes wide open.

"You have to get Berla! If all this is true, that I am truly here out of prison, you have to do the same thing for Berla! They are going to execute her today!"

Canli told them that Berla was the leader of a group of particularly strident females opposing the current government.

She was arrested the same day that the Global Police Force came for Canli. Berla had put up a fight. She injured a GPF officer and a trooper before they subdued her. They used their shock sticks on Berla and beat her before they brought her into the same GPF station where Canli had been taken.

There had been a short trial. Canli was sentenced to three years imprisonment. Berla was given a life sentence. Since her arrest, Berla was constantly arguing and fighting with the guards, and was beaten for her insolence. A short time ago, when she was attacked by one of the guards, she killed him. Another trial was held, and Berla was sentenced to be hung in a public place. That sentence was to be carried out today.

Jesse acted quickly, this time using Canli as the reassuring voice. Jesse brought Berla to the Thahll 2 meeting room. Berla also wore a ragged and dirty prison uniform. The difference was that Berla also bore the marks of the cruel treatment she had lived through. There were numerous, barely healed cuts on her head and face. One of her lower arms hung crookedly as if it had been broken. In spite of that she stood erect as she surveyed the new surroundings and unusual group of beings in the room. She appeared ready to take on everyone in the room. Only when it became clear that it wouldn't be necessary to defend herself did she succumb to her weakened state. She leaned on the table, and sought a chair to sit in.

"Berla, do you need something?" Canli asked.

"A little water, for now. Thank you."

Jesse went to the sink in the room, filled a container with water, and gave it to Berla.

Berla drank the water and paused to look around the room.

"Thanks, for bringing me to your meeting," Berla said, with a wry smile. "I'm glad for the improved quarters. I'm also glad to see the male Sudahlli in a pile against the wall. I've come to hate the males of our race."

Berla looked at Arlut in his fleet uniform.

"Why is this one still alive?" she asked.

"His name is Arlut," Set Li said. "He is Canli's brother. He helped us get Canli out, and she alerted us to your situation. So far, Arlut has been helpful. The others on the floor were not. They are not dead, merely unconscious."

"Too bad," Berla said, with a snarl. "Nothing personal, Arlut. Thanks for helping."

Berla turned to Set Li. "You seem to be the one in charge. Perhaps you can explain all this."

"First let me introduce myself. I am Set Li, First-Born Mother of clan Parlac, and Master of the Sudahlli ship Chantlasec."

Berla's eyes widened. "Your name has not been heard on Sudahlli for a very long time. You are dressed as if you were in a museum exhibit. Are you from some unheard of Sudahlli colony on a distant planet?"

Set Li looked at Berla and gave her an understanding smile. She thought this one would have been a strong clan leader in Set Li's time—one she would have been proud to call sister. It saddened her to find Berla in such a state. Pity wasn't Set Li's way, and Berla would have been insulted if Set Li had offered it.

"Wait until you hear the rest," Set Li said, and told Berla what she had just told Canli

Berla laughed, wincing slightly from the pain. "That was the best entertainment I've had in a very long time, sister. I can't believe it, but as I look around at the beings in the room, I'm thinking that I might have to open my mind to consider the impossible."

Set Li smiled. "Don't try to understand everything at once."

"If I could suggest…," Arlut said, reluctant to interrupt these two powerful females.

All eyes turned to him.

"What is it, Arlut?" Set Li asked.

"I was going to suggest, that if there are no other guests that need to be brought out of prison perhaps you might want to consider your next steps on the station."

"What does he mean?" Berla asked.

"We arrived in Sudahlli space a short time ago," Set Li said. "When we came aboard the station, Prime Officer Neylec tried to disarm my mate and me, with the apparent intent to take us into custody. I objected. Prime Officer Neylec is on the floor over there with his three guards. There are more guards unconscious on the Bridge. Before we can continue our discussion, Arlut is wisely suggesting that we finish the task of taking over the station."

"Oh." Berla's regard for Set Li went up a notch. Taking over the space station that the current Sudahlli leaders are so proud of without killing anyone was quite an accomplishment.

"What should we be concerned about, Arlut?" Set Li asked.

"Several things all at once. Most urgent are the other twenty crew members aboard. What are you going to do about them? A shift change is coming up. Then there is the fact that the ship you arrived in probably showed up on screens in fleet operations on the surface. This station has not reported anything about your arrival. I imagine that we have been contacted with questions from below. If so, they haven't received a response. They will be anxious about that, and who knows what they will do. How do you want to handle that?"

"What do you suggest regarding a response to the surface?" Set Li asked.

"We could say that Prime Officer Neylec is meeting with the new arrivals and will report shortly. That kind of response won't keep them happy for long, but it will give you some time to think about your next steps."

"Thank you, Arlut. I appreciate your help."

Set Li turned to the two escaped prisoners and said, "Please bear with me. Arlut is right. There is more to do before we can make our plans. I will take care of these immediate needs."

"Arlut, is there a place for Canli and Berla to clean up and rest before we continue?" Set Li asked. "We'll also need food for them and some clothes."

"Yes. We'll show them into Prime Officer Neylec's quarters on our way to the Bridge. When we inform the rest of the crew about the new order of things some will object, but others will try to help. We'll ask one of the helpful ones to bring food and clothes for them."

Set Li was pleased with Arlut's attitude and hoped she would gain other recruits like him from the rest of the crew.

When they returned to the Bridge, Jardut was happy to see them. It had been a while and he was wondering what had happened. Arlut went to the communications station and saw that it was lit up with messages. He opened one from a tech he knew in fleet ops and found what he expected—curiosity about the new arrival. Set Li watched him close as he opened a channel to that tech.

"Hi, Sardat, sorry for the delay."

"An unidentified ship arrives in Sudahlli space and there's no word from the station. You can imagine the concern. What's going on? Who are they?"

Choosing his words carefully, Arlut said, "As I understand it, the ship belongs to a race called the Lorengi. You can tell those concerned that the Lorengi seem peaceful. Prime Officer

Neylec is in a closed session with the new arrivals. I will get back to you when I know more."

Arlut shut down the system, and looked at Set Li.

"Thank you Arlut. Now let's see to the rest of the crew. Is there a gathering place close by that is large enough for all of the crew?"

"Yes, shall I ask the crew to gather there?"

After Arlut had announced the meeting over the station comm, Set Li looked at the three other Bridge staff who had sat back down at their stations, looking at their monitors. "How about these techs? Can their workstations be abandoned for a short time?"

Arlut looked at his colleagues for an answer.

"How long?" one of them asked.

"About as long as we were gone just now."

That seemed to be agreeable. They were uncomfortable with what was going on, but they wanted to be at the meeting where they might get an explanation.

Set Li asked the Lorengi, Gordi, to stay on the Bridge in case anything new came up. Then she let Arlut and the other techs lead the way to the meeting with the crew. She turned to Jesse on the way.

"We can talk later about how you make people drop to the floor, Jesse, but please be ready to do that again in case some of the crew get unruly when I tell them things have changed."

"I'll be watching," Jesse said.

Some crew members were awakened by the urgent call from Arlut to come to a meeting, and they grumbled at him a bit when he came into the room. Others murmured about what could cause this rare all-crew meeting. All the grumbling and murmurs ceased when Set Li, Jardut, Atala, and Jesse entered.

The murmurs started up again when it became clear that Prime Officer Neylec wasn't coming.

"Thank you for coming so promptly. My name is Set Li. My companions and I recently arrived in Sudahlli space. We asked Prime Officer for permission to come aboard Thahll 2. He granted that, but soon after he attempted to disarm us and take us into custody. He is now unconscious, as are his security chief and guards.

"We came in peace, glad to be back to Thahll after being away for…a long time. We were saddened by the reception but would not submit to Prime Officer Neylec's brutish behavior. As a result of these recent events, we thought it would be a good idea to talk with the rest of the crew."

"Do you mean you are taking control of this station?" an older member of the crew asked.

"I see no alternative at this point," Set Li answered. "That certainly wasn't my idea when we came aboard."

"But you're a female," another crew member said in disbelief.

"Yes." Set Li was not one to explain herself.

There were additional murmurs as the crew tried to make sense of what they heard and what they saw before them.

"I could have just left as I came, but in my short time aboard Thahll 2, I have found that females are treated terribly under the current government. That bothers me, as it should you."

A number of comments flew around the room, ranging from "That's how it should be," to "It's wrong, but what can we do about it?"

Set Li let the commotion go on for a while, and then got their attention again by introducing Jesse and Atala. Atala nodded and drew amazed looks and more discussion in the crowd. Jesse went further by addressing the group telepathically.

"Hello. I am a Human from the planet we call Earth. I am glad to be among you. I am sad that things have taken the turn they have, but I hope that you will support and help Set Li as she works through this difficult situation."

When Jesse was young, living on the streets of Seattle, he pretended to be mute to hide what he was capable of as an H2. He was successful with the ruse then. He thought that it might be a good idea to remain silent in this situation. It might be enough to restrain the crew from violent behavior.

As Set Li often said about male Sudahlli, some of them have difficulty accepting new and unusual situations. Most of the crew members were mulling things over, but one large male in a mechanic's uniform let out a loud growl from the back of the room. He charged toward the front. Jesse raised his hand, and the brute fell to the floor.

"I am sorry I had to do that," Jesse said, addressing the crew, *"but I couldn't have him disrupting this meeting. He is only unconscious, but he might have hurt himself when he fell. Will some of you please check to see if he needs medical attention?"*

The shocked looks on the faces in the audience increased Jesse's confidence that the ruse was a good idea, though he had never thought of himself as a mysterious alien before.

24 Flustered Fleet

Fleet Operations, Taxlan Base, Thahll

In the headquarters of the Sudahlli Space Fleet it was usually just as quiet as aboard Thahll 2. There hadn't been any 'fleet operations' to manage for some time. The World Council was on the verge of cutting Fleet's budget again. Fleet Commander Meritac was eager to show the Council that Fleet was still needed and useful. He needed some meaningful projects, some commercial enterprise like mining on the moon that would demonstrate the Fleet's importance—something to get the Council excited about space travel again. Having some crazy female take over Thahll 2 was not what he had in mind.

"What, by all the stars is a First-Born Mother?" Meritac shouted at Sardat, the tech that relayed the message about who took over the Thahll 2.

Sardat began to explain his understanding of the title.

"Oh shut up! I don't really care. What else?"

"She says that she is Master of the Sudahlli ship, Chantlasec."

"There is no Sudahlli ship by that name! Females are not masters of anything, except causing trouble."

"Yes, Sir." Sardat said. He wished someone else had been on duty when Arlut sent the message from the station.

"Did you talk with her?"

"No, Sir. The tech aboard the station said that she wanted to talk with the Fleet Commander. Shall I set a time?"

"Not right away. Let her wait. I need to talk with the Defense minister at the Council. He's going to love this. Get him for me."

"Yes, Sir!" Sardat was glad to shift the focus off of himself for the moment.

A short time later the screen on Meritac's desk blinked indicating an incoming call. He pressed the accept button and the face of Defense Minister Hartac appeared."

"Did I hear right?" Hartac demanded. "Someone has taken over the space station?"

"Yes. She apparently hasn't injured anyone in the process."

"She? She! Are you telling me that you have let a FEMALE take over Thahll 2 and all of the Fleet vessels docked there?" Hartac shouted.

"I didn't let her do anything."

"Your staff did. You say no one was injured. It sounds like they didn't put up a fight. Sounds like the Fleet officers and staff just let her take over the station. They're 'your' staff."

"Can we please get beyond whose fault it was, and on to what to do about it?" Meritac asked.

"You expect me to tell you how to fix this?"

"No, of course not."

"This is your problem to fix, and you better find a way to fix it quickly. By the way, two terrorists have escaped from prison. This mysterious female doesn't happen to be one of them does she? This isn't somehow connected to those escaped prisoners is it?"

"What? How could that be?" Meritac asked.

"I don't know. You tell me. A short time ago, we were in control of 'our' station. Now some female has control of it at the same time that female prisoners escaped. You better hope the two events are not connected. If they are, this situation may be taken out of your hands, and you may be taken out of your position just as quickly. Contact me when you have a full report of the situation and a plan to fix it!"

When the screen went blank Meritac raised his upper arms, and ran his fingers through his top fur, while his lower arms hugged his mid-section in an attempt to quell the growing unease in his innards. A few minutes ago he was worried about how he was going to manage operations with yet another budget cut. Now he had been told that he might not have to worry about that or any other aspect of Fleet operations. He wouldn't let that happen. No female was going to ruin his career! He pushed the comm button.

"Sardat, connect me with Thahll 2."

Meritac's screen next showed a male in Fleet uniform.

"What's your name?"

"I am Tech First, Arlut, Sir."

"Tell me what has happened."

"Wouldn't you rather hear it from…?"

"Answer me!"

"Yes, Sir." Arlut told the Fleet Commander what he knew of the events, beginning with the unknown ship appearing near Salana, but leaving out the part about bringing the female prisoners aboard. He didn't know how it was done and didn't want to be the one who told the Commander about it.

"How many came aboard with her? She must have had quite a crew to so easily take over the station."

"Only her and her mate, Jardut, two Lorengi and one Human."

Meritac set aside the mention of two races he didn't recognize. He would investigate that later. "Were they heavily armed?"

"Set Li and Jardut had hand weapons only. The others were unarmed."

"How did they do it?"

"Pardon, Sir?"

"How did they overcome the Prime Officer and his security guards with so few weapons, and not injure anyone in the process?"

"I'm unsure of what happened in the meeting with Prime Officer Neylec. I believe Set Li may have used the califa to render them unconscious. Now that I've seen him in action, it could be that the Human may have helped."

The "califa"? Meritac hadn't heard that word since his time in the academy. It was part of what females had used centuries ago to maintain their control over males. Since the Change, when females reach maturity they were forced to extend their califa and have them clipped off. Training on how to use them, or even discussion of the califa was strictly forbidden. Violations were severely punished. Who is this female that she could use the califa? Perhaps she didn't. The tech mentioned something about a Human having a role in the takeover, whatever a Human was. How it was done wasn't the issue. The problem was that the intruders had control of his station. To remedy that, he needed to talk with this Set Li.

"Tech First, connect me with the female, Set Li."

When the face of Set Li came on the screen Meritac controlled his anger. He had never had to negotiate with a female or ask one for anything. He would begin in a business-like manner and get her to give up control of the station.

"Am I addressing the person Set Li?"

"I am Set Li. Are you the Commander of Sudahlli's Fleet?"

"I am Fleet Commander, Meritac. I am told you have taken over Thahll 2. I must ask you to stand down and put Prime Officer Neylec in his rightful role as station master."

"I tried to talk to Prime Officer Neylec in a civilized manner when we came aboard this station. Instead, without any provocation from us he became hostile, and demanded we give up our weapons, with the obvious intention of restraining our movements. He will remain unconscious until a more rational leader can be provided, and our continued freedom is assured."

"You will immediately turn over the station to the crew. We will see what to do about the position of Prime Officer in the future, but for now, you must relinquish control of the station."

"Actually, Commander, the crew is running the station at this time. It's just the Prime Officer and his security staff who are not on duty."

"So I can send a new Prime Officer and security team to the station and you won't interfere?"

"I don't want your station, Commander. My mate, my crew and I have been away from Thahll for a long time. We simply wanted to come home. Your Prime Officer's attitude toward me and what I've found out about how females are treated by the current government have made it clear that we can't come back to the Thahll we knew. Things have changed, and we are still considering what to do about it."

Meritac couldn't make sense of what Set Li was talking about. She claimed an ancient title and that she was master of a Sudahlli ship that didn't exist.

"How long were you gone? Where were you?"

"I'm not sure we should discuss that."

"Why do you say that?"

"I told Prime Officer Neylec how long we had been gone. He laughed at us. That was when he became hostile and tried to take our weapons. He didn't believe me and didn't wait for an explanation. Just as well I suppose, he wouldn't have believed the explanation either."

"At this point, your story is probably exactly what we should discuss."

"Alright. You have probably heard that I have arrived with members of two other races in my party—two Lorengi and one Human. They are part of my story."

When Set Li finished Meritac tried not to laugh. What she said was preposterous, but she obviously believed it. Also, though he hadn't seen them, she was accompanied by two races he hadn't heard of before. Something unusual was in play here, but not anything like what she claimed.

"I don't know what to make of what you have told me. Setting that aside, why don't you and your newfound friends just leave?"

"I would have done that. My crew and I would have been disappointed about not being able to visit our home planet. Then we learned that it was common practice to beat and imprison females for merely protesting the abuses laid upon females in your current society. I felt the need to join their cause and change the conditions that allow such abuse."

"You can try if you wish, but you will suffer the same fate as those you expect to rescue."

"Thank you for your clear answer. Though I don't want your station, I think I will keep it awhile longer."

"I cannot allow that."

"How do propose taking it back? This station apparently has weapons and can defend itself. I don't think you want to fire weapons at your station in any event. I have your station, and I believe most of your Fleet vessels are docked here."

"I can stop the shipment of food and supplies."

"That will only harm your crew. My people are amply supplied by the Lorengi ship that brought us here."

Meritac had heard all he was going to from this female, and his ability to control his anger failed him.

"I will see you hang! You and all who support you will die a painful and very public death. Those who might be tempted to join the 'cause' you speak of will shrink back in fear, leaving the cause to wither away in obscurity."

He slammed a fist on the comm, spraying small pieces all over his office, which ended the conversation.

25 Sisters Awake!

Aboard Thahll 2

Set Li was troubled, but not surprised by the Fleet Commander's arrogant rant at the end of the conversation. She had held hope that Prime Officer Neylec's attitude was his alone. Now she knew that it was endemic, at least among the leadership of Fleet. It didn't take much of a stretch to assume the same was true for all the current Sudahlli leadership. If it turned out that almost all males felt this way, the task of changing the social situation on the planet would go from merely overwhelming to impossible.

At the end of the meeting with the crew she asked that they continue with their duties. They seemed willing, if grudgingly, to do that. Perhaps they were swayed by the mysterious way that Jesse had dropped one of their colleagues to the floor. After the meeting Set Li made sure food and clean clothes had been brought to Canli and Berla, who were now resting in Neylec's quarters. She decided that it was time to talk with the others who had boarded the station with her before initiating any other actions on her own.

She asked Arlut where they could put all of the unconscious crew. He showed them a small room that would be adequate for keeping them out of the way. Jardut and Arlut dragged the ones from the Bridge. Jesse teleported those from the meeting room. Once there, they were arranged in reasonably comfortable positions. Set Li asked Jesse what they should do with them if they woke up. Jesse said they wouldn't wake up until it was time to do something with them. She just looked at him. He just gave her another of his unrevealing smiles and walked to the meeting room.

"Now what?" Jardut asked when they all were seated at the table in the meeting room. "Dear Set Li, what have you gotten us into?"

"A valid question, mate of mine. Although I'm not sure all the blame for this can rest on my shoulders. I would suggest that Neylec's actions started us on this path. I have reviewed what has happened since and believe that the steps we have taken have been the right ones so far. So let's go back to your first question, 'Now what?'"

"One option is for us all to leave," Set Li said. "We have set Canli and Berla free. They could probably give us a location on the surface where they would be safe for a time. I would be forever troubled if we chose that path. Sudahlli are suffering under this government. I don't see how we can choose to do nothing and leave."

"What can we do if we stay?" Jardut asked. "We are so few."

"That is true, Jardut," Atala said, "at this time we are few, but Set Li is right. It would be wrong to leave."

The Sudahlli and Jesse looked at Atala's image. They were surprised by her comment. All through their actions on Thahll 2 the Lorengi had been silent.

"I know that, Atala," Jardut said. "I just can't imagine what we can do." He turned back to Set Li. "I'm sure you are including this in your thoughts, but the Chantlasec crew need to have a say in our decision."

"Of course," Set Li said. "We will seek their views. Over half are female. I think I know what they will say when they get done cursing after we tell them what is happening on the surface. I think I know the male members of my crew well enough to believe that they will support us as well. We will talk with them shortly. Jesse, what do you have to say about all of this?"

"To begin with," Jesse said, "I am going to continue my role as the 'mysterious alien' and communicate only telepathically, at least for a while. Atala and Gordi are mysterious, too. They can speak out loud, but the Sudahlli don't know what to make of the fact that they can see through them. I think these mysteries will give us an edge when we need it.

"In terms of what I think about this situation, I won't support an armed revolt. I imagine the Lorengi feel the same way. We are few now, but there are probably Sudahlli all across Thahll that will join us if we can show them that it is possible to accomplish what we are trying to do. We will need to talk with Berla about that. I'm not concerned about our numbers, or how we will go about it. My question is what 'it' is. What do you want to accomplish, Set Li?"

"I want to create a balance in the society," Set Li answered. "It appears that the males have created an unnatural bias against females. It's not right, and their actions are very cruel and unjust. Even if we don't intervene, the current situation won't last. If Berla is a representative example of the female population, the war you and I want to avoid will erupt spontaneously, and it will be terrible for all Sudahlli. I want to keep that from happening and assert the proper role of female Sudahlli."

"Like before?" Jardut asked. "Females running everything?"

Set Li gave her mate an understanding smile. "I understand your resentment, Jardut, and I don't blame you. The society you and I knew was unbalanced in the other direction. As I try to understand how what we see on Thahll today could have happened, I believe it must have grown out that resentment the males felt within our society. Something must have caused that resentment to surge to the fore, allowing the males to take over. I'm seeking to make a non-violent transition to equal roles for males and females."

"Good," Jesse said. "I will support that, and the others from Earth will as well. Technological help from the Dhara'chee might be useful. We'll have to ask if they are willing to help here as they are on Solan. Ontoron, what can the Annli do to help?"

"I have been watching what has happened since you came to the Sudahlli home world. I agree that it would be good to accomplish what Set Li has outlined. The Annli have chosen to avoid interfering with those living in the material world. That is changing with recent events. I think I can say that we will help your efforts, but our ability to affect the material world is diminishing. So let us see what is needed, and what help the Annli can provide toward that."

"The Lorengi will support this, too," Gordi said. "Like Ontoron said of the Annli, I am not sure what we can do in our current form. I believe our ships may be helpful, and I think they will be eager to help."

"This sounds very promising," Set Li said. "Thank you everyone. Let's get started."

Set Li took the shuttle back to Jannida, leaving Jardut aboard Thahll 2 to keep things under control in her brief absence. She led her crew back aboard Chantlasec, and then docked her ship at the Sudahlli station. Since the Thahll 2 crew had been held to a minimum, there was room for members of the Chantlasec crew on the station. Set Li asked the Thahll 2 staff to help the Chantlasec crew to become familiar with the station. Most of the Thahll 2 staff were eager to learn about their visitors, and willingly told the newcomers what they needed to know about the station. The Chantlasec crew found that technology had made surprisingly little progress during the millennia of their absence.

Seeing the two crews working well together, Jesse felt comfortable leaving for a while. He asked Atala and Gordi if they would like to go to Earth with him, and they did.

Jesse spoke with another friend as well when he arrived at Sunaj.

"Martha, I've undertaken a project on a distant planet. I was wondering if you might be able to help."

"Janus has been keeping me posted on what we are doing out in the galaxy," Martha replied. "Fascinating! Athena has kept me up to date on her activities when she leaves Earth. Between her and Janus, I feel well informed, almost as if I had shared their experiences—almost. This time I would like to go myself."

"I was hoping you'd say that," Jesse said.

Jarruda had chosen to bring the Lorengi to Earth while the others were working on Solan and Thahll. Their arrival and news of their rescue and new races discovered, created considerable excitement among the people of Earth. There were many requests for Lorengi to visit various countries. Even though it kept Jarruda very busy, Atala and Gordi were able to discuss the Thahll situation with her before they went back to the Thahll 2 with Jesse.

Jesse loaded supplies he thought might be useful and a few volunteers aboard the Jannida. Space was provided for Martha to store herself. On their way back to Thahll 2 they stopped at Solan. Jesse took the opportunity to get together with Carmen. Then he spoke with Orlyn.

"Oh, young Jesse, we Dhara'chee don't take part in conflicts," Orlyn said.

"What I'm asking is can you devise a method to render the Sudahlli weapons harmless? You wouldn't actually have to take part. Your technology would keep people from getting killed."

"What kind of weapons?"

"I've brought some examples. They are energy weapons of some sort."

"We have had to defend ourselves in the past from this type of weaponry, though that usually has been to thwart attacks by other spaceships. Perhaps the same principle can be scaled down to affect the weapons the Sudahlli use."

They learned that the Dhara'chee device might be useful, but they couldn't figure out how to make it practical for tactical deployment on land. Still, the experiment gave Jesse an idea.

"Ontoron, I think I have a suggestion for how the Annli can help."

Returning to Thahll 2 a few days after he had left, Jesse found Set Li talking with Berla and Canli about conditions on Thahll and possible ways to make changes. Berla wasn't convinced it would work. Her doubts increased when she learned that Jesse had only brought fifty volunteers from Earth and that they were unarmed.

"There are three billion Sudahlli on our planet. We only have your crew of thirty, Set Li, and Jesse's fifty Humans who have no weapons!"

"We cannot possibly win an armed conflict, Berla," Set Li said. "So we will have to approach it in a different way."

"The opposition is armed," Berla said, "and they like to use their weapons."

Jesse took one of the Sudahlli hand weapons and fired it at the wall, shocking everyone in the room. It made a hole in the wall. He then asked Berla to try it. She took it in her hand. She had used this kind of weapon in the past even though it was forbidden for females to have weapons. She lifted the weapon, aimed at the wall near where Jesse had made his mark, and fired. Nothing happened. She attempted to fire it again with the same result. Just before Berla had tried to fire the weapon the first time everyone in the room had felt a small disturbance in the air.

Berla looked at Jesse, lifting up the weapon with a questioning look on her face.

"What did you do to this before you handed it to me?"

"I did nothing, but something was done to it before you fired. Its energy cell was drained, as was the cell in all of these sample weapons on the table."

Berla picked up a rifle-like weapon and fired it against the wall. Nothing happened.

"Can this be done to a large number of weapons, big and small?"

"Yes."

"How is it done?"

Jesse explained about the Annli. Berla was shaken and dubious until Set Li calmly reassured her that it was true.

"We Annli have the ability to absorb energy of various types," Ontoron said. *"We just focused on the energy cells in the weapons and absorbed the energy from them."*

Berla shook her head, trying to take in these revelations. She took a deep breath and said, "This will make a difference. What else do we have?"

Set Li was glad that Berla was beginning to see the how this could work.

"A number of things which you will see soon," Set Li said. "Before we discuss them, I would like to talk with you about what we have in mind."

"Isn't it obvious?" Berla said indignantly. "We make those wretches pay for what they have done."

"Justice will be done, Berla," Set Li said, "but we cannot adopt their ruthlessness, or their cruelty to achieve our goals. You have seen that our team will be unarmed for the most part. That means that we are not planning to win this with weapons. We want to avoid injury or death on both sides. If we can do it this way, we have the best chance to establish a new rule of law that is good for males and females. We are aiming at a better society, a healthier way for all Sudahlli."

"So you expect the government and their police to just give up? You are expecting those who have suffered under this government to forget about their injuries, set aside their need for revenge?"

"Yes," Set Li confirmed.

Berla laughed.

"You continue to entertain, sister. Were Sudahlli all pacifists in that ancient time you say you come from, Set Li?"

"If anything we were more violent, Berla, and it was the females who had control. Terrible injustices were done to the males of the time. I do not want to repeat those mistakes. I don't want to kill any Sudahlli. What I have described is what we have planned. I'm sure it won't all go smoothly, but it's what we will strive for. This is what you, our sisters who have suffered, and those who continue to resist have to agree to. After we get started, anyone attempting to use violence, male or female, will be set aside and taken out of the picture."

"I thought you said that you weren't going to kill anyone."

"I'm not, Berla. Those people won't be killed, they'll just be immobilized."

"How?"

Set Li looked at Jesse. He nodded. Canli, who was in the room fell forward onto the table where she was sitting.

"What have you done?" Berla gasped.

"She is unconscious, but unharmed," Set Li said, and then looked at Jesse.

Canli stirred, sat back in her chair, looked around, and said, "I'm sorry. Did I just fall asleep? Oh, wait. Is that what you intend to do to those you were speaking of?"

"That will be the first step," Set Li said. "If they continue to be violent, they will have to be put in the cells that we plan to empty by releasing those who have been unjustly imprisoned."

Berla was conflicted about Set Li's plan and unsettled by the novel things she had just witnessed. She quickly got over both feelings, sat down at the table and said, "Let's get this going before any more of our sisters are harmed."

It took another day to develop a plan and choose how to proceed. When they were ready they asked Janus to reach out telepathically to all Sudahlli females and make it possible for Set Li to address them first.

"Sisters Awake!"

26 A Change in the Wind

Aboard Thahll 2

Upon returning from Earth, Jesse had asked Jannida to dock with Thahll 2, and had asked to have a link forged between Jannida and Thahll 2, so that Martha could get into the Thahll 2 systems.

"What are they like?" Jesse asked Martha.

"Foreign, but understandable. There! I'm in. What do you want me to do?"

"I would like you to set yourself up to be able to control all Thahll 2 systems. Let the technicians do their work for now but be ready to take over. Cut off all communications between the station and the surface. If one of the technicians feels the need to communicate on some routine matter, have them check with me. Get control of the weapons systems. Finally, learn how to get into the systems on the surface. Our ultimate goal is for you to be able to find out anything we need to know and make any 'adjustments' we need to make—like you were able to do on Earth.

"What you want on Thahll 2 should be easy. Getting into the surface systems from here...well let me explore what can be done."

"Thanks, Martha."

"You're welcome. This will be the most fun I've had in a long time. Oops! There's a search and destroy security program looking for me. I'd better concentrate."

Jesse let Martha do her work and went in search of Set Li. Set Li's message to the females on the surface was enthusiastically welcomed by those who received it. Having Berla and Canli on hand as local validation helped. Many grumbled and complained when Set Li told them of the non-violent approach that they must adhere to. Set Li wasn't surprised and resigned herself to the fact that they wouldn't totally accept anything until they saw their plan in action and working.

Her telepathic message to the population at large through Janus was chaotic. The females had the advantage of having heard Set Li's plan already and liking the change it promised. The males had a harder time with it. Disbelief, outrage, and fear that it might actually unfold as the voice in their heads said it would, were the reactions of many of the males. Others were calmer and accepting.

"Well, we have let them know we're coming," Set Li said. "We better follow up quickly with some visible activity on the ground. Berla where are you known? I would like to start with a smaller community to see how this will work."

"My hometown has a population of about ten thousand, and it is remote from other population centers. The local government leadership is as bad as elsewhere, but the male workers and police are a mixed lot. Some support the government. Others follow orders, but don't like it."

"Sounds like a good place to find the flaws in our plan," Set Li said.

"What's the name of your town?" Martha asked.

"Who is that?" Berla demanded.

"Her name is Martha," Jesse replied.

"Where is she? I haven't met her. Is she one of your volunteers?"

"Yes, but a little different than the others. You see, Martha is…"

"I'll explain, Jesse," Martha said. "Berla, I am a cyber-based intelligence. From your perspective perhaps 'smart system' would be a better description. It's my job to break into the computer systems on the surface to help with our non-violent rebellion. If you let me know the name of your town I will get into your town government and police systems and take them over."

Berla looked at Set Li.

"Jesse said something about it, but I don't know any more than that," Set Li said.

"While we are on Thahll 2," Jesse said, "Martha can communicate with us through the station comm. In the field, you will need these small implants to communicate with her."

He showed them the implants and how they're applied to the neck behind their ears. The Sudahlli went along with it but were shocked when Martha spoke to them through the implants. To their credit, they didn't let this additional marvel unsettle them.

"The more I see of what we will have on our side," Berla said, "the more hope I have for our success. The name of my town is Denalla, Martha."

"So are you able to connect with the surface, Martha?" Jesse asked.

"Yes. I've found Denalla, and through the city systems I've found a way into the systems of the World Council. It's not as strong a set up as I'd like, but I'll work on strengthening it as we go along. It will be sufficient for our work in Denalla."

With Martha's help Jannida was able to locate Denalla on the surface. The first ground team was made up of the Sudahlli Set Li, Jardut, Berla, Canli, the Lorengi Atala, and Jesse. The other Lorengi and Human volunteers would remain aboard Jannida observing and ready to help if needed. Ontoron was observing for the Annli. Martha said she was ready. Janus said he was ready.

Berla directed Jannida to hover over a field just out of town. There were a few Sudahlli working in the field when they arrived. Through Janus, Set Li communicated with them to reduce their shock before they set down on the ground.

The first team members to exit the ship were the four Sudahlli. Set Li and Jardut had left their hand weapons on Jannida. Jesse and Atala came after them. The heat and humidity were like a wall that Jesse bumped into as he left the ship. He began to sweat immediately. The Sudahlli in the party seemed unaffected, but then this was their home world. Set Li and Jardut were in their most formal uniforms, which were plain hide breeches and close-fitting vests. The only adornment being colorful patches identifying them as members of Clan Parlac.

Some of those in the field ran toward town. Others came closer to investigate.

One of the females asked, "Are you the one who spoke in our minds earlier?"

"Quiet!" a male standing next to her said. He raised one of his hands as if to strike her. He fell to the ground before he had the chance.

Another male in the group said, "My name is Tonkat. Thank you for taking care of Belagar. He is always trying to push us around. Is he dead?"

"No," Set Li said. "As I have said in my messages we will strive to avoid injuries as we proceed. Will you walk with us Tonkat?"

He looked around at the three males and four females of the local Sudahlli.

"We all will walk with you!"

With that, Set Li communicated with the rest of the town with the help of Janus as they walked in that direction.

"I hope our ship hasn't disturbed you. We have chosen your town to begin our effort, because one of yours, Berla, is with us. Some members of your community are walking with us. I hope you will greet us as courteously as we will greet you. Belagar of your community began with a disrespectful approach. He is unharmed, but unconscious. We have left him in the field. Perhaps some who are close to him could go retrieve him. He will remain unconscious for the time being. We will be entering your town shortly."

Their small group came upon a street with residential structures lining it. In the distance they could see taller buildings which, according to Berla, were in the center of town and included the government offices. As they walked along Sudahlli came out of their homes to watch. Some males and many of the females joined the procession, sometimes bringing their children with them. The adults were somber, unsure of what would happen. The children thought the strange Sudahlli and the two new races represented by Jesse and Atala were great fun and chattered as they walked along.

As they approached the town center they could see that a crowd had already gathered. It parted to allow them to continue to the main municipal building. An air car flew in above the plaza and hovered over the crowd.

"You are instructed to disperse!" demanded a voice broadcasted from the hovering vehicle.

"We are a peaceful assembly," Set Li asserted. "We will remain here at the steps. Please send out a representative of the town government to meet with us."

"You will disperse or be fired upon!" the voice asserted.

"Please land your vehicle and talk with us on the ground. We are unarmed, so you are in no danger. Surely you don't want to fire into this crowd of your citizens."

Apparently they agreed with Set Li. The vehicle landed in the nearby plaza. A door opened and six Sudahlli police came storming out. Five had shock sticks in their hand. They pushed their way through the crowd, not waiting for the Sudahlli to get out of their way. Some in the crowd were knocked to the pavement in the process. Seeing that, the crowd moved more quickly to let them through, but began to grumble.

Seeing the anger of the crowd beginning to rise, Set Li spread out her upper hands with her palms down, gesturing for them to remain calm. Then she lowered her arms to her side and looked directly at the leader of the police squad who was storming toward her. When the leader got a closer look at Atala and Jesse, he stopped before he reached their small group, which was now standing alone. Those who had accompanied them from the neighborhood had blended back into the spectators. A hush came over the gathering. Even the police were silent as they tried to assess what was going on.

The police officer who apparently was in charge, turned to the crowd, and ordered them to disperse. They pulled back a bit but stayed where they were. He could have ordered his squad to forcefully move the crowd, but he looked uncertain. He turned to Set Li.

"Who are you, and what are these?" he said, pointing at Jesse and Atala.

"I am a Lorengi," Atala said. "I am interested in learning about the Sudahlli."

He was shocked when the apparition before him spoke. He was even more surprised when Jesse addressed him, those in the crowd, and the Sudahlli in the Administration Building.

"I am Human. My name is Jesse Chavez. I have accompanied these Sudahlli to lend my support. Who are you?"

The lead officer didn't answer Jesse, but turned to Set Li.

"What do you want here?" he demanded.

"A short answer to your question is change—change for the better for all Sudahlli. I will give a more detailed description when I am talking to the leaders of your town."

"You won't be talking to anyone, female," the officer said through gritted teeth. "You and your group are under arrest and will come with me to the cells."

"That won't be convenient," Set Li said. "Please direct me to the mayor, town council or whoever is in charge."

"Take them!" the officer ordered his squad. Three troopers rushed forward to carry out the order. Two held back. The three charging toward Set Li suddenly dropped to the ground. The other two remained where they were.

The officer saw what happened. He looked at the two police still standing. "Get them, I said!"

They didn't move. The officer pulled his weapon first pointing it at them and then toward Set Li. He reversed position a couple of times, and apparently decided that Set Li was his target.

"What have you done to my officers?"

222

"They are unconscious and will remain so until we are out of danger," Set Li said. "Now please stop this senseless posturing and take us to the leaders of this town."

"I am coming to you," a new voice from the top of the steps said. They all looked up and saw a tall male Sudahlli, with graying fur dressed in a tan suit of linen-like material. "Put away that weapon, Shatoc. Can't you recognize when it's time to think instead of act?"

"Councilor Mentan, I was about to..."

"You were about to attempt to shoot these visitors. Can't you see the futility of the path you are on? You should check your weapon. I'm guessing that it cannot be fired."

Shatoc looked at the energy level in his hand weapon and looked a second time in disbelief. He then sheepishly put it back in his holster. He looked at Set Li as if expecting an answer, but the answer came from Councilor Mentan.

"It has been reported that all the weapons belonging to our police have all been drained. Perhaps we should listen to these visitors to learn what they have to say."

He turned to Set Li.

"Am I addressing, Set Li, First Mother of Clan Parlac?" Mentan asked.

"Yes."

"Would you be willing to revive the downed police if Shatoc took them away with him in his air car?"

Set Li nodded. The downed officers stirred and struggled to regain their feet. They were about to attempt to follow through on the last orders they received, when Shatoc stopped them. He glared at Set Li, and then herded his squad back toward their vehicle. On the way, he slapped the two reluctant officers on the back of the head.

"Am I addressing the leader of Denalla?" Set Li asked.

"I am Councilor Mentan. I serve as the head of this town council. I also am a member of the World Council. You have created quite a stir on our world, First Mother. I see Berla is with you. You'll have to tell me sometime how you managed to extract her and her companion from a high security prison, and how you also managed to take over Thahll 2 without firing one bolt of energy. Those discussions will have to wait, as I'm sure you want to talk of other things first. I sense a change in the wind."

"True, it is changing, Councilor," Set Li said. "It is signaling the end of one season and the beginning of another."

27 Counselling the Council

Denalla, Thahll

Set Li liked the civilized manner of Councilor Mentan but didn't believe that his civility indicated that he would agree with her demands. The look on his face gave away nothing. Did the smile indicate he was just humoring another crazy female? Did the stern look that came to his eyes when she mentioned a "season coming to an end" mean that he would oppose making the changes that Set Li knew were needed? She couldn't tell, but she would rather deal with Mentan than Shatoc.

"Shall we go inside and discuss matters?" Mentan asked.

"That would be better. Before we leave, do I have your assurance that this crowd will not be harmed?"

"I can see why you would ask that given Shatoc's behavior, but they will not be bothered. They are free to stay or go. You have my assurance."

Set Li turned to the crowd.

"Friends, I don't know how long this will take, but I will tell you the results of my talk with Councilor Mentan when we are done. Thank you for your support."

There were murmurs as those in the crowd discussed their next step. Some moved to leave. Many decided to stay.

Set Li and the rest of the ground team followed Mentan up the steps and into the three-story Administration Building. He led them to a large, window-less meeting room on the first floor. As they entered, they saw four other male Sudahlli enter from another door. Set Li and her group sat together on one side of the table. Mentan sat at the head of the table, and the four new Sudahlli, who were introduced as the rest of the town council sat across from Set Li and her group.

Mentan suggested refreshments. Set Li said that water would be appreciated. When water had been provided Mentan opened the discussion.

"When I first heard of the incident on Thahll 2 I did some research. I am a student of ancient history. The name seemed familiar to me. Millennia ago there was a Set Li who figured prominently in the history of that time. That Set Li was instrumental in the forming of the original Council of Clans which resulted in a reduction of the bitter inter-Clan conflicts. Is that the reason you chose that name when you announced yourself to our world? Do you see her as your role model as you seek to make changes now?"

"I don't know what the historical record says, but I am that Set Li."

The other four at the table laughed out loud. Mentan looked at them disapprovingly and the laughter stopped. Set Li was untroubled by their laughter and looked straight at the four councilors.

"That has been the response every time I have introduced myself since I arrived. I realize it is difficult for you to believe. If you are interested, I can explain how it has happened that the historical person Mentan spoke of is before you today. If not, let us continue with our discussion. It is of little importance to me whether you believe me or not."

Her confident tone took the smiles off their faces. Mentan said he was interested. So she told them the story, which also explained the presence of Atala and Jesse. She finished with a description of the presence of the Annli and the role they played. The Council Members began to express their disbelief again. They were silenced by the appearance of Ontoron. He materialized before them as an amorphous volume of light that shimmered and changed shape constantly and introduced himself.

"We Annli are thought of as mythical creatures, if we enter any being's thoughts at all in these times. We still exist, but in a unique form as pure energy. The rest of the Annli have sanctioned my participation in this process on your world. We generally avoid interference with the material world, but to keep this from turning into an armed conflict, I have taken the energy from your weapons. I will continue to observe and help where I can."

"We are honored you are with us during what is likely to be a significant moment in the history of the Sudahlli," Mentan said.

The other four council members looked at Mentan as if he were insane. He smiled in return.

"If you have alternative explanations for all that is claimed at this table today, my fellow Council Members, then present those explanations. If not then let us treat our guests with the respect as is due those they claim to be."

He turned to Set Li.

"First Mother...?"

"Thank you, Councilor Mentan, but please call me Set Li. The title First Mother is no longer relevant on Thahll. As to why we are here, we seek to eliminate the abuse the females are experiencing in Sudahlli society. We ask that their place in that society be on equal footing with males. They are to be educated and have an equal opportunity to play any role in society. We must act quickly to make sure no more females are mistreated as my two companions have been or harassed because of their gender. As a first step you will release the following Sudahlli who have been imprisoned merely because they protested current policies."

Set Li read the list given to her by Martha.

"Relatives or friends close to these prisoners are to be contacted so that they can bring appropriate garments and support the former prisoners as they reenter the lives you have taken from them."

"Impossible!" one Council Member shouted. "Who are you to come here and tell us what to do? Those prisoners broke the law and were rightfully imprisoned!"

"Change the laws and release them."

"How could you know of these prisoners?" another Council Member demanded.

Set Li didn't respond.

Mentan let the Council Members fume for a while before he addressed them.

"You might note that Set Li has brought Berla with her. When I learned that Berla had escaped from prison, I looked into her case. She refused to submit to the prison guards demeaning treatment. She was beat frequently, but she fought back. At one point she killed one of the guards and was sentenced to be executed. When I examined the situation more closely, I found that male guards often used their positions to sexually abuse their female prisoners."

"One instance of abuse does not justify changing the whole system," another of the Council members said. "She killed a guard."

"She was defending her life!" Mentan declared. "This treatment of prisoners is pervasive in the system. It shows how little respect we have for females in our society. It is time for a change!"

"You cannot do this on your own authority, Mentan. We have to agree to the action, and we aren't in agreement. The laws these prisoners broke are the same across all of Thahll. Changing them must be sanctioned by the World Council."

"As a World Council member, I have certain prerogatives. One of them is to pardon prisoners if I find an injustice has occurred. I am not changing the laws with this action, but merely pardoning a few prisoners."

Mentan pushed a button on the console in front of him. A moment later an aide came in and took down the names of the prisoners Set Li listed. The aide was astonished when Mentan added two additional names and told him what was to be done. There was a pleased smile on the aide's face when he left the room to put the new order into effect.

Mentan turned to Berla and Canli.

"Berla, Canliot, my apology is insufficient to make up for the treatment you received in prison, but I do apologize. I have added your names to the list of prisoners to be pardoned. A formal record of those pardons will be entered into the system."

Mentan ended their meeting so he could address those who remained outside on the plaza. He asked the visitors to join him. A hush fell over the crowd as they appeared at the top of the steps. Mentan stepped forward.

"As you are aware we are in the midst of extraordinary events. Historical figures have appeared accompanied by races unknown to us. They are holding up a mirror for us so that we might see ourselves as we are today. I have looked into that mirror, and I am ashamed of what I have seen."

He provided an outline of the earlier discussion and told about the prisoners being released. Representatives from the media had come to see what the gathering was all about. They recorded the event including visual images of the strange visitors and Mentan's speech. The media sought to talk with Set Li and her group afterword, but Mentan stepped in to become the focus of the media's attention. After the interview he brought his guests back inside the building, and in the lobby he turned to Set Li.

"Would you be willing to come with me to address the World Council?"

"Will it take time to gather them together?"

Mentan laughed.

"No, Set Li. Your recent actions have already accomplished that."

Berla and Canli asked to remain behind to help with the transition of the newly released prisoners. Mentan gave instructions to the Town Council staff to help Berla and Canli.

If they were going to address the world body, Jesse thought that male and female representatives of the Human and Lorengi races should attend. He asked Melba Thomas, one of the H2 volunteers on Jannida and Gordi, the male Lorengi, to join them. There were gasps among the Sudahlli when Melba and Gordi appeared out of thin air. Even Mentan was taken aback.

"More things for you to explain to me, Set Li, if you are willing at the appropriate time."

"I'll do my best Councilor, but I will need help from my companions when the time comes. Where is the World Council meeting?"

Jesse asked Martha if she knew the location.

"Yes." she said through his implant. "I know where it is, and I am in their system. I have also had time to do some research on the Councilors. The actions of some Councilors border on criminal. I will have the information handy if we need it."

Jesse also asked Janus if he had identified the Councilors and their staff.

"Yes. Being able to sense and work with the minds of the three billion Sudahlli at such a distance is far easier than I would have imagined a short time ago. I think I am growing apace with the continuing development the H2s."

"Stay tuned," Jesse said. *"There's more fun on the horizon."*

Set Li was looking at Jesse when he returned his attention to those in the lobby.

"Councilor Mentan has told me where the World Council meets."

"We also have the location. We could go back to the ship, walking or teleporting and ride in Jannida to that location, or we could just pop in as Melba and Gordi did here a moment ago."

Mentan watched the one-side discussion Set Li was having with Jesse.

"May I be included in your plans?"

"Yes, of course. I was just about to ask you to join us. I'll let Jesse explain."

"We have several options for getting to the World Council meeting, Councilor Mentan." Jesse said still using only telepathy to maintain the role he chose for himself.

Jesse went on to explain the options he saw. Mentan laughed.

"I prefer the 'pop in on them' option. Though it would be good to alert them ahead of time. Some of my colleagues are older and in poor health. Even after being alerted, this will be quite a shock."

Jesse made arrangements with Jannida to travel there and remain airborne over the World Council building. He asked Mentan to picture an area in front of the Council that was large enough for their group, and then asked Janus to alert the Council members, and ask them to make sure that area was clear. He waited until he was assured by Janus that the area had been cleared, then he and Melba teleported the group to the World Council.

The walls of the room they arrived in were covered with dark wood panels. There were tall windows along three of the walls, but the light from them seemed to be absorbed by the dark wood so the room remained dark.

At one end of the room there was a raised stage, where six members of the World Council were sitting. Mentan's place was empty. He stood on the floor with the visitors. The ceiling lights over the Council provided the only artificial light in the large hall.

Council staff and armed guards stood to both sides of the stage on the floor level. Behind the new arrivals there was a large seating area for the audience and petitioners waiting their turn to speak before the Council.

Mentan's voice broke into the complete silence in the hall that followed the startled reactions to the group's arrival. "Good morning, Council Lead Chanut."

The Council Members were not only astonished by the apparition, but they had also just received telepathic communication from Janus before the group had appeared in front of them. The head of the Council, Artan Chanut struggled a moment to gain his composure.

"Councilor Mentan, what have we here?" Chanut asked, only being partially successful in his attempt to present his usual officious manner.

"Visitors, and two Sudahlli who have returned home after a long absence."

"I would say 'welcome,' but hardly seems an appropriate greeting for those who have broken the law. Have they come to turn themselves in for judgment?"

"No. They wish to petition the Council for changes that they believe are needed."

"We have a full schedule before us today. Ask them to talk with our staff to see when we can accommodate their request. In the meantime, I believe we will confine them to the cells while we decide to do about their criminal acts," Chanut said, arrogantly.

Set Li smiled at the pompous Council Lead and his apparent indifference to the presence of the Humans and Lorengi.

"We have seen what happens to those you put in your cells," she said. "We won't be going to your cells."

"Guards, remove this female!" Chanut said. "Females are not allowed to speak in the Council Chamber."

"If I might suggest…," Mentan said.

"What do you suggest, Mentan?"

"I suggest that we make an exception and let her speak."

"Denied. Guards!"

Two guards from each side of the hall took a step in the direction of the group and fell to the floor.

"As I was saying," Mentan said, "I think you should hear what she has to say. I am not sure how they do the things they do, but they render any aggressor unconscious, and as shown by our arrival today, they can move about without mechanical aid."

Chanut was visibly frustrated. He slammed his two lower fists on the counter before him. "You will not take over this World Council!"

"Our aim is to work *with* the World Council," Set Li said. "Since arriving here we have observed things that are objectionable, and we would like to see them changed."

"Who are you to make such demands?"

Set Li told him who she was, provided a synopsis of events since their arrival, what she had seen and what changes she wanted.

"And you expect us to comply with your demands?"

"I know it won't be simple, but we expect that you will work with us toward the goals we have."

"What if we refuse?"

Set Li let his question remain in the air for a time. She stood and calmly looked at the Council members. She began again without answering his question.

"In the short time we have been here, Council Lead Chanut, I have observed that most Sudahlli, both male and female, will favor the changes we advocate. If you are seen as the body behind these changes the bulk of the population will praise your efforts. Those who see their positions threatened might oppose you, but most will be glad to support you. Also, my friends you see with me and their colleagues have agreed to help.

"There is one other present who I would like you to meet," Set Li said. "Ontoron, would you introduce yourself to the Council?"

A bright, shimmering patch of light energy formed in front of the Council. A voice from within the brightness spoke into the Council Members' minds and the minds of the others in the room.

"Hello. I am an Annli. My name is Ontoron. Thank you for allowing my friends to speak before you today. The changes they are proposing are heartily supported by all Annli. We will help however we can as you go through this cultural shift. We

Annli are an ancient race. Even though we are no longer corporeal we have learned many things and are willing to share anything that will help the Sudahlli during this challenging time."

The World Council of Thahll sat in stunned silence. No one in the room spoke. Feet shuffled and chairs creaked as Council Members and some in the audience shifted their positions. Council Lead Chanut cleared his throat and prepared to speak, but no words came. He tried again with more success.

"Uh, thank you, Ontoron. You are correct in thinking that what has been proposed would present a significant challenge for our people. It seems that several races have concluded that they can dictate how we Sudahlli should live. You do not have that right!

"Having made that clear, I must acknowledge that we recently have witnessed extraordinary events and have met beings with abilities that are beyond our experience, beyond our imagination. This kind of experience alters any conscious beings' perspective. It has caused me to pause and consider. Seeing my fellow Council Members' expressions leads me to believe that they also may be thinking about the implications of what we have experienced."

Chanut looked at the Council Members. They all nodded their heads as if agreeing with his previous statement. He also assumed it meant that they would support what he had in mind. He turned to where Ontoron shimmered before them.

"This is not a time for a wise leader to stubbornly refuse to consider suggestions just because they don't conform to previous norms," Chanut said, trying to sound like he was in control of the situation, but failing. "Therefore, we invite you and the other races represented here to work with us as we evaluate how to proceed."

28 A Dangerous Experiment

Sunaj, Frazier, Washington State

Rosalind entered the main Sunaj building and went to her office, where Jamal was waiting for her. They had encountered so much in their recent travels that they had plenty to talk about. Two of their new acquaintances joined them in Rosalind's office to share in the discussion—the Lorengi scientist Nassada in holographic form and Gerana from the Annli as a telepathic voice in their heads.

"So we are agreed that it is likely that the dimension the ships were trapped in seems to be a very useful part of our universe," Rosalind said. *"It may be the dimension though which we are able to teleport and communicate telepathically. It may also be the dimension used by those who travel faster than light aboard powered ships. We agree it is likely, but 'likely' is not a satisfying result to me. Is there a way we can become more certain about our conclusion?"*

"Our ships and the others were trapped there when we attempted to travel in those ways you list," Nassada said. *"We were able to communicate telepathically within the dimension, actually that was the only way we were able to communicate."*

"We weren't able to communicate with those in the dimension from the outside," Jamal said.

"True," Gerana said, *"but that doesn't disprove what we are thinking about the dimension."*

"I agree that it doesn't disprove it, Gerana," Rosalind said, *"but little items like that make me less comfortable with our assumptions."*

"What did the Annli do to create the 'window,' Gerana?" Nassada asked. *"We might understand more about the dimension by learning what you had to overcome to open up a window into it."*

"I am not sure my explanation will help you," Gerana said. *"We are very different from both of your manifestations— Human corporeal and Lorengi digital. Does it help the discussion to say that we can sense the dimension and that those ships were in it? Does it help if I tell you that we used our personal energy to create an opening in the window between the observable universe and the dimension so that the trapped ships would be visible to Carmen?"*

"Actually, that information might help," Rosalind said. *"Perhaps we can better understand the dimension by learning more about the Annli 'manifestation.' Gerana can you describe yourself to us?"*

Before Gerana began Theron contacted Sam in his office at Sunaj. Sam had years of experience of Janus suddenly contacting him. He couldn't see him, but he had become accustomed to the telepathic voice of Janus coming into his thoughts out of the thin air. It seemed he would have to get used to the same thing with Theron, the Annli. He welcomed the new experience.

"Sam, you've asked me about the Annli. Gerana is about to describe us to Rosalind and Nassada. Gerana has always had the best understanding of what happened to us and what we have become. This would be a good opportunity to learn about the Annli. You might want to connect to the conversation."

"Thanks. I will check in."

Sam announced himself telepathically, and Gerana began.

"As you probably have surmised, the Annli began our existence as physical creatures with our own particular form of evolution. It began eons ago and continued to the point where we became a technologically advanced, space-faring society. Our evolution went further than others and seems to be continuing. I think the part of our evolution that you are most interested in is the process where we left our physical bodies.

"The change began in an alarming way. Some of us started fading, becoming translucent, like how you appear Nassada. The condition wasn't permanent at first. We went in and out of the state. We didn't understand what was happening, and we became frightened.

"The next phase was even more alarming. We would be conversing with a friend, and they would disappear. Often they would keep conversing not noticing they had become invisible and had switched from verbal conversation to telepathy.

"Once the immaterial phase began, it spread rapidly until all the Annli were no longer physical. We became pure energy. We believe that our individual consciousness binds our personal energy together, much like we think matter is shaped into various forms by the conscious intelligence in our universe.

"The conversion process required external energy. Each time an individual converted to this form, part of organic and inorganic mass surrounding that individual was converted to energy to support the process. When we all had converted, we had consumed our entire planet and its one moon.

"This was not a premeditated change. We had not been concentrating on becoming pure energy. We were conducting our affairs as we normally did. We were concerned about the fact that some of us were periodically becoming translucent. Our scientists were looking into that when we became

completely invisible. It just happened, and it happened quickly. One moment we and our planet were material. A very short time later we were energy.

"We were panicked by the change at first, not knowing what to do with our outmoded way of thinking and living— up/down, hot/cold, occupation/vocation. Many of these familiar concepts no longer had a role in our existence. Family and friends as concepts had changed. Before the conversion we had been conscious bits of matter associating with each other. We became, and remain to this day, an amalgamation of individual conscious bits of energy. As far as we know we are unique. We had to form new ways of associating with each other.

"We draw energy from the cosmos to sustain ourselves, much as our planet used to absorbed sunlight. We found that we could travel around the galaxy in a way that was similar to how your two races teleport. We could travel as individuals or in groups. In these travels, we never lost contact with each other. As you are finding, telepathy is not weakened by distance. We are convinced that telepathy and teleportation are accomplished through the dimension we are discussing.

"We learned how to interact with and influence things in the material world. We were tempted to interfere with races on other planets, trying to make things better. We found that our good intentions didn't keep us from making mistakes and decided that adopting a non-interference policy was best. Deviation from this policy is rare and is something that must be discussed by all of us. We deviated from this policy in this case for reasons that will be clear once you understand what happened.

"After spending millennia exploring the galaxy some of us wanted to try something else. Some wanted to travel to another galaxy, but we decided that we probably would find more of

what we had in our galaxy. Some wanted to find out if we could travel to another universe and back. That idea was dangerously intriguing. Surely we would be able to find something new in another universe. The idea gained enough support that those who wished to explore the concept were allowed to proceed."

"Interesting concept indeed," Rosalind said, *"but where would one start?"*

"We had studied the idea of multiple universes before we had gone through our transition. One idea was that our universe and the others are each bound by separate membranes of some sort. We wanted to see what would happen if we could discern that membrane, could break through it, and go through the membrane of a neighboring universe. We recognized that the potential threat to our universe was enormous, so we proceeded very cautiously.

"Then the moment arrived when we believed that we had finally come to sense the membrane boundary of our universe. We thought to influence the smallest portion of that membrane to move toward the membrane of a neighboring universe. So we pushed."

"You WHAT?" Rosalind exclaimed. *"That is about the most dangerous and arrogant thing I've ever heard of. What about potential harm to this universe?* Rosalind calmed herself by recognizing that the universe had survived whatever experiment they had tried. Then Rosalind the scientist asked, *"What did you find out?"*

"We learned, as you say, that it was an extremely dangerous thing to do. There was a tremendous burst of energy in that micro instant when the two membranes touched. Luckily the damage was contained to a small portion of the universe, only a limited number of beings were affected, and thankfully

not injured. I speak of those ships that were trapped in that dimension while in transit."

"I think that over three billion Lorengi and other beings is more than a 'limited number,'" Nassada said.

"I apologize, Nassada," Gerana said. *"Of course, you are right, and we regret that we so dramatically impacted all your lives. My poor choice of words was influenced by our thoughts about how many of the uncountable beings in our universe that could have been affected by our action."*

"Why didn't you rescue those ships right away?" Sam asked.

"We didn't know they were there at first," Gerana said. *"We pulled back from what we had done. We looked around and were relieved that we couldn't detect any damage from the event. Time was taken attempting to understand what had happened. During that period we found that there was an anomaly in the dimension we are discussing. Something material was within a dimension that was formerly empty. As we understood that dimension, it had to be empty! Yet something was there, and we knew we were at fault.*

"We studied the situation for some time trying to create a way to find out what it was that was trapped in the dimension. We learned how to create an opening between our four-dimension frame of reference and this other dimension. Putting it in a way that would make sense to you, we created the opening and 'looked in.' We found that we had trapped ships in the dimension while they were in transit using either FTL ships or teleportation.

"Before you ask, Sam, we saw what we had done, but knew we were unable to do anything about it. It would take a physical intervention that we were incapable of performing. We were

241

deeply saddened. We closed the window and began a desperate search to find a way to undo what we had done."

"But eventually, something was done," Rosalind said. *"What happened, Gerana?"*

"Something highly unlikely!"

29 Deeper Meaning

La Jolla, California

When the discussion with Gerana shifted to the physics behind the transformation of the Annli Sam chose to bow out. He teleported to La Jolla and the home he shared with his wife, Senator Lesley Anderson.

Carmen reported that feeding and educating the Garduk, creating a sustainable infrastructure, and introducing technology at a prudent rate on Solan was going to be a very long project. Sam hoped that Carmen could create a project management team that would free her to move on to other things when the time came.

Jesse said that once it was apparent that the government was going to go along with the societal changes Set Li was advocating, the bulk of the male Sudahlli embraced the better treatment of females. Everyone demanded that Set Li be positioned to oversee the changes, and many wanted her to be appointed to the lead position of the World Council. She agreed to monitor the change process but declined to lead the Council. She did fill one of the vacancies on the World Council which became available when the inappropriate activities of certain Council Members became public. She was instrumental in getting a female appointed to another of the vacancies. Those developments sounded promising to Sam.

Sam discussed all that had happened with Lesley and told her about the new races that had been discovered. He introduced her to Jarruda, the Lorengi leader, and Lesley took charge of introducing Jarruda to the President and Congressional leaders. Sam was pleasantly surprised how readily Lesley accepted the notion of beings made exclusively of energy when he introduced her to Theron and told her about the Annli. When he asked her about it later she said that it was no more astounding than when she had learned of Janus and conversed telepathically with him.

Lesley was pleased to have met Jarruda and Theron and was supportive of the efforts on Solan and Thahll. She applauded Sam's continued exploration of the metaphysical future of Humanity but declined joining him in his search for answers. Lesley's main focus remained on helping those on Earth adjust to the inevitability of the population becoming dominantly H2, and to the concept that Humans were not alone in the universe.

So Sam was often alone at the beach house while Lesley was working with her staff at her San Diego office. He didn't mind. He had a lot to think about. On one of those warm sunny solitary days, Sam was sitting on the deck overlooking the ocean. He decided it was time to continue the conversation with Theron about the deeper implications of the matters that had been discussed in the conversation with Gerana. He invited Janus to join him.

He contacted Theron telepathically and asked what Gerana had meant when he said something "highly unlikely" happened. Theron said he was glad to have the opportunity to tell him.

"When we saw that our experiment trapped the ships," Theron began, *"we learned at the same time that there was nothing we could do to rescue them. We theorized that they*

were trapped in a dimension where they would not experience the passing of time. We hoped that was true. The alternative, that they were trapped and would age and die in that abysmal situation was too horrible to consider.

"So we believed we had time to search for someone who might be able to help. We searched over an expansive part of the galaxy and found nothing promising until we happened onto the Lorengi. We admired the work they were doing. They were seeking out life on planets, studying whatever forms of life they found, and intervening in rare circumstances where a small change might make the difference between extinction and survival."

"Like they did with the Cheneshi?" Sam asked.

"Yes. In that case, enabling an innate ability the Cheneshi had for telepathy allowed them to warn off the herbivore species that was eating their young saplings. That one change made it possible for the Cheneshi to thrive and develop into the mentally powerful and gentle race that they have become.

"We were observing the Lorengi when they came upon your ancestors. We saw what they saw in your ancestor's DNA. After all our searching we finally had happened upon a race that might be able to help."

"I don't understand," Janus said. *"How could you see all that simply by looking at the DNA of prehistoric version of Homo sapiens?"*

"You wouldn't know this, but the DNA we saw was unbelievably similar to ours. What's more, there was an additional level of complexity woven into it, which seemed to include a dormant ability to make further changes in your DNA.

"Humans were the only other race we had come upon in our galaxy-wide search that we thought might evolve as we had, and possibly even go beyond us. We wanted to do something

with you right away but knew that we had to wait until you developed as a race.

"It was excruciating to wait, and watch you stumble along on your path toward civilized behavior. We could influence your development only in a small way. We were able to communicate with some and inform their thoughts. Most Humans were unable to accept what we were trying to tell them. They treated the 'voice in their heads' as an aberration and would not listen lest they were thought insane.

"Humans made progress. There were small instances of enlightenment. Those were soon overrun by barbarism. Then another effort to bring light into your world would occur, and again fear and darkness would overwhelm the effort. Humans went through cycle after cycle of this for millennia. Gradually, the number of enlightened people began to increase.

"After all those millennia, we Annli began to change. We were becoming less substantial. We were sensing that we were less able to have an impact on the material world. Our feeling of urgency increased once we recognized that eventually we wouldn't be able to open the view into the dimension that you called the 'window.' Still we forced ourselves to wait.

"Near the end of what you call the Twentieth Century we observed that the percentage of your population who were acting in a mindful way, with love and kindness toward others was increasing significantly. Their actions seemed to threaten people who were fighting desperately to hold on to a different vision of reality.

"We knew that we had to act soon, or fear might overwhelm the mindful ones again. We were concerned that we might lose our ability to intervene. The Annli had learned more about the dormant aspect of your DNA, which if brought to life

might make further changes. We decided it was time to activate it. We had no way of knowing what the outcome would be."

Sam was fascinated by Theron's brief description of Humanity's struggle to emerge from barbarism and a fear-based society. The process took thousands of years with many thousands of generations of Humans struggling to survive. The Annli were watching the whole time, patiently waiting for Humans to get through a dangerous time. The difference in perspective was unsettling to Sam.

"You triggered the start of the births of what we call H2s?" Sam asked.

"Yes."

"How did you do that?"

"The Annli population is made up of billions of individual energy beings, Sam. We can concentrate our energy wherever we wish. We focused on the necessary cells in Human males, and shifted information in the DNA, which brought about the change. That's not a detailed description, but that was the essence of it."

"Our scientists will want to know more, but it is sufficient for me," Sam said. *"So you started the change process, but you didn't introduce the features into our DNA in the first place?"* Sam asked.

"No."

"Do you think the complexity of our DNA was a natural development, or an intervention by some other entity?"

"The Annli have been around a long time. We haven't encountered anyone that gene engineered a particular species."

"You said our DNA was similar to yours. How do you think your DNA became what it was?"

"We assumed that it was just part of our evolution."

"We certainly began to think about it when you triggered the development of a new version of Humans," Sam said. *"Humans being born with a new version of DNA all seem to be driven to do things that support the survival of our race and the rest of life on our planet. We speculated that there must have been some intelligence which intervened to achieve this result."*

"I would agree with the conclusion that there was some intelligence behind the change, Sam," Theron said. *"I don't think you have to look for some race of altruistic gene engineers who introduced these features in your DNA. I would look no further than the consciousness in the universe that we think shapes matter and energy into forms that all move toward a higher state. The Annli believe that the universe needed you, so it created you."*

"That is difficult to believe," Sam said.

"I understand," Theron said, *"consider your collective consciousness, Janus, and what it is doing. That is easier for you to accept because you can see some of the things Janus is doing on the macro level. The consciousness of the universe within which we are all included, must work at the micro level, influencing micro amounts of energy within all matter. It works behind the scenes, making incrementally small adjustments."*

"So somehow during the eons we took to develop our DNA was modified to include some unusual ingredients?" Sam asked.

"That's how we see it, but you seem disappointed at the prospect."

"A super race doing gene engineering experiments makes a better plot for science fiction fans."

"Humans are special, Sam, but we haven't seen any evidence of a 'super race.'"

"What does all this mean?" Sam asked. *"We were able to rescue those trapped in the dimension. Is that rescue the 'role' you were hoping we would be able to fulfill?"*

"Rescuing everyone in the ships was important. It is also representative of the broader role you might play in the galaxy. Over the millennia we have been observing life in the galaxy. We have seen many situations where the right kind of help, at the right time, would improve things. We were unable to provide the needed aid in our current form, but Humans could. In several ways, you have leaped beyond us when we were material beings. We see that as meaningful."

"What do you mean?" Sam asked. *"From our discussions it sounded like your technology was further advanced than ours."*

"That part is true, but that is the only way in which we surpassed you. At the time we were still material beings our technology allowed us to communicate with anyone verbally and visually, anywhere our system had expanded to, including the full reach of our explorations at that time. We could travel anywhere on our planet instantaneously, and our FTL ships brought us to faraway places rapidly.

"With these aids, we didn't pursue development of telepathy. Some were capable of it, but it was seen as unnecessary, given our level of technology. We did not explore the possibility of being able to personally move ourselves with our minds. We did not see the need. The Lorengi were capable of both telepathy and teleportation, but we were satisfied with our technological means to accomplish the same ends.

"Had we explored these things, done more with our minds as you have, it is possible that we might have developed a form of global consciousness. Even now when we are fully aware of each other, we know our experience is nothing like what Janus

is. The development of Janus separates you from all other races we have encountered in the galaxy.

"The Annli were surprised when we changed state as we did. Before we were happy, perhaps even smug with our technological advances. We were expecting a continuous stream of technological changes to enhance our future existence. Then, to our surprise, we suddenly changed into the beings we are now.

"We were shocked and humbled at the same time. We quickly learned that even though our technology was interesting, it had been a barrier to a deeper understanding of the universe. It supported the illusion that we were separate— separate from each other, from other life forms, from the rest of the universe. That we were wrong in our belief became crystal clear when we found ourselves in this new form, as drops in the immense ocean of the universe."

"Why are you telling us this?" Janus asked. *"We see the differences you speak of, but you are making more of them than we see ourselves."*

"We have a perspective quite apart from yours," Theron responded. *"We have explored a significant amount of the galaxy and can draw a comparison. We are aware of our own evolution as well. You may be headed toward our state of existence, but we predict that is far, far in your future. As individuals you are able to travel and communicate over galactic distances with your minds. Perhaps Humans are more than the Annli will ever become.*

"Look what you are already doing. You are helping the Garduk revive their race which was on the brink of extinction. You are helping the Sudahlli re-civilize their culture."

"You, the Lorengi and the Dhara'chee are helping," Janus observed.

"True, but the Annli would not be able to accomplish what you are doing. You have the vision, the drive, the initiative, the wisdom, and the love necessary to make it all happen.

"Ask yourself, why are Humans on those planets, doing what they are doing? Most races are concerned with their own matters. Some help others as they conduct their affairs, but the needs of others are nearly always second to their own needs. Not you. You are acting as if the needs of others ARE your needs, as if other beings are not separate from you. You see that helping them is the same as aiding yourselves."

"Well," Sam said, *"they need help."*

"Are you helping these people for your own gain?" Theron asked. *"Are you lending your aid now with the expectation that you will be paid back some time in the future?"*

"No." Sam said. *"The Garduk need help so we do what we can. The Sudahlli are struggling to re-define how to live together. We offer support without telling them the answer. The Cheneshi asked for our help. We went to their planet and helped them find the answer to their problem. We don't expect anything in return. We enjoy meeting new races, helping where we can, and especially value the friends that we make."*

"Exactly." Theron said. *"What I am saying is that there will be many opportunities in the galaxy for you to repeat these experiences."*

Sam understood what Theron was saying. So far, happenstance had been the provider of the opportunities. In the future would a new, more formal, purposeful enterprise of coming to the aid of others be the dominant role of Humans? Sam smiled at the prospect and hoped it was true.

Epilogue

La Jolla, California

The sun was setting, shining brightly through the western windows when Lesley arrived home after a long day in her office. She was proud of the accomplishments she had made during her tenure as a Senator. Congress and most State Legislatures were aligned with new priorities—allocating budgets to improve the quality of life for everyone and mitigating the impact of Human activity on the planet. It wouldn't work if other countries in the world weren't on board, but more and more of them were. It also helped that many of those who had accumulated great wealth were, like Sam, dedicating that wealth toward these same ends. There was still a lot of work to be done, but it was gratifying to see the momentum going in the right direction.

She received no answer when she called out upon entering her house, so she walked out the back door to the deck, where she found Sam gazing into the distance over the Pacific Ocean.

"Are you asleep out here?"

"Huh?"

"You looked like you were either lost in thought, or your mind was a million miles away."

"Light-years, Les. Light-years. We're a race that's traveling around the galaxy now, and according to Theron, we have work to do."

Lesley had "met" Theron, if you could use that word for meeting someone as a voice in your head. She had been told about the Annli and their current state of existence. With Janus as a close friend, Lesley had become accustomed to telepathic voices coming from thin air. She didn't see any difference if the air was energized. She sat down in the deck chair next to Sam.

"Oh? What has the Energetic One been saying?" Lesley asked.

Sam told her what Theron had said.

"Hmmm."

"Exactly what I thought," Sam said.

"What does Janus have to say about all of this?"

"I'm at the 'Hmmm'" stage, also," Janus said. *"Like Sam, I'm not sure what to think about the history Theron has laid before us, or what he has suggested for our future."*

"I haven't been agonizing over these issues, as you two have," Lesley said. "I know they are important, but I've been focused on things here at home. Still, I have a viewpoint that might be helpful. Let's think about what we've lived through here on Earth during this century.

"H2s began showing up at the beginning of the century. Their numbers increased, but gradually. The gradual growth seemed to be part of the design. Currently there are about one and a third billion H2s. That's about 14% of the total population of Earth.

"We H2s found we could improve things on our planet and have been able to help those on other planets as well. The projects on Solan and Thahll will take time and resources.

"My colleagues and I, as well as other leaders across the world have plenty to keep us busy. There remain a multitude of issues and situations that need resolution as we manage the shift toward an ever-increasing number of H2s.

"My point is we don't have to look for more work. If it comes, fine, but let's focus on developing our Humanity in the meantime."

"Hmmm…," Sam said.

Lesley gave him a punch to the shoulder and laughed. Sam laughed too and went inside to the kitchen. When he came back out, he brought a tray of fruit, cheese and crackers, two glasses and a chilled bottle of white wine. He poured each of them a glass of wine. He raised his glass in a toast.

"Here's to…," Sam paused not sure which part of all this he should be toasting to.

"…an interesting future," Lesley finished for him.

* * *

Janus left his two friends to enjoy their afternoon by the ocean. He agreed with what Lesley had said about their future. A lot had happened in a very short time. It was wise to help the Human population adjust to what had already occurred and get ready for what was to come.

Sorting out what Humans were becoming was critical for Janus, too. Human consciousness was a major part of what Janus was. All consciousness and life on Earth were thriving and growing, but Humans were dynamic, creative and changing into what they apparently were meant to be. Janus would grow along with them, and help them in their noble tasks, but that wasn't all he would do, or all that he was.

What was he? What was *his* future? It was time he stopped to consider these questions anew in the light of the recent revelations.

The Annli, the Lorengi, and even the Cheneshi said Janus was unique. The Annli said Janus was more powerful than he knew. Janus had already roamed widely in the galaxy with the Humans, Carmen and Jesse in particular. He not only traveled, but he was also able to act, have an impact on those distant planets.

He had experimented and had learned that he could travel to other star systems even further away by himself. It wasn't necessary to have one of his components, such as a Human, to go there in order for him to reach those locations. He was able to sense life and consciousness at those locations, if he found any, and knew he could interact with what he found if he chose to do so. He had learned he could act independently.

So what was he? Was he a new kind of life form? If so, he was the only one of his kind as far as he or the Annli knew. Janus had encountered a variety of forms of consciousness. There were cyber-based, artificial intelligences like Martha. The Lorengi were another conscious life form—stored personalities of previously-organic beings. Lorengi had also created self-aware ships. The Annli were another life form. So many forms of conscious beings, but no other like Janus, like himself!

The Annli believed that there was a consciousness that shaped matter and energy in the universe, and that it had formed the unique H2 Human DNA on purpose. Had the universe expected Janus to emerge as a result of Human development? Was he, a being comprised of only consciousness, to play a greater role in the universe as well?

A gentle whisper floated into his awareness. It wasn't like anything Janus had experienced before. It expressed one thought only, "*Yes.*"

Be sure to look for the other books in the

Janus Unfolding Series

Emergence
Factotum
Inheritance
Ancient Agendas
The Urritan Legacy

<u>Reviews Matter!</u>

I would like to know your thoughts about my book. Please consider taking a few minutes to write a review.

at

Amazon

C. A. Knutsen was born in the Pacific Northwest with its mountains, rivers and rugged ocean coast. Enjoying the natural beauty, he is especially drawn to the shores of Puget Sound with its majestic, rocky bluffs and forests. This setting inspires his speculations about the wonderful life on this planet and its possible transformations in the future, as well as the role Human beings have in sustaining life and caring for each other.

Knutsen has a Bachelor of Science in Electrical Engineering and a Masters in Business Administration from the University of Washington. His background in science and business, as well as his passion for the environment, now inform his visionary fiction.

caknutsen.com